ALSO BY JEFF HOWE

INTO THE ROARING FORK

THE SILVER PIGEONS

A Novel

JEFF HOWE

Published in the United States by Cameron & Greys Publishing

ISBN: 978-0-578-65424-9

To my mother, Marjorie Macke Howe

CHAPTER ONE

IN THE YEAR 2000

Tethered to the scent, his nose yanks him hard left through the golden prairie grass, where he stops on a dime and points like a compass needle in the direction of a pheasant. They had told me Truck would do this whenever he caught wind of a bird, but to see it firsthand in the endless realm of Big Sky Country far exceeds my expectations.

"Good boy, Truck," our hunting guide, Orrin, says to his dog. I trail on Orrin's east flank; Hollis is beside him on the west. In the brisk October morning air, which dilates the blood vessels in our faces, the three of us walk the field. Two of us carry twenty-gauge shotguns. Orrin, unarmed, pivots my way. "Garrett, I want you up even with me and Hollis."

An hour ago, back at the lodge, Orrin had gone over the rules that Hollis and I acknowledged and agreed to follow. Safety is paramount, and with that in mind I quicken my step toward them. As I do, I remember what Orrin had instructed regarding our formation: travel parallel to each other and maintain our own line of sight with Truck's. I have the shot if the bird flies toward the single digits past twelve o'clock, and Hollis has the doubles. From one of the pockets on my hunting coat I produce two shells and place them into the upper and lower barrels of my twenty-gauge, close the break action, and check the safety. It's on. It's a

1

top-of-the-line field gun; the safety automatically resets whenever the firearm is broken open—a helpful feature for a beginner like me. Hollis has loaned it to me for the hunt. He holds the exact same model in his hands. Beretta, I recall.

Truck is a German shorthaired pointer, a beautiful dog with a brown and gray coat like an Appaloosa. His front right paw is off the ground and curled backwards; the classic canine hunting stance I've seen in magazines at Hollis's house. Truck stands as still as the sun while I shoulder my gun.

But it's premature.

"Not yet," Orrin tells me, and I lower it. "Easy boy," the guide whispers to his dog and, possibly, to me as well. "Nice and easy."

I look over at Hollis and see he has his gun down at his belly. It's apparent I'm too anxious, so I hold my gun like his. He's done this many times before. Best to imitate him from now on in order to stay on Orrin's good side.

Truck stamps his paw on the ground and begins to move through the tall grass once again. Orrin lets him go. "The bird's running," he informs us. "Follow Truck."

And that's what we do—with man and man's best friend to lead our way.

Smart pheasants won't fly unless they're forced to; otherwise they become a target once they're airborne. Their preferred method of escape is to run. This keeps them concealed and takes less energy than the repeated flapping of their wings. Unlike the two of us, who are guests for four days and expect to burn a few calories while out in the field, the birds desire the exact opposite.

Hollis has filled me in on the nature and history of game birds. The rest of my knowledge comes from bits and pieces I've picked up here and there on my own. For example, the grouse is indigenous to North America, but the ring-necked pheasant isn't. They were imported from China, much the same way brown and rainbow trout in the streams west of us were shipped in from Europe over a hundred years ago.

Truck disappears into the hula skirt of waist-high grass. Hollis breaks open his gun—rendering it harmless—and carries it over his shoulder as he would a small child, a firm grip on the barrel where ankles would dangle. I follow suit. Orrin looks back at us and nods to display his approval of our safety measure. On our invisible legs, we weave our way through the field searching for the dog. The golden grass stretches on as far as the eye can see, like crops of wheat in Kansas, toward the firmament of cobalt blue. Big Sky is a good name for Montana. Big Land would be just as relevant. I wish we could stop for a moment. I'd like to take a picture of Truck when he's on to a bird. But the others keep moving, and so do I.

"I see him," Orrin says. "He's on point." Despite the occasional limp, Orrin moves well for a gray-haired man. He's older—in his mid-fifties—but in much better shape than Hollis or myself. Unlike the two of us, he never sits at a desk, which gives him stronger legs from his daily walks in these fields every autumn. This also allows him to travel faster and farther on foot than either of us, even though we are all similar in height (six feet), and three in gait. He is impressive to look at, with his fit body—flat stomach, square shoulders and jaw—donning camo with patches of orange blaze, and carrying only what he needs to hunt game that's as well suited for its environment as he is. Less the dog, I consider the sides to be even.

Hollis and I hustle up to Orrin, where I assume my proper position next to him. I'm winded, still recovering from last night's libations; Hollis, not as much.

"Where is he?" Hollis asks Orrin. I realize I can't see where the dog is, either.

Up ahead on our right, there's a dense thicket that seems to be the object of Orrin's focus. Truck must be somewhere near it.

"See him?" Orrin asks me.

"I don't," I reply. "Do you have him, Hollis?"

Hollis takes two steps forward. "Now I do."

Orrin moves forward and I follow. I see Hollis close the action on his gun and hold it out in front of him with the barrel pointed away from Orrin and me. I can now see the dog and Orrin instructs me to ready my gun. I snap the action shut and double-check the safety.

"We'll walk forward together to flush the bird," Orrin says, outstretching his arms to keep us separated but parallel—the opposite of school children walking single-file, hand in hand. As we approach the thicket I can't help but realize the obvious juxtaposition between hunter and prey—the bird practically invisible attributed to the camouflage nature gave it, the three of us wearing our hunting caps and jackets displaying bright orange patches for all to see. But there isn't anyone else around to see us—not for miles. This place feels more isolated and remote than the dirt roads we traveled to get here.

I notice Hollis raising his gun a few inches with each forward step we take. I feel I should do the same, but first I ask aloud: "Should I mount my gun?"

"Not until I tell you to," Orrin says. "I told you that back at the ranch."

His tone makes me uncomfortable, as I must make him. I brush it off—brush *him* off—but it's not that easy to do. I've agreed to pay him and his employer—Little Wing Ranch—three thousand a day to walk their grounds, hunt their wild birds, dine, drink, and sleep in their exclusive confines that cater to only six hunters at a time. Hollis said we were lucky to get in on such late notice, although it required him to pull some strings with the owner with whom he had some sort of connection. Return customers get first dibs, he'd said, and those who have been here before always come back. I imagine my own customers would never return if I spoke to them the way Orrin just spoke to me. *He is who he is*, I say to myself. *Put yourself in his shoes. He knows a gun is in a beginner's hands.* I get where he's coming from and try to focus on where we're headed, which is straight for the bird I still cannot see.

"Get with the program," Hollis says, and he winks. In reply, I flip him off.

From where the dog is on point, the pheasant should be less than twenty feet away. But it's veiled to me, and my sight is almost as good as Hollis's, a forty-six-year-old man—spectacles free. It's that well camouflaged in the brush. Truck, though, seems to have x-ray vision in his nose, which tunnels his eyes like a scope on a rifle.

Aware of each other's presence, the bird and dog now play the hand they've been dealt. The bird chooses to run. It sounds like more than one. Or it could be the slight wind out of the north that rustles the grass and undergrowth. There is still much for me to learn. The dog gives chase. "I saw them," Hollis says. "It's a pair of grouse."

"They're pheasant," Orrin says, correcting him. "Two hens." From the sound of it, he doesn't much like Hollis, either. This makes me feel better only in the sense that misery loves company.

"Getting sloppy in your old age, H-Bomb," I say in reference to his "undisclosed" nickname from college whenever I want to even the score, like our late-night ping-pong battles on Daufuskie Island, when (on rare occasions) I've gotten the better of him.

The terrain becomes hillier, with patches of grass as thick as horse mane. It doesn't slow Orrin down, though. Not a bit. I scramble to keep up with Hollis who scrambles to keep up with man and his best friend. Before Orrin has a chance to look back at me, I remember to break open the action on my gun and carry it over my shoulder. I'm a good student, and I'm now one step ahead of my friend in gun safety and terrain coverage. In preparation for the climb up the hill, Hollis breaks open the action on his gun. Orrin is already at the top, waiting for us.

"Hustle up," he calls below. "Truck's on point."

It's turning out to be more work than I thought. Hollis told a tale of birds everywhere that we'd shoot at all day long. In truth, we have walked much more than we have shot. In fact, we haven't fired once, and it's been an hour. *That's okay*, I reassure myself. *I'm not here for the hunt. It's not what this is all about. Enjoy the moment, the time with your friends, the food and drinks soon to come, including Wes and Rob's arrival.* I reach Orrin at the top of the rolling hill, where all of Montana comes into view once more.

Hollis joins us, and we hurry down the backside of the ridge. In the flatland near a solitary tree, Truck has either located the hens on the run or an entirely new bird. Orrin repeats the drill with his outstretched arms, and we make our approach parallel to each other.

"Go ahead and close your gun," Orrin says to me, and I do as he instructs.

I come to the conclusion that Truck amazes me even more than the landscape which I already find so out of this world. At a forty-five-degree angle to us, he faces our quarry, and this time I see it too: a ring-necked pheasant. It's not the hens. He's onto a different bird. I like this. Out with the old, in with the new. It's a good-sized animal, with a long tail equal in length to its body. Its ruby, copper, and sapphire markings are beautiful, and the white ring around its neck gives it the collared look of a cleric. For a moment, I question my ability to shoot it; not my talent, or lack of talent that involves a firearm and an object flung into the air. I know the answer to that question: three out of twenty-five on the skeet course at Hollis's gun club. But I've never killed anything in my life, not counting the lightning bugs we caught as kids and smeared on the sidewalk of our Detroit suburb to make them glow.

"See the rooster?" Orrin asks me.

His drill-instructor voice ends my internal debate. "I got him."

I assume Hollis has it in his sights too. Orrin doesn't question him. At least, not in the same way he questions me. The man must sense that he doesn't have to hold my friend's hand, or perhaps, for some other reason, he prefers to leave him be.

The stationary bird takes a step forward and stops. The movement of its head, neck, body, and legs is similar to that of a chicken, which makes my decision to shoot it less guilt-ridden. I eat chicken twice a week. I'll eat this one tonight.

Dressed to the nines, the pheasant doesn't want to fly, but he doesn't want to run, either. Just like Truck, he stands his ground. But unlike the stationary animals, the three of us advance toward the dog and bird.

"Mount your gun," Orrin tells me. Hollis still holds his out in front of his chest and belly. I assume Orrin knows Hollis is a seasoned veteran and with one quick motion can mount his gun, aim, turn off the safety, and fire. But to do all of that in a moment's notice is too much for me to think about and accomplish as a rookie, so he simplifies things for me. He knows how fast wild birds can get up in the air and be gone; I don't.

We are now almost parallel with Truck. Orrin stands by his side. I'm astounded that the bird hasn't made a dash for freedom, and that the dog has remained motionless for as long as it has.

"Pretty cool, huh?" Hollis says.

I make no reply. There are too many other things for me to concentrate on. For better balance, I reposition my feet to withstand the kick of the gun that I know is on the horizon. As I plant my left foot, I step on a fallen twig that's buried in the grass. It cracks. The crackle spooks a nearby rabbit from its hiding place. It runs toward the bird it doesn't know is there. The dog runs toward both, and the bird takes off. I take off the safety. The bird is now under the bead at the end of the upper barrel on my gun; the way Hollis had taught me to aim. It flies to the right of twelve o'clock, which makes him my target. In my excitement, and my desire to not miss and earn the praise of my companions, I squeeze the trigger. But I squeeze too early and I know it, but it's too late. Orrin had instructed us to wait until we could see the bird completely surrounded by blue sky before firing at it. A moment before I pull the trigger I see grass in my field of vision and, without warning, the top of Truck's head as he leaps for the bird. There's nothing I can do. I can't retrieve the birdshot any more than I can change its trajectory. In less than a fraction of a second I hear and feel the explosion of the gunshot, but it is nothing compared to the sound that follows: the simultaneous wail of the dog and flutter of the bird's crippled wings as both animals go down.

The dog is louder than anything I've ever heard. Even louder than the jet engines on the planes I sell. It yelps and yelps as Orrin rushes toward him. Blood shoots out the left side of his head and mouth as his hind legs kick into nothingness as if he's trying to run for his life. But he's on his side and doesn't go anywhere. Orrin reaches him and falls to his knees, blocking my view. I remain standing behind him, watching the blaze orange shoulder patches of Orrin's camo jacket rise and fall in unison with the man's sobs. At least, I think he's sobbing. At this moment I can only hear Truck's siren-like howling. The sound is gut-wrenching.

"Oh my God, Orrin. I'm ... so ... sorry." I'm in shock at what I've done. Nobody hears me. Truck is all we hear. I say it again and look at Hollis who's focused on the man and his dog.

"I'll run and get the four-wheeler, okay?" Hollis says to our guide, then turns to begin the journey for the makeshift ambulance.

But before the man answers the question he doesn't hear, he gets to his feet and storms toward me. There's no time to react. With his burly hands, he grabs for my gun. Out of instinct, I pull back and hold it firmly.

"Give me your fucking gun," he says over the yelp of the dog.

Hollis hears him and rushes to my side. "Don't give it to him."

"Stay out of this," Orrin demands of my friend.

As he continues with his attempt to pry the gun from my hands, my index finger slips through the trigger guard and now I can fire my second shot—in self-defense. But I can't take another man's life unless I'm one hundred percent certain he wants to take mine. Right or wrong, foolish or not, I let go of the gun to avoid another accidental shooting. To defend me, Hollis points his shotgun at Orrin. Orrin looks at Hollis with rage in his eyes for going so far as to bear down on him with his firearm but turns and heads for Truck. With the dog below him, he aims the gun at its ribcage, fires, and the dog's wailing ceases.

Now it's the man's turn to wail. He sobs and lowers the shotgun to the ground. Again, he drops to his knees and lays his body over Truck, the black soles of his boots on full display. I pray with him. I am heartbroken for what I've done and the sorrow I've bestowed upon this man—an infliction of grief as unbounded as this land and sky. I can feel it both inside and out ... where the hair has risen on my arms and the back of my neck.

Hollis and I remain silent and shaken. I sense relief in him—perhaps he senses the same in me—now knowing that the man wanted the gun only to put his dog out of its misery. But my heart still pounds. Maybe it perceives something I don't. It won't slow down. I take several deep breaths while we continue to observe Orrin. He stands up with his back still toward us. He looks down at the dead animal at his feet before he turns and locks eyes with me. His eyes are tinted with fury. Hollis notices this and steps between the two of us, holding his gun near his belly like he'd done while stalking the bird.

"What did I tell you about low shots?" he says to me, as he leans his large body against my friend's.

"I'm sorry. I'm truly, truly sorry." I've never been more sorry.

"You sonofabitch. I told you no low shots!"

"Hold on, Orrin," Hollis says. "It was an accident. Let's be rational about this."

Hollis tries to stand his ground, but Orrin's weight, strength, and rage assist him in pushing Hollis backwards toward me. As stealthily as a professional pickpocket, Orrin reaches into the pouch on Hollis's coat and pulls a shell from it. Hollis doesn't notice Orrin do this, but I do, and it alarms me. I reach for Orrin's hand and grip him by the wrist, which puts the three of us halfway into a bear hug.

"He's grabbed one of your shells," I say to alert my friend and put Orrin on notice.

"Drop it!" Hollis demands.

CHAPTER TWO

Lisa and I never thought we would miss the ocean equally as much as we did our friends, but some things become inseparable over time. Savannah, Georgia, was our home for nearly fourteen years, and Daufuskie Island, South Carolina—a few miles east of us as the crow flies—had been our idea of heaven. That was where we met Hollis and Helen Baumgartner, owners of the cottage next to ours. We spent summer vacations and numerous weekends throughout the year with them. The ages of our children were nearly identical. Our boy, Will, was the same age as their son, Graham. They were three when they met and twelve when they parted ways. Our younger daughter, Jenny, and their daughter, Aimee, had January birthdays, one year apart.

It was a perfect setup there on the island. The only negative was suffering from the aftereffects of alcohol the morning following our occasional evening excesses. The kids had each other for playmates, and Lisa and I had Hollis and Helen. On Fridays, we'd meet at the dock with coolers filled with food and drinks and take the ferry over to the island that was the next one in that barrier chain south of Hilton Head. The mostly undeveloped isle is only accessible by boat. We fell in love with the place because zero bridges meant zero cars, and therefore zero crowds. Daufuskie was rustic, isolated, full of charm, and quiet. The only vehicles with motors on the island were golf carts and lawn mowers. In time, our pair of families became a quartet. Farther down the road from our cottages lived Rob and Jami Henry and their three kids. On the backside of the island was the second home of Wes and Vickie Reardon. At the time of our meeting, Vickie was pregnant with their first child, Brooke.

I'd worked (clawed, actually) my way up the corporate ladder to become an executive of the Gulfstream Aerospace Corporation in Savannah, a town that adopted Lisa and I after we moved there from Grand Rapids, Michigan, where the two of us originally met. Back then, we were both fresh out of school and employed by Steelcase. She designed the furniture, and I sold it—lots of it. One day I was on a plane— bumped up to first class—and struck up a conversation with a guy in the seat next to me. He turned out to be a fellow alumnus of the University of Michigan, as well. He also happened to be the Senior Vice President of Gulfstream. He gave me his business card and asked me to stay in touch. One thing led to another—including my relationship with Lisa—and three years later I was married and on the payroll at Gulfstream.

Hollis was a commodities trader who'd put in his time on the Mercantile Stock Exchange in Chicago, as well as the NYMEX in New York. It was common belief that he'd made a small fortune in futures contracts that involved everything from soybeans to light sweet crude. But he never boasted. He was humble and generous, and lived a semi-retired lifestyle—one we were all jealous of—as a trader who worked from home. I'd never seen an office setup like his; so many computer screens for just one person.

Hollis's path originally began westward across the southern United States. A native of Atlanta, Georgia, he graduated from Millsaps College in Mississippi, and later moved to Houston, Texas, where he worked in the oil industry for ten years. From there, he made a career change and crossed the Mason-Dixon Line to brave the North's harsh winters and the occasional lash of the rough-and-tumble futures business. When he'd had enough and, I presume, made enough, he and Helen scampered home to Georgia to raise their family. "From one jungle to another," he liked to say of their move from the Big Apple to Savannah and Daufuskie. I take comfort in saying it was the best move he ever made. Without him, Will may have never made it out of a riptide that weekend on the island when I was away on business. And for that I'm forever indebted.

That was our life. Those were our friends. As inseparable as forty-somethings raising families could be and as close in ideology and genetics without being related. We all worked hard and played hard, all the time. Until, at the age of forty-eight, I uprooted the family to move to St. Louis to lead a new division of the Boeing Aerospace Corporation. I'd become well versed in the trade of private aircraft sales to individuals and corporations with enormous net worth, and now Boeing wanted me to do the same with 737s. The Saudi kings and the mega rich were no longer content with Gulfstream IVs and the new V. Boeing saw the trend as a cash cow and hired me to milk it.

We were sitting around the Henrys' fire pit on Daufuskie one April night, while the kids chased crabs on the beach with their flashlights, when I broke the news. I think they all suspected something as soon as I pulled out the bottle of Patrón and the eight rocks glasses I'd rounded up from the Henrys' kitchen.

"Lisa and I have some news," I said as I began to pour a couple ounces into each glass.

"Hey, not to steal your thunder or anything, but Helen and I have some news of our own," Hollis said. "Yesterday marked the day that she's one year cancer-free."

Wes was the first person to raise his glass and say "Cheers." We all followed suit and knocked back the liquor with rounds of congratulations and big smiles, Helen's being the largest.

"Sorry for the interruption, Garrett" Hollis said.

"Quite all right," I replied.

"Now tell us your news," he said. "Is it good or bad?"

"Both," I replied. "Kind of like this tequila."

I poured another round, and when all the drinks were ready and in the hands of our best friends, Lisa began to tear up.

"Is Garrett pregnant?" Rob chimed in. Everyone laughed. Lisa wiped her eye.

"I wish," I told them. "We're moving to St. Louis." Except for the crackle of some old timber, there was dead silence. "Bottoms up."

I threw back the poison.

"No . . . fucking . . . way," Hollis said in disbelief.

"Boeing made me an offer I couldn't refuse."

With some hesitancy, everyone else knocked back their own shots. Lisa began to cry and the other girls joined her.

The wives formed a huddle on the south side of the fire. We husbands took the north.

"Congratulations," Wes said, then Hollis and Rob each gave me a pat on the back as I went into more detail regarding the Boeing opportunity. Being businessmen themselves, they understood why I consented to leave Georgia for the unknown on the banks of the Mississippi: money, and lots of it. That's the honest truth. I never thought I could be bought, but apparently I could.

"We're keeping our place here on Daufuskie, though," I informed them. That was the only condition Lisa required to agree to Boeing's offer, which was perfectly fine with me. She could take the kids there in summer and I could fly back and forth to be with them as much as possible.

Unfortunately none of this came even close to happening. And I have lain awake a century of nights in search of some sort of explanation, other than the one I will always accept full responsibility for. My family had everything they could've possibly ever wanted, and more. And for more of what we didn't need, I chased a dream that turned into a nightmare; the kind you have with one eye open. In time, this came to be how every member of my family would sleep.

After our better halves went inside, the four of us walked down to the beach to put a bigger dent in the bottle and check on the kids. We plopped down in the sand. As I looked up, I saw that the stars were out by the millions, like dollar signs at Boeing. But as I look back, all that glitters isn't gold.

"I propose a toast," Hollis said. We raised our shot glasses. "To a Montana hunting trip every fall."

"Mandatory attendance," Wes said.

"I'm in," Rob announced, and he raised his glass higher than everyone else's. It was easy for him, being six feet, four inches tall.

"Wouldn't miss it for the world," I declared.

"It's about the only thing he won't miss," Hollis said. "I've seen him shoot."

CHAPTER THREE

Orrin breaks free and backs away from us. Sweat streams down the side of his face. His hat lies on the ground, knocked off by the scuffle. Silver-streaked, his long hair shines like tinsel in the sun. He stands there in his camo jacket and pants, catching his breath. I try to calm him down.

"Orrin," I say, "I will do whatever I can to resolve this for you."

"There's no dog like Truck. You don't fucking get it, do you?"

"I understand where you're coming—"

"No, you don't."

I don't reply. He is in an irrational state of mind and I'm convinced any attempt on my part to pacify him will fail. Far better to say nothing and just leave him alone.

He turns and looks at Truck. I imagine he is also looking at the gun lying next to the carcass.

"Please put the shell down," Hollis says.

Orrin looks like he's standing on the edge of a cliff, trying to make up his mind about what to do next. He sways back and forth in the light wind like the prairie grass which surrounds him and continues looking back and forth between his dog and my gun. I'm convinced that lodged in his mind is the thought of lunging for the twenty-gauge because he still holds the shell in his beefy left hand.

He squares up to us, and seemingly out of left field says, "You owe me ten thousand dollars."

"Fine," I reply without batting an eye, in an attempt to defuse the situation and safely make it back to the lodge.

"And a new dog."

"Okay."

"No," Hollis says, "that's not okay, Orrin." Hollis's pride has gotten the better of him. "Ten thousand and a new dog is out of line. You know that."

"What do you know about dogs?"

"Enough to know that the replacement cost of one is only five grand."

I get nervous all over again when Orrin turns his back to us and once more gazes down at the spot where the dead dog and the firearm lie next to each other. It wouldn't disturb me as much if the ammunition wasn't in his hand. But it is, and the sunlight flickers off the brass part of the shell, reminding us of what could be.

I can tell by Orrin's body language that he is upset with Hollis's position on the matter. I want to intervene to let Hollis know that I will write the check. It's just money and I have plenty of it. Besides, we could always renegotiate back at the lodge, or in a court of law. Anything would be better than the situation we're in right now. But, right or wrong, I say nothing, and keep my thoughts to myself, thoughts that include my knowledge of Hollis's Deep Southern lineage that's a breed apart when push comes to shove. He's in his element here; I'm not. Mine is the office tower or hangar, so I remain silent and let Hollis negotiate fair compensation for Orrin's loss.

"No amount of money can replace what you've taken from me," Orrin tells us.

Then why did you ask for the ten grand? I can tell Hollis is thinking the same thing. But I'm quick to answer my own question: he's outraged and can't think straight. I understand this. He's in tremendous pain. I feel it too, for what I've done to him. Lisa and I love our own dog. Our kids love him. To lose Friday would crush us. There is no need for me to walk a mile in this man's shoes.

"I don't know what to say," I tell him, "other than I'm sorry and I'll make restitution."

"We can work this out," Hollis adds.

"He was everything to me," Orrin says, not in sadness but in anger, as he turns to face us. "The hours and hours I spent training him, and all the days we spent in these fields together for the last nine years. And every night curled up at my feet as we slept. Tell me what that's worth." While he vents, we say nothing. He gives Hollis a long, cold stare, then me. "You come out here with all your money and think you can do whatever you want. I know your type—especially you, Hollis."

What Orrin specifically means by this, I don't know, but he's going in the wrong direction and Hollis tries to prevent him from going any further. "It's time to head back to the lodge," Hollis says. It's slight—only an inch or two—but I see Hollis's gun barrel rise. Perhaps a subtle reminder to Orrin that we aren't defenseless.

Orrin takes a deep breath, exhales, and steps backward—away from us and closer to the gun. He rotates to face Truck's body once more.

"I know there's got to be some way to settle this amicably," I say.

Orrin's shoulders slump, which seems out of place for a man like him, and he looks up at the sky. I think he says, "There's only one way." But he speaks his words upward and without much force, so I'm not entirely sure. He takes two short steps and drops to his knees next to Truck and the gun, still holding the shell in his hand. In a language that sounds tribal, he begins to chant with his arms outstretched toward the heavens and tilts his head back. When the chanting stops, he returns to earth from his ceremony and leans forward toward the gun next to his right knee.

"Don't you dare touch that gun," Hollis warns him.

He ignores Hollis. With his left hand, he reaches for the stock. He lifts it from the ground. While still on his knees, he uses his thumb to push the lever on the action to break open the gun. In this position, it can be loaded to harm us . . . or himself, which I now consider to be a possibility. I assume Hollis does, too.

"Last warning," Hollis says. He switches off the safety to his own gun, and the click punctuates his command.

I can't believe things have escalated this far; as far as life and death. I begin to panic. Unarmed, I don't know if I should rush Orrin or run away from him. Hollis trains his gun on the man like a bird he wishes would fly. But I know that's the last thing he wants to happen. We both want to resolve this in a peaceful manner, though it appears our thoughts have become the past tense of wishful thinking, because Orrin chambers the round and snaps the barrel to close the action. The gun can now be fired. It's a time bomb with a lit fuse. He's a time bomb. A simple twist of his body and a pull of the trigger—should the man choose those actions—is all it would take to end Hollis's or my time on this earth as a husband and father.

"Put it down!" The agony in Hollis's directive is palpable.

Orrin's movement of his arms and torso to reposition the firearm—a position we're uncertain of—forces Hollis and me to make a split-second decision. I try to speak, to plead with Orrin one last time, to plead with Hollis to consider all the possibilities of what might be occurring, but I can't put my thoughts into words because my mind is only concerned with my body, and my body has begun to run for its life at a full sprint. On the balls of my feet I hear the explosion but don't see it. The sound of the shot seems to propel me through the air as I leap, like that pheasant I dropped. Stunned to be unharmed and still able to breathe after landing, I turn to see that Hollis is unscathed as well.

Everything now feels as if it's happening in slow motion. I come to a complete stop and face what I had hoped to leave behind. My eyes follow the direction Hollis's barrel points, zeroing in on a man with a bloodied back lying face down on the ground. Like his dog, Orrin has been mortally wounded, but I won't know this until three incredibly long seconds pass. Time seems to stretch out around me. Instead of the moment it takes to call out "Mississippi" between numbers, I feel I'm crossing the river itself. When the moment finally arrives, I witness Orrin's body breathe its last, deflate, and become lifeless. The sight is grim. What's worse is how his body is slumped over Truck, giving the appearance of some awful deceased human-animal hybrid, the dog's limbs sticking out from underneath, and the barrel of the gun looking like a fifth leg. Hollis and I stare with our mouths open in disbelief. We glance at each other, frozen in time that we know will never pass the same for either of us ever again. Until, as though the flip of a switch, everything reverts to Greenwich Mean Time and Hollis beats me to Orrin's side, lays his gun in the grass, and turns the body over, revealing closed eyes and parted lips, where blood drips from the corner of and drops onto the soil.

"Jesus Christ," I murmur.

Hollis feels the neck for a pulse, but there is none. With one hand over the other he begins to pump the chest in order to try and start the man's heart. Over and over, my friend labors with the emergency procedure while I pray that Orrin can be brought back to life.

"Come on," Hollis pleads. He straddles the man's abdomen and presses up and down just below the sternum. "Come on, come on."

But his efforts are in vain. The man has been dead for well over two minutes, all the while having his chest pumped by Hollis. He's not coming back. Not to this earth. Still, something tells Hollis not to give up. He carries on, to the brink of exhaustion, then catches his breath and gives it one last attempt. After five quick pumps, he leans in close to listen to the man's open mouth, but there is no sign of life. He then removes himself from atop Orrin's body and collapses on the ground next to him.

This can't be happening. The sky is too blue, the grass too golden, the breeze too gentle, the sun too kind. As he lies on his back, Hollis covers his face with his hands. I squat down to be nearer him, to comfort him. He sits up and meets me at eye level. I drape my arm over his shoulder; a shoulder that trembles.

"You did everything you could."

"I don't know . . ."

"No, you did."

He removes his hat and runs his fingers through his straight brown hair. "Fuck." With each stroke, he repeats the expletive more loudly.

"It's going to be okay, Hollis."

"What did I just do?"

"It's all right. We'll work it out."

"Oh shit, this is really fucked up."

"Just take it easy for a second."

"I can't. I can't believe what just happened," he says. He places his fingertips against his temples. "No, no, no. This is not good, Garrett. You have no idea how bad this is."

He's correct. I don't have a clue. But my outlook isn't as ominous. I don't see an act of self-defense in that light. "Take a deep breath," I say. "You didn't have a choice, right?"

"What do you mean by that?" he asks.

"By what?"

"You said 'right'." He looks at me like an acquaintance instead of the close friend that I am. "Didn't you see it?"

"Yeah. I mean, I saw him turning toward us with the gun."

My reply doesn't appear to satisfy him, so he asks: "How far did he turn?"

"I don't know. That's when I started running."

"Oh, this is fucked up."

"It's not."

"Yes it is, because in my defense you can't say whether or not I was justified to shoot a man in the back, can you?"

"You did what you thought you had to do and so did I. That's why I ran." We are face-to-face. "There's no questioning we were in fear for our lives."

"But there will be."

"Well, if that happens, then we'll just tell the truth." He stares at me, expressionless. I've never seen him this way. "We need to dial 911."

"And what are we going to tell them? That I shot our hunting guide in the back because I thought he was going to shoot you for killing his dog?"

We are both shaken. As shaken as I am, I understand the hesitancy on his part to call the authorities. But I don't want to do anything other than get them involved as soon as possible. The sooner the better.

"You were protecting me and had no other choice," I say with conviction. "It's the truth."

"We need to think about this."

I don't think there's anything to think about other than to report what has just taken place, to be truthful and explain why Hollis had no choice but to defend himself—and me— against an armed man who was enraged by the accidental shooting of his bird dog. I'm stuck on the truth. A loss of human life has occurred. I see no other avenue to go down. "We did what we had to do," I say, careful to choose *we* instead of *you*. I will not abandon my friend like that.

"I pulled the trigger," he says. "And I don't even remember squeezing it. It just went off."

"Either way, you were acting in self-defense." I console him, the friend who possibly saved my life. The man who saved my son's. The man who recently lost his father.

"I don't know."

"What do you mean?" But I do know what he means—at least, I think I do.

"I can't say for sure what I was doing."

"Are you saying that because you aren't sure what *he* was doing?"

"Maybe so."

"Do you think he was suicidal?" I get it out on the table. It'd been in the back of my mind too.

"He could've been, I guess."

"Hard to believe a man would kill himself over the loss of his dog."

"I know," he replies. He pauses, looks down at the grass, and picks a blade. "Then maybe the outcome was inevitable."

I hadn't thought about it like that, and the thought pushes me even further into my friend's corner and strengthens my belief we've done nothing wrong and should do nothing other than call 911.

"You had every right to pull the trigger. Let's make the call."

"I think you might be too naïve about this, Garrett. I could be in some serious shit."

We both stand and move away from the corpse and the carcass. But the added distance only fuels the remorse for the loss of life I feel responsible for. Tremors set in. I bend over and place my hands on my knees. I'm overwhelmed with guilt and sorrow and pity, and remnants of alcohol from the previous evening. The intensity grows as I imagine the family that the man belongs to—the family members who will be far more distraught than Hollis and I are—when they learn of his death. A sensation of nausea followed by another round of shakes keeps my hands on my knees, and when I glance at the hole in Orrin's back, the contents from my stomach shoot out of my mouth. My abdomen contracts and expels several times.

I wipe my mouth and nose with my coat sleeve and return to an upright position. "Sorry."

Hollis comes to my aid. "No, *I'm* sorry," he says. We lean on each other. We need each other. Then he steps back and reaches out to put his hand on my shoulder. "We need to think about this clearly, okay?"

"Okay," I respond. But there's nothing to think about other than what happened. "Hollis, you saved my life. It's the truth." I pull out my phone. I want to call 911. Time to do it.

"Hang on a second," Hollis says.

There's no signal. We're in the middle of nowhere Montana. Even at the lodge the reception is weak.

"You're thinking the worst," I say. "You didn't do anything wrong."

I try to reassure him that we need to do the right thing and get in touch with the authorities right away. We need to head back to the ATV and return to the lodge to get help.

"Nobody is going to help anyone who's shot a man in the back," he says. "This is Montana."

"And Montana is part of the United States. We're not in some third-world country."

"Okay, let's say we tell them what happened. We tell the truth, and for whatever reason they doubt our story."

"I hear you. Go on." I'm confident that whatever he says I can refute.

"And the big doubt being the hole in Orrin's back that screams for retribution from a jury of our 'peers.' And they all live around here, and they're up in arms over what's happened. And they don't take too kindly to our kind from back east who come out here with the kind of money they can only dream of ever having. See where I'm going?" I nod and he continues. "And the prosecutors think, at the minimum, it's involuntary manslaughter and they could win a conviction against me on this and bring justice for their constituents."

"Hold on, Hollis. That doesn't make any sense. Think about it. There's no reason for us to shoot our hunting guide. There's no motive. It makes no sense that we would intentionally harm the man, or even involuntarily, unless we had reason to fear for our lives. They'll understand this. I'm sure they will."

He looks at me. I imagine I see more of the man of reason I've always known than the irrational person talking nonsense to me. And at the same time, I see we've drifted beyond the scene of the accident as we crest a slight ridge where the grass plains spill into a valley with a river and railroad tracks zippered down the middle of it.

"I'm not so sure of that at all," he says. "How would you feel if you were in my shoes?" I have no response. "Can you imagine not being able to return home to Lisa, Will, and Jenny? To be incarcerated and having to stand trial? To lose everything? And what about Helen's remission? I can't put her through something like this. It would be too much. No way, Garrett. No way."

"I get where you're coming from," I say, and I do, which makes it tougher and tougher for me to do the right thing. I love the man. He's one of the best things to ever happen to me. His wife and kids, too. And because of this I become more emotional and less logical, though not without a fight. "I would never let anything happen to you guys. We're in this together."

"I don't want to chance it."

"It's not about chance. It's facts and reason and I saw what happened. You have a witness."

"One that can talk, and one that no longer can," he replies. "I worry about what that says. And you didn't see all of it."

"I saw enough to know there's nothing to worry about. We need to call the police."

He reaches for my arm and takes hold of it. We stop. He shakes his head. "We can't do that."

"Why not?"

"We just can't."

"Are you talking about getting cellular reception out here, or something else?" I don't want it to be anything other than a technological inability to use our phones, but it is. I can see it written all over his face.

"It's something else." He stands and puts his hat on. I straighten as well. "Let's talk over here."

Hollis finds a small patch of prairie where the grass is stunted, and he sits down. I join him there, arms locked around bent knees, our backs to the deceased.

"Tell me what's on your mind, Hollis."

"This goes no further than the two of us, okay?"

"I promise."

He takes a deep breath and momentarily holds it as if to clear his mind. "There's more to the Little Wing Ranch than meets the eye. The same goes for me."

Chapter Four

Hollis plans the trip. He's hunted birds all his life, so he knows where and when to take us. It will be the third week in October. That's the best time, he tells us. The weather is perfect because it's not too hot and not too cold. The dog and hunter can go all day. He sends us an email with a link to the ranch's website. From a structural standpoint, the lodge at Little Wing is smaller than expected, but it's stunning in design and architecture. Hollis says it's one of the best upland hunting lodges in the entire West, if not the world. Luxury accommodations on 12,000 acres of prime hunting grounds and caters to a maximum of just six guests at a time. Each hunter has the equivalent of almost two thousand acres all to himself. It's more than anyone needs, but better too much than not enough, Hollis implies. From the pictures, the stone-and-timber lodge and six guest cabins sit in the middle of (nowhere) Montana in a sea of golden grass, only three and a half hours from Little Bighorn Battlefield National Monument—a place I'd always wanted to visit. The domain is like something out of a fairy tale, and so the junket is an easy sell to the four of us. The package includes transportation to and from the airport, four days hunting/five nights private cabin lodging for each of us, three gourmet meals per day, and open bar nightly in the lodge. At three thousand per person per day, it's by no means an inexpensive "boys' trip," but we're all doing well financially and none of us balk at the price. The trip will be good for us; even better for Hollis, whose father has lost his battle from complications of a stroke. The two of them made an annual pilgrimage each fall to the fields in the Dakotas and Montana, where they spent a week together hunting birds, for twenty years straight. And now the torch will be passed to us. We're happy to carry it and become part of that legacy.

Hollis and I meet in Sidney, Montana the night before Wes and Rob are due to arrive the next afternoon. They have last-minute business to attend to and can't make it out there until Thursday, which causes them to forfeit one day's hunt and one night's room and board. But it's clear the negotiations they're engaged in are profitable enough for them to afford the $3,000 loss. In truth, we all could afford it. That's not to be taken as conceit or bravado. It's just that we'd all worked hard to become successful and this was how we conducted ourselves. Within reason, we could come and go as we pleased. But eating three grand would never sit well enough for me to in fact do something like that, so I'm there on time, forty minutes after Hollis's arrival at the airport, and ready to get what I paid for so handsomely.

He stands in his worn corduroys and barn coat with his hard-shell gun cases under each arm like crutches and a large beige duffle at his feet. He sees me and waves. There's an older man beside him wearing a green plaid long-sleeve shirt under a suede vest, jeans, and a tan cowboy hat. A thick mustache is as white as his hair. Hollis smiles back at me. It's the best smile this side of the Big Muddy (and the other side when he's on it).

Traffic is light in the baggage claim area as we approach each other and embrace. It's so good to see my old friend.

He still looks the same: the epitome of success. Over the last six months his chestnut brown hair has thinned a bit, but he compensates for the loss with an increase in length. In a well-trained manner, it stays combed behind his ears—where a hint of gray shows—ending in baby curls. We are twins in this regard. But I am two inches taller and twenty pounds heavier than his six-foot frame. It's not muscle, though. Or not as much muscle. He's solid; I'm not. But I was at one time. We step back and look each other in the eye. His are the steel blue of aircraft skin. Mine are dark brown and weathered like my wallet. I'm the product of an Italian mother and have more of her Roman features than the Anglo-Saxon ones of my father. Hollis looks more related to my father than I do.

"Great to see you," I tell him.

"The pleasure is all mine," he replies. "Lawton, this is my good friend, Garrett Ingram."

Lawton Mills is the owner of Little Wing Ranch. He's come to pick us up and take us back to the lodge. His grip is firm, and after he releases my hand, he leans over to help me with my luggage. But I insist on a self-portage of it out to his car. I appreciate good service, but not at an older man's expense.

We load our bags into his Grand Cherokee and off we go. There's a cooler next to me in the backseat and he invites me to open it to grab some drinks. It contains wine and beer. I reach up to the front seat and hand Hollis a Coors, then pull one out for myself.

"There's cheese and crackers, too. Don't be shy," Lawton says into the rearview mirror.

A tray covered with foil rests on the seat next to the cooler. I peel back the Reynold's Wrap.

"I'll take one," Hollis says.

I make two: one for Hollis, one for Lawton.

On the way to the lodge the sun begins to set. It's my first time visiting this part of the country and I absorb it all through my window before the sky blackens. I've never seen any place like it—wide open land shag-carpeted with prairie grass out to the horizon. Clusters of trees dot the landscape but are extremely few and far between.

"How long have you owned the lodge?" I ask Lawton.

"Thirty-five years. But the land's been in my wife's family for a hundred."

"Homesteaders?" I imply.

"Something like that," he says, smiling. In the reflection I can see the ends of his mustache stretch out to the edges of the rearview mirror like the wingspan of a wise old owl.

Hollis changes the subject. "The forecast looks great this week."

"You couldn't have picked a better time to visit," Lawton says.

In what seems like a short amount of time we travel beyond the reach of any municipality, where horses and cattle outnumber homes and people. The surrounding landscape continues to be endless fields of grassland as far as the eye can see, disappearing as it reaches the twilight of the horizon. I'd hoped to glimpse the lodge and our private cabins before nightfall—to put a face with a name upon introduction—but that might have to wait until morning. Thirty minutes into our ride we turn off the paved two-lane county highway onto a single-lane dirt road. We approach a wooden bridge only wide enough for one vehicle to cross at a time and Lawton slows down—almost to a stop—until he's sure there's no oncoming traffic. He honks, then proceeds to cross the span.

"What's the name of this river?" I ask Lawton, pulling the beer away from my lips. I lean towards my window in an attempt to view the river itself, but all I see is the hint of the water's surface, a shade darker than dusk.

"It's the east fork of the Redwater," Hollis says, before Lawton has the chance to answer. "It'll be my eighth straight year of fishing it, right?"

"Eighth or ninth," Lawton replies.

"Figures you'd pick a ranch where you can hunt *and* fish," I say.

"Field and stream: the best of both worlds . . . and, of course, nothing but the best for my friends."

"Thanks for 'looking out' for us." He knows I would rather play a set or two of tennis than play a fish. Wes would feel the same way. Rob, on the other hand, would be happy to join Hollis.

I see the corner of Hollis's smile on the left side of his face, illuminated by the instrument panel, and realize I can read his mind like a book. His thought is that each day, when our hunt is over, he'll get Lawton to outfit us with gear from the lodge so we can all head down to the river to fish, which I'm okay with, since literally I'm just along for the ride. It's all about being together, I remind myself as I bring the beer back to my mouth. After two big swallows, the bottle is almost empty.

After traveling for five miles along the dirt and gravel road, I spot what appears to be the lodge up ahead. It's now completely dark outside and only the silhouette of the structure is visible until our headlights get close enough to light it up. The stone-and-timber building is an architectural masterpiece. The pictures I'd seen do not even come close to doing it justice. The cabins—still in the shadows—are on its right flank and appear to be of similar design. Miniature duplicates, perhaps.

As we approach the compound, the road returns to asphalt, quieting our arrival and making our ride in the vehicle smooth once again. A flagpole—outfitted with the stars and stripes—sits in the center of a grass island that we begin to circle. A quarter of the way around it counterclockwise, we exit onto another paved drive that leads toward the cabins. Now center stage, it's clear the accommodations are replicas of the main lodge, which provides for a nice welcome. The "home away from home" intent is much appreciated.

In front of each of the six cabins is a small parking space and Lawton pulls into the first one. He parks the Jeep and we all get out. Hollis, still holding his second beer, begins to stretch. Like a contagious yawn, I do the same. It's been a long day of travel for both of us.

An older woman with ivory hair steps through the front door of the lodge and walks our way. She travels along the edge of the circular drive where the landscape lights dot the perimeter of the grass island, their beams trained on the flag. She joins us by the rear of the Jeep.

"Hollis and Garrett," Lawton says, "I'd like you to meet my wife, Dolores."

She smiles from above the collar of the red wool coat wrapped around her. Being somewhat plump and rounded like her husband, the image of Mrs. Claus comes to mind.

"I have a wonderful supper for you tonight," she tells us in the glow of the front porch light of Cabin #1. "Sure hope you gentlemen brought your appetites."

We did. Rack of lamb, wild rice, asparagus, and lobster bisque are on the menu. There's also trout, should either of us prefer fish for the main course. She hands us the keys to our respective cabins and lets us know the bar is open.

I'm placed in Cabin #2. It's not a cabin. It's plush. *Well done, Hollis.* I wheel my duffle to the bedroom. Along the way I stop and grab a beer from the fridge. Everything's inclusive, and they truly have everything. Several bottles of bourbon and vodka are on the counter next to the fridge, as well as every type of snack and cheese you could want. The furniture has a slightly western feel, but with a greater touch of Ralph Lauren. It's all high-end bark frame and fine leather on the chairs and sofa, with thick wool blankets draped over them. The stone fireplace is the centerpiece. Made of river rock, it towers up and through the vaulted ceiling.

After a quick shower, I head to Hollis's cabin, but he is at my door before I can exit mine.

"What do you think of the place?" he asks.

"First class, just like you promised."

Dressed in jeans, old duck boots, and a black Patagonia fleece, Hollis stands holding a bottle of Woodford and insists we do a shot before we head for the bar.

"What time do we have to be up in the morning?" I ask, the hint in my words loud and clear.

"Eight-ish," he replies. He sees the fearful look on my face and smiles. "Don't worry, I'll go easy on you."

His hollow leg gives him the usual advantage. The last thing I want is to be hungover in the morning and walk mile after mile with gun in hand like a wounded soldier. But I knew going into this that could be the case, thus I succumb and grab two glasses. Hollis pours.

"To lots of birds," he says. "Bottoms up."

CHAPTER FIVE

I hear something. This happens sometimes when I dream, but dreams are rare for me due to what little sleep I get. As with most interrupted nights (to the best of my knowledge), I lie awake. The sound is faint but increases in volume as it climbs the ivy, which clings to the exterior stone of our home, and enters our bedroom through the lead-paned window—perhaps having traveled all the way from the foundation.

Our home—in the St. Louis suburb of Ladue—has a stairwell outside that leads down to a basement door two levels below the bed Lisa and I share. A drain—covered with pine needles, twigs, and early-spring droppings this time of year—is centered at the bottom of that landing and can back up in heavy rains. It's raining, and I debate whether or not to get out of bed and go outside to remove the debris so the water doesn't back up. When that happens, it seeps underneath the door and floods our basement like it did last autumn. I shouldn't have to deal with this, though. Not in the middle of the night, at least. The stairwell should've been swept clean days ago by one of my kids. It's their job to do this. It was mine at my home in Northville—a suburb of Detroit—when I was their age. Our Tudor is large and needs to be maintained, more than ever in spring and autumn when the droppings clog the gutters and drains. I could pay to have the home serviced, but I have two kids who need to learn to be responsible and help around the house.

They aren't as responsible as I'd like, though; and I know they haven't swept the stairwell.

I sit up when I hear another sound. *This is not a dream.* By routine, I feel my face. It's dry and I welcome the peacefulness of an evening without cold sweat. Still, something has awakened me. Lisa is asleep and doesn't respond to my whispering her name. Apparently she also doesn't hear the rain on the slate roof and copper gutters that diminishes my ability to hear most anything else. But with perfect stillness and great concentration I pick up on the sound that isn't part of the storm: the muffled thump of a heartbeat that isn't mine, or my wife's. I turn my head and am able to zero in on the sound, filtering through the noise of the downpour and determine its source is the basement door. Something is attempting to force it open. I hear it again. Thirty seconds later, as I am sitting in the dark on the edge of the bed trying to determine if maybe I'm just hearing things, the home alarm erupts into a high-pitched wail that echoes the yelping of the dog I shot five months ago.

Someone is in the house. While the alarm continues, I spring to my feet in my boxers. Lisa, now fully awake, is one step behind. My first thought is the kids, but they've beaten me to it as they race through the darkness of the second-floor hallway and into our master bedroom. We corral them there. From the safe on the lower shelf of the nightstand, I grab the gun and turn on the lamp.

I can see the fear in Lisa's eyes having to do with Will and Jenny's proximity to the firearm. I firmly hold the grip of the gun and am sure to point the muzzle in the opposite direction of my family. On the nightstand by her side of the bed, she reaches for the key fob that controls the home alarm.

I tell her not to turn it off. As disturbing as the noise is, I know it's our best defense.

"What's going on, Dad?" my frightened baby girl asks.

"Everybody, stay here."

Just as I begin to head toward the door to confront the threat before it reaches the second floor, the phone behind me rings. I turn and see Lisa answer it.

To be heard over the alarm, she shouts into the receiver, "Send the police right away!"

Will sits next to his sister—who's begun to cry—on the bed and wraps his arms around her. He shakes his head at me and beckons me to come back. I silently tell him no and open the bedroom door. Just before stepping through, I twist the latch on the doorknob, locking it from the inside, then step through and pull the door shut behind me.

Outside the bedroom everything is pitch-black, which is good. This gives me the advantage. I'm nocturnal because I know every part of my home's interior blindfolded. I know the layout of the rooms and the placement of the furniture. I'm in my element. In just a few seconds, my eyes adjust, and I'm ready to continue down the hallway to the steps. Our home is large and contains two stairways. The rear one is located across from the spare bedroom—the original maid's quarters—and leads down to the kitchen. It's narrow, with sharp bends. The other leads to the foyer. I choose the latter because it's less confined, and it's the first one I come to.

At the top of the stairs, I lean over the oak railing. I wait there and watch and listen as the howl of the alarm rises from below and reverberates off the plaster ceiling of the two-story foyer. It's so loud I can't hear anything else, even our dog who I assume is barking in his crate, which (unlike the darkness) puts me at a disadvantage. The loss of one sense, however, necessitates my use of another. I switch the gun to my left hand and place my right on the railing to search for vibrations like an ear resting on a railroad track. I think I can feel his footsteps. Yes, he's running across the wooden floor that rumbles up the handrail to the inside of my chest.

I let go of the rail, grip the gun with both hands, and extend my arms in front of me. From where I stand, it's clear the only route to my family is through me, no matter which stairway he comes up. As I move the gun back and forth to cover both of his possible approaches, I'm charged with adrenaline and ready to fire.

Red, white, and blue lights begin flashing rhythmically through the window above the front door as well as the ones on either side of it. They grow in brightness, and soon the foyer lights up with the colors of the American flag. To avoid becoming a visible target, I lower myself to the floor. From the vicinity of our circular drive I can hear the sound of sirens and screeching tires join the chorus of the alarm. Even though I am visually unable to tell exactly how many vehicles have arrived, I can tell from the cacophony of sounds that there's an army of police out there.

To get a better look, I peer over the rail and can see flashlight beams scurrying across the front lawn. Uncertain of what the police are up to, I stay where I am.

I hear a knock—actually, more like the pounding of a bass drum than a knock—at the front door. To answer it I would have to desert my post, leaving my family vulnerable to anyone who might come up the back stairway. I pause, trying to decide the best course of action to take. A second pounding of the drum (followed by the quick succession of a third and fourth) sends me down the steps.

When I begin to unbolt the door, a voice from the other side demands that I identify myself.

"I'm Garrett Ingram. I live here."

I swing the door open, and two policemen standing in the pouring rain draw their sidearms.

"Drop your weapon!" they both scream over the noise of the alarm. The light from all the vehicles blinds me and I can only think to shield my eyes. But I've forgotten that I am holding a gun. In my moment of disorientation I accidentally raise my hands slightly higher. It's the opposite direction they want my arms and hands to go, and they remind me: "Drop it! Drop it now!"

Before it's too late, I remember what I'm in possession of. I stop the movement, and reiterate, "I'm Garrett Ingram. This is my home." Standing there in my boxers, I must look the part. But they don't care. They just want the gun out of my hands. "My family's upstairs and someone's in the house," I shout, and then lower my firearm, setting it on the floor.

Swift as leopards, they pounce on it and enter with their guns and flashlights leading the way. As I move to the side, the upstairs hallway light turns on, and the siren of the alarm deadens. From the bedroom Lisa calls out to me. Instinctually I rush for the stairway, but a policeman—a large black man—grabs me and prevents me from going anywhere. As he holds me, his partner heads up the stairs two at a time.

"We're coming," I yell up to her.

CHAPTER SIX

With fear and remorse and guilt—for what I assume stems from pulling the trigger—Hollis says, "I've made one too many imprudent trades, Garrett, and I've put myself and my family in deep financial trouble. That's why we're here."

Possibly more startling than the news of my friend's economic dire straits, is the unusual look of defeat in his eyes. Never did I think I would see him this way. Not Hollis, of all people. "Tell me what's going on," I say.

Before he speaks, he looks in the direction of death, as if he can still see it. But he can't. Neither of us can. It's on the other side of the ridge. Maybe its scent though is what tugs at him. Either way, he knows it's there. We both do. As his eyes well up with tears he wipes them away and turns back to me. "I'm in talks with Lawton and Dolores Mills to purchase the Little Wing Ranch from them, with the intent to lease its mineral rights." He further composes himself and awaits my reply.

I take my time digesting the information before responding. "You're a little ahead of me."

"Maybe you've noticed, or maybe you haven't, but all the activity going on around here in Elm Coulee is because Halliburton and Lyco drilled a well 10,000 feet below our very own and struck pay dirt."

"Pay dirt?"

"Yeah, the good kind of dirt—black gold."

"Oil?"

"Shale oil, to be exact." He then stretches out his arms to their extent with his palms facing upward as though testing for rain. "This is all part of the Bakken Formation—millions of barrels of shale oil and billions of cubic feet of natural gas."

I see nothing but prairie grass but know that what Hollis says isn't impossible. In fact, if I didn't know about the dead bodies of the man and his dog just over the crest of the ridge behind us, I would probably doubt their existence as well. But to literally be sitting on a gold mine is the last thing I would ever envision.

The act of dialing 911 continues to repeat over and over in my brain. However, my thoughts become further scrambled as I attempt to calibrate what Hollis is telling me, while in my mind I imagine hearing Orrin's voice from beyond the grave. I do my best to focus on Hollis and try to convince myself that if it weren't for him, it might have been me lying dead on the ground instead of Orrin.

"Okay, I understand the amount of money involved. Connect the dots for me."

"Do you know what a landman is?"

"No."

"When an oil strike occurs, they go around knocking on the doors of property owners to work out leasing deals for their oil companies. If everything goes right, the farmer gives the oil company permission to drill on his property—for a certain amount of time—and in return the oil company pays a royalty to the farmer on all the oil they pump out of the ground."

"I'm following you."

"Well, I've put together a group of investors to purchase Lawton's ranch from him. He knows that he could lease it to any number of the oil guys that have come calling, but he also knows that being on the edge of Elm Coulee creates the risk of them finding lower amounts of oil than expected, or even drilling dry wells. And if either one of those happens, he'll end up with the short end of the stick."

"But you're willing to take that risk?"

"Yes," he replies. "We've offered him an above-market price for his land. And since he's ready to retire and sell the ranch that none of his kids have any interest in running, he's opted for the sure bet. I even pitched it to him in a language I knew he'd respond to: 'a bird in the hand' and all that."

"Okay, I understand the deal. But how does all this relate to that"—I point toward the ridge—"and your reluctance to call the police?"

"Orrin is a Sioux, and I'm bidding against them for the ranch," he explains. "The Fort Peck Reservation, which is home to the Sioux, abuts Lawton's property on its western edge."

I remember seeing it on the map before leaving to come out here. What I didn't know was the ranch was adjacent to it.

"It's one of the largest reservations in the country," Hollis continues. "But the reservation is just northwest of Elm Coulee. There's no oil on reservation land."

"So the Sioux want a piece of the pie, too?"

"They do. But regardless of the oil and gas, Lawton verbally committed to the Sioux years ago that he would sell them the ranch—to own and operate the business—in exchange for them allowing his hunters access to their lands." Hollis once again spreads his arms out toward the horizon and says, "All this prime habitat is what makes the Little Wing the best in the world for pheasant."

"How far along with Lawton are you?"

"Beyond what the Sioux can afford," Hollis replies. "We're almost at the finish line, which I desperately need to cross."

"I see."

"Can you 'see' how the hole I put in Orrin's back is going to look to the Sioux, and those sworn to protect and serve them? Does the phrase 'with intent to do bodily harm' come to mind?"

"I get where you're coming from—I do—but there's a man lying dead thirty feet away from us and I still think we need to report this accident—as tragic as it is—to the police. From everything you've told me, you'll nevertheless end up getting everything you want, and we'll end up having done the right thing. Let's make the call."

"But I haven't told you everything."

"What else is there?"

"Indians are protected by the FBI. If we call the police, they'll notify the feds and there'll be a federal investigation as well, which could take months. During that time my investors walk, and so does Lawton. There's too much at stake for me to let that happen. It was an accident. I was protecting you. Both of us. What's done is done, and nothing can bring him back or change any of this, so let's salvage what there is by burying him and the dog and pretend this never happened." He pauses. "If you want, I'll cut you in on the deal."

"I want to help you, Hollis. I really do, and I'd never want anything in return for doing that." I have zero interest in his business proposition. My interest lies with Hollis's well-being. "It hurts me to see you like this, but what you're asking me to do is something I don't think I'm capable of."

"Then I'll do the digging."

"You know what I mean."

"Garrett, I pulled that trigger to save your life. Think about that for a second." I do, and I see him thinking about it too. "Is it too much to ask you to save my family and me?"

His point is well taken, and then some. His plea is gripping. I think long and hard before finally speaking. "What about Orrin's family?"

"He doesn't have one. He lost his wife and only child years ago in an auto accident."

"How do you know all this?"

"My dad and I heard Lawton talk about it over drinks one night."

With our heads turned away from each other, we silently stare off into the distance. I fight it. Fight him and his plea. "Listen to me," I say, shifting to face him. "If we do anything other than go to the police and tell them the truth, everything we have will be at risk."

"Everything already is for me."

"It isn't. You just think it is. Be rational."

"You're not standing in my shoes. You have no idea what this feels like."

Even though I don't, I think I do. "I won't let anything happen to you."

"That was my exact thought about you a few minutes ago."

I say nothing because there is nothing else I can add. I'm once again overwhelmed by his words and the actions he took to back them up. I lower my head, deep in thought, and stare at the soil and the grass sprouting from it like hair on a scalp. "This is really hard, because I know what the right thing to do is." I reach down and break off a blade the same way Hollis had earlier. "And what makes it even harder is that you mean as much to me as doing it."

He leans toward me. The sun is in his eyes. He squints and they become crescent moons. "I need your help." He speaks with such sincerity that his words chisel and penetrate deep inside me. I love the man—a man I can tell is hurting like never before. "Will you help me?" Again, I am drawn further to his aid by the plea. By the pity. I cannot walk away from him. He did not walk away from my son. He already possesses my heart and soul. It's my guilt that forces me to challenge him orally instead.

"I just can't see myself doing what you're asking me to do."

"Then look at it another way."

"I would if I could."

"You can, Garrett," he says. "The choice is yours. You can choose to help me; Helen, who has fought and battled so hard these past two years; and my children; or you can choose not to. I had to make the same decision when I was on the beach and saw Will in distress. His arms were waving for help. He was struggling to stay afloat. I'm not much of a swimmer, but I didn't hesitate to put myself and my family in harm's way when I swam out to him in that current."

I remember how I cried on the phone when Lisa called and told me the news that day. In my Seattle hotel room, I wept like a baby from the guilt of not being there and the love for Hollis. I was broken then. I am broken now.

"What do you want me to do?"

"I want you to pretend this never happened. We went hunting with Orrin. When we were through, he went his way in his pickup and we went ours in the four-wheeler."

This is the hardest pill to swallow, but I feel myself committing more and more to helping him; to put him first, not myself or my family. I'm so torn, but he continues to present the appearance of a man in need of mercy—which he is—and because Orrin is well beyond that point, there is no reason for the potential for two lives to be lost, excluding Truck's.

I cannot say no to my friend. That's what it all boils down to there in the golden field with the bluest of skies I've ever seen. He stands as he sees the change in my eyes, and I rise with him. He wraps his arms around me and hugs me as though we are father and son. He sheds a tear, and I feel his body shudder—this great, strong man—and it brings me to my knees. I well up too, as we both know each of us is committed to the other for the rest of our lives. But what we don't know is what will happen to us between now and the unforeseeable future, and that alone almost feels more unnerving than the recent events of our day—especially something we could never have dreamed would happen.

He lets go of me and we stand face-to-face. "We need to bury him and the dog, and then drive his pickup down the road and abandon it somewhere."

I see his plan take shape. "How far down the road?"

"At least five miles."

The area is strewn with trails for SUVs and various other off-road vehicles. Where they stretch on to, though, is anyone's guess. In the Little Wing's Polaris, which we drove with the intent to go fishing afterwards, we passed handfuls of them while following Orrin from the ranch to the starting point of our hunt.

"I think we should drive it farther away," I say.

"How far?"

"As far as we can go without the likelihood of being seen."

"How far do you think we are from the lodge?"

"Seven miles."

"And we didn't see anyone on the road the entire way here."

The thought is supportive. There is no one around for miles. We are on the moon. If we drive the pickup far enough away from the bodies, the prospect of the grave ever being found is as remote as the land we stand on. There's too much ground to cover in Big Land Country for that to happen. Hollis takes it a step further to cover our tracks even more, and suggests we drive the pickup into a secluded stretch of the river, which might keep it hidden for weeks, months, years, or forever. And when (or if) they find it, we are long gone and so are the bodies and so is the evidence.

"How deep is the river?" I ask.

"The Redwater has some good pools. The problem with rivers, though, is they attract people. That increases the odds of someone seeing us."

Hollis is the outdoorsman and knows these things. But I still lean toward his idea to drive it into some godforsaken stretch of the river where it might never be found. "What do you think those odds are?"

"I don't exactly know." His wheels turn some more. "Probably slim to none after sunset."

"And if his pickup is ever found, wouldn't it appear to be an accident?"

"It would, especially if a window is rolled down or shattered, and it looks like a drowning or impact-related death. Maybe a combination of the two. The likely conclusion would be that he wasn't wearing his seatbelt and his body got sucked out and taken downstream by the current, and the dog drowned too."

"Where does the Redwater flow?"

"Into the Missouri just up the road. Missouri to the Mississippi, Mississippi to the sea. Get my drift? No pun intended." I do get his drift, but I am also feeling the onset of cold feet. *Stop wavering!* Hollis looks beyond me into the vast expanse of the Montana grasslands. But I know I'm the one he is sizing up, not Big Sky Country. With a turn of his head, he shifts his gaze from the great wide open to the box canyon of my soul, and says, "No turning back?"

"No turning back."

CHAPTER SEVEN

We huddle together as a family. Lisa, in her robe, and the kids, in their pajamas, are still shaken and confused, like Friday, who has been let out of his crate. Half a dozen police officers gather nearby in the kitchen. They assure us the house is secure and that we are the only ones in it.

After I throw on a pair of jeans and a sweatshirt, I'm escorted by Officers Powell and Jankowski down to the basement. Lisa, Will, and Jenny remain behind with the others. As we pass the kids' playroom, the basement turns cavernous and I hear the sound of a deluge. Beyond the ancient Williamson boiler, I see the water in question penetrating our home and flowing to the drain near the washer and dryer. It's a stream, ankle high and a body-length in width. We wade through it to reach its source, the wide-open door which leads outside. *So much for the secure house.*

"We found it open when we arrived," Jankowski says.

We inspect things further and detect splintered wood on the jamb where the deadbolt fits.

"It was forced," Powell adds.

As suspected, the drain at the bottom of the stairwell is clogged with nature's debris. Water pools there and threatens to fill the basement as the heavy rain refuses to let up. We stay just out of its reach inside the covered bridge of the basement, but I lean out and reach into the flood to remove the debris. Like magic, a whirlpool forms and the water level begins to recede. The river soon runs dry, which leads me to ask, "If the water backed up high enough, could it have pushed the door in?"

They both take their flashlights and give things another look. Jankowski rubs his hand up and down the area that has been splintered. He peels away a few pieces of the wood and drops them to the floor. He turns to me. "This wood doesn't feel firm. Kind of rotted." He bends down again and pries another piece off. "It definitely could've been the water."

Like the drain, I release the breath I'm holding and exhale with relief.

"You should probably have that repaired," Powell says. "And there should be a strike plate, too."

"What's a strike plate?" I sell planes. Home repair is not part of my repertoire.

"It's the metal plate that reinforces the deadbolt."

It's an old home. Lisa and I had it inspected before purchase, but I can't remember if this was brought to our attention on the report. If it had been, I would've considered it minor. Now I don't. After what my family has just been through, I realize the importance of the basement door is equal to that of the roof over our heads. I plan to have Lisa call the carpenter first thing in the morning.

Powell shuts the door and deadbolts it into the damaged lumber. He pulls on the doorknob to test the door's strength. It's weak. With the slightest amount of force it could be opened. Yes, the alarm is my backup, but I'd prefer to put the door on steroids. Jankowski suggests we nail it shut with a two-by-four until it can be fixed by a professional. I like that idea. They help me rummage through the basement for a piece of wood. There's a nearby work bench left behind by the previous owner. I kept it because I thought I could find some use for it. Tonight, I have. It's made of two-by-fours. I grab a saw from the tool chest and cut a leg off, and Jankowski uses it to nail the door shut. Now the house feels secure.

"Bit of a fire hazard," Powell says.

His partner looks at him, and replies, "It'll be getting fixed tomorrow. You're fine, Mr. Ingram."

We return to the first floor. I again question the wet prints on the hardwood there, but they ease my worry with common sense: they are most likely from the six policemen who entered my home.

One by one, the first responders who came to protect and serve dwindle in number. I remain with my family in the kitchen until the last of them departs. My wife and children are still frightened. They know something's not right. They've known it since I purchased the gun and safe a few months after returning from the hunt in Montana. The nine-millimeter rests on the counter next to the paper towels. From where we are seated at the breakfast table, we all can see it—the stainless steel elephant in the room. As I look at their faces, I can tell how much it bothers them, more than the thunder and lightning that now accompanies the rain. There's much to explain. I want to explain. I feel they are ready to be told and old enough to understand. After all, Jenny is twelve and Will is nearly fourteen.

The time has come for me to tell someone, but only Lisa can know the complete truth.

She heats up two cups of milk in the microwave and serves them to Will and Jenny. With their hands wrapped around the warmed ceramic, they sip their drinks like royalty to delay their inevitable return to their bedrooms. I can't blame them for not wanting to go. I myself do not wish to return to mine, either, but for an entirely different reason. The kitchen is the heart of the house, and I feel I can protect my family much better here than I can from upstairs in the master suite.

It was much appreciated of the police to provide rational explanations for the events this evening: the idea that the basement door was merely forced open by the pressure of the pooling water and the subsequent eruption of the home alarm caused my imagination to run wild. But as much as I would like to believe we have nothing to worry about, I know things the officers don't and can't convince myself of their assessment in our safety. Therefore I will be here through the night, vigilant in my defense of those I love.

"Can I sleep in your bed?" Jenny asks, looking back and forth between Lisa and me. Her eyelids become heavy, threatening to cover those big brown eyes of hers like window shades pulled down for the night. It's already two minutes past 1:00am and my little Roman girl in her lilac pajamas is on the ropes.

Lisa reaches over and rubs Jenny's head. "Of course."

"How about you, Big Man?" I ask my son.

Will, with his elbows on the table and wrists under his chin, proudly takes the high road and replies, "I'm fine in my own room, Dad."

I can tell he's as tired as his sister and it's just a matter of time until his lanky forearms collapse beneath his face, causing his head to drop like a coconut.

"The good news is you can sleep in tomorrow," Lisa says, expecting the kids to take the hint.

It's Friday night and we all can sleep in. Most Saturdays I head into the office for a few hours, but tomorrow I will stay home. I'm in no hurry to leave my family.

"Let's head up," I say.

We exit the kitchen and climb the back stairs. On the second floor, we separate. Jenny is Lisa's ward; Will is mine. He leads me into his room and right away gets into bed, a bed he nearly fills in length. My son is tall for his age, the sapling in pursuit of sunlight. There is no Roman in my boy that I can see. Unlike his sister, he is cut from Lisa's cloth with Nordic features of blue eyes and skin that will tan, though it shouldn't. His hair, now in the catcher's mitt of his pillow, is butterscotch—equal parts mother and father. I run my fingers through it, and in moments he's asleep. With a pull of the chain, I turn off the lamp and tiptoe into the afterglow of the hallway toward the back stairs which lead to the kitchen.

I wait for Lisa at the kitchen table, where she agreed to reconvene with me. It may be a while until she shows because Jenny is a thoroughbred at bedtime; often it's a struggle to get her in the gate. But since she used her bargaining chip to sleep in our bed, I'm optimistic she'll uphold her part of the deal and go down without too much of a fight. A few minutes later, Lisa's footsteps on the back stairs confirms my little girl's business acumen, and the MBA that is sure to come as I learn of her negotiation to sleep in her own bed on the condition that Friday be allowed to sleep with her.

Lisa takes a seat next to me at the table, and I adjust my chair so that we are face-to-face. I love this woman. She represents everything good in the world, which I can say with the competency of someone who has traveled on business to every place in it. I see it in her blue eyes, bordered with faint lines from a lifetime of laughter. I see it in her soft lips that could calm a baby with one kiss; the shoulder-length blonde hair, radiant as a Carolina moon; those high cheekbones. And that smile of hers that I can never say no to.

But it's currently absent and has been for some time. Not the physical smile itself. That still comes and goes like it always has. These days, though, it is more veneer than truthful expression, which I take full responsibility for. As husband and wife for over twenty years, like any two people who live together for that long, we've become reflections of each other. We know when something doesn't look right. And as each of us looks into the mirror of our significant other, both of us see the smoke. I see it rise from the cigarette that she's lit and holding between the first two fingers on her left hand, an inch from her wedding ring. Dressed in a white wool sweater and flannel pajama bottoms beneath her robe, she's ready to hear what I need to tell her. She's been ready since November.

"I'm sorry for the way I've been acting lately."

"Lately?" she replies. "Try months."

I leave it at that, because I know whatever the length of time, it's been too long. "You're right."

"What's going on with you?"

"It's not an affair or anything like that. You know me well enough to know that's never been, or will be, on my radar."

"Really? I always thought you had a thing for Anna Kournikova. I kind of saw you two ending up together." Her smile returns—the one that's been truant.

"Not her, it's the newest Russian phenom, Maria Sharapova."

She gives another genuine smile before it's erased by a puff of the cigarette as she gets up and goes to the white farmhouse sink to put it out with water. That's the drill when it comes to her late-night smokes: after a few drags, extinguish the guilt of the carcinogen and fire hazard as much as possible. When she became pregnant with Will, she quit cold turkey. In between Jenny and after, it's the occasional alcohol-tainted social cig or after-hours decompression like it is now. But this time there is more on her mind. And I should know; I put it there.

She returns to her seat, leans forward, and places both hands on my knees. Through the denim of my jeans, I feel the caress of her warm touch. "What is it?"

In my direct line of sight beyond her, I see the handgun on the counter. Then I see the dog, the man.

"This is the hardest thing I've ever had to tell you," I say. She tenses and I feel her nails tighten on me like pincers. "Because what I'm about to say not only will put you at risk of aiding and abetting, or accessory after the fact—maybe even both—but it might also cause us to lose everything we have."

"What are you talking about, Garrett?" She releases both her hands from my knees.

"If you want me to continue, I will."

"You sound like you're advising me of my rights."

"In a way, I guess I am."

"That's absurd. Why would you say something like that? To me of all people?"

"I'm just trying to protect our family."

"From what?" Her hands clasp my own.

"From the repercussions of taking a man's life."

She pulls away. I chalk it up to mere instinct.

"What have you done?"

I straighten in my chair. "This all goes back to the hunting trip in Montana."

"Go on."

"On the first day, when Hollis and I were out with our guide, I accidentally shot his bird dog." Her head turns up and away to the right, like there's more to come and she would rather it graze her than meet her head on. "The poor thing is wailing on the ground and the man takes my gun from me and shoots it to put it out of its misery." Her eyes begin to water. "I didn't mean to do it. It was an accident." She nods. Of course, she knows I wouldn't intentionally shoot a dog. "I love dogs. I love Friday."

"I know you do," she manages to say.

"The man's name was Orrin, and he knelt on the ground sobbing over his dead dog for what seemed like hours." I stop and wipe away tears from Lisa's cheeks. "Then, in a fit of rage, he got up and came storming towards me. But Hollis jumped in front of him holding his gun. The guy was so upset and we were all pushing and shoving, we didn't see him reach into Hollis's coat pocket and grab a shell until it was too late. He broke away from us and went back to where his dog was lying on the ground next to a shotgun. Hollis told him to drop the shell. He kept telling him while I told him that I'd do whatever he wanted. I was willing to pay him $10,000 and buy him a new dog. But he was out of his mind with anger, and he loaded the gun."

"Oh my God."

"Hollis ordered him to drop the gun. I begged and pleaded with him to put it down. I just didn't know what to do and all I could think of was you and the kids and that I never wanted to be without you. And the next thing I knew I was running away to avoid being shot and I heard a gun go off."

CHAPTER EIGHT

The ground is hard; it won't be easy to dig. And without shovels it will be even tougher. We begin walking back to the ATV. We're about two miles from where we parked it. As we cover the terrain, we both look for pointed rocks that we can use to dig with. But there isn't much in the way of that. It's grassland with an occasional tree or grove of them. As a result, we pen our hopes on what we can find in the back of the Polaris ATV or the bed of Orrin's pickup.

We walk at a swift pace and reach the vehicles in less than a half hour. In the back of the Polaris we find a six-pack of bottled water and some sandwiches in a cooler, a rolled-up vinyl tarp, our fishing gear, and a five-gallon bucket containing a first-aid kit. It's disappointing to say the least.

We walk over to the pickup. Hollis walks around to the driver's side opposite me. Each of us keeps a watchful eye on the dirt road. The first thing I notice is the empty dog crate located behind the cab. Elsewhere in the bed, though, are several things we can use. Next to a small stack of firewood is an axe. I put on my hunting gloves and reach in to grab it. Hollis does the same and pulls out a sledgehammer and a log-splitting wedge. Hopefully it's enough to work with.

We hustle away from the vehicles and head back toward the bodies. With the extra weight of the tools we're carrying, the return trip takes a bit longer, but thankfully not too much. When we make it back, we choose a spot to dig a grave. At one end Hollis pounds the wedge into the ground with the sledgehammer, loosening the dirt. At the other end I use my axe to do the same.

Little by little we increase the size of the hole, scooping up the dirt with our hands and throwing it off to the side. The pile of excavated soil grows large. After two hours, exhaustion sets in. We set down our tools and examine our work. So far we've managed to carve out a grave six feet in length, three in width, and two in depth, as per Hollis's boot.

"Want me to go back to the Polaris and get the water?" I ask. I could definitely use a drink and I'm disappointed that we didn't think to bring any back with us.

"I'm good."

Hollis picks up his tools and resumes digging; I follow his lead much the same way I did during the hunt. An hour later the hole is three feet in depth. We both agree that it's enough. Hollis removes the keys and wallet from Orrin's pockets and slides them into his own. He then slides the deceased Orrin into the grave. The dog goes in next.

It is far easier to push the dirt back into the hole than it was to remove it. But the excess displaced soil has formed a slight mound when we finish. While I use the sledgehammer to tamp it down, Hollis blends the backfill into the surrounding grass and soil with his boots and hands. Our work is almost through, but not quite. We fan out and uproot small sections of sod to transplant on top of the grave. When this final task is finished, we stand back and observe our work. We can barely see any evidence that the ground has been disturbed, and even that would require a long hard examination to notice anything's out of place. The job has been done well. To me, the footprint of man is as far removed from this area as the presence of the buffalo. Hollis agrees. The two of us gaze for a moment upon the far-reaching prairie grass as it gently sways in the light and variable winds. Same as it always has. Same as it forever will.

With the bird I shot stuffed into the rear pouch of my hunting jacket, we hustle back to the vehicles, clean the tools, and return them to their proper places. Hollis wants to get the pickup and ATV off the road and keep them out of sight until nightfall. We drive them across the prairie until we find a ridge with a rocky overhang and park beneath it. It's a good spot to bide our time discussing further details. We exit the vehicles and sit together in the shade.

"I'm having second thoughts about the river," Hollis says.

I'm having second thoughts about everything, but I look away to hide any sign of hesitancy on my face. However, I can't look away for too long, or he'll catch on. As I fight it—something I will learn to do often—I turn my head to face him. "Why?"

"It might come off as looking staged, which is exactly what we don't want."

"What will they think if they find his pickup abandoned on a dirt road, miles from here?" I get no reply from Hollis. He just stares out onto the Great Plains. "That he and his dog went for a walk and never came back? I think that will have them combing the fields more than anything."

It bothers me that Hollis's gut instinct bothers him. He's as brilliant as they come. What does he sense?

After a long pause, he says, "I'm good with the river."

"You sure?"

"Yeah, I'm sure," he replies. "You're right. It's better than leaving it abandoned in a field."

When the sun begins to dip below the horizon, we return to the driver's seat of each vehicle and start the engines. Without turning on our headlights we drive to the main road then eastward toward the Redwater River. Hollis drives the Polaris as fast as it will go while I follow in the pickup. After four miles, we make it undetected to the one-lane bridge and continue onto the dirt road to our right. The road parallels the river for at least a mile to a small clearing where Hollis slows down and comes to a stop. I pull up behind him. He gets out and walks over to the nearby riverbank. I join him there and can see a large bend in the river.

"I like this spot," he says.

Hollis knows rivers. I don't. "Why?"

"A sharp bend like that means a deep pool of water."

"How deep?"

"I'll bet it's fifteen to twenty feet."

I like the look of the sharp bend in the road as much as the one in the river. Hollis does too. We both agree it's a place where someone could accidentally miss the turn and drive off the road. We scout the area and inspect it as best we can. Convinced it's as good a place as we could find, and that we are alone, we evaluate the angle and speed needed to get the pickup into the deepest part of the water below. But as the darkness increases, our time becomes limited. As fishermen, we should be on our way back to the lodge by now.

Hollis volunteers to drive the truck towards the edge and jump out at the last second. Before I hand him the keys, we go over the details one last time. He gets into the pickup, makes sure both windows are rolled down, and drives it about thirty yards back the way we came. While he positions himself like a plane getting ready for takeoff, I walk over to the place at the edge of the embankment to mark the spot where we want the vehicle to go airborne. I wave my arms above my head, and he waves back, acknowledging my signal.

Hollis opens the driver's side door and stands on the running board like a garbage man, holding on to the truck's cab with his left hand and gripping the wheel with his right. He leans in and stretches his right leg to push down on the gas pedal, and the engine rumbles. The vehicle moves forward. As it gains speed, man and his harnessed pistons, axels, and gears zero in on the bull's-eye, and, at the last second, I jump out of the way as Hollis leaps from the pickup.

While I role, I catch a glimpse of the Chevy as it launches off the embankment, followed by a tremendous boom when it smacks the water beneath the area where Hollis and I come to a stop. He has rolled a bit farther, though, and almost goes over the edge; but I'm able to grab hold of his jacket to prevent this. We assist each other to stand and together look down at the scene below us. There is nothing but darkness on top of darkness, and soon it becomes one—to our relief—as the river closes its mouth to swallow the pickup whole before Hollis tosses in Orrin's wallet like a penny into a wishing well.

We waste no time climbing into the Polaris and getting back on the road. While I drive, Hollis reaches behind us and grabs some of the fishing gear. The boots and waders will need to be soaked in the river. Two fly rods and reels, and an open bale spinning rod need moistening as well. The packed lunch will have to be discarded.

"Anything else?" I ask.

He takes another look. "I'll wet some of the flies and lures, too."

I park the ATV just before we reach the bridge, where a short trail leads down to the river. Hollis hops out with all that he can carry, and I take the rest. At the water's edge, Hollis ladles each piece of gear into the Redwater, and then hands it to me. As soon as my arms are full, I head back up the trail and dump my load into the bed of the Polaris. Hollis does the same. We return to the front seat and head for home through the biting wind of the cool country air. I keep it at twenty-five miles per hour while we talk.

"Let's go over it one more time," I suggest.

"After Orrin came to the ranch," Hollis says, "we followed him for about five or six miles to where he turned right onto another dirt road. About a mile or so on that one, we took a right again and about a half mile farther, we parked and began our hunt. Right turns, right?"

"Right."

We nearly shout at the top of our lungs to be heard over sound of the wind, the engine, and the rough road.

Hollis continues. "We hunted for several hours, flushing six birds and missing every one of them. I insisted on you getting your first bird, so each time the dog pointed, I moved in behind you to give you the honors. No matter which way the bird flew, it was yours."

I'm a bad shot, which will make the one bird we have—all that we've got to show for our efforts—from our time in the fields of Montana believable. Hollis assures me slow days happen, more so with beginners.

"For lunch we all ate the club sandwiches Lawton provided for us, then we hunted for a couple more hours and you finally got a bird. When our hunt was over—about midafternoon—Orrin left with his dog in his pickup and headed toward the bridge. We followed suit in the Polaris, but drove slower and eventually lost sight of him. We fished the river upstream of the bridge."

"How far upstream?" I ask. This was a detail we'd not yet gone over.

"A quarter mile. But nobody is going to ask that."

For the sake of consistency, and to demonstrate I've memorized the script, I finish the recital. "You caught several fish and released them. I'd never been fly fishing and was skunked. The sunset was beautiful, and we watched it while taking nips from your flask. The entire day, we never saw anyone."

"What kind of fish?" Hollis says, double-checking to see how much I remember the more minute details of our story.

"Northern Pike."

He'd explained to me earlier that the Redwater wasn't a trout stream. But there were plenty of hungry Northern Pike that would be more than happy to devour a streamer fly. He referred to them as "northerns."

We know we will receive questions. Lots of questions. None of them, though, will be more significant than where it was that Orrin took us hunting, because the lie we tell will determine the distance from the truth, and the further the better. On the way back to the lodge, in an area we estimate to be about five miles away from it, we find a dirt road that we nominate as the one where we took our first right turn and continued following Orrin. There are plenty to choose from, which is to our advantage. It would be easy for a visitor to be inaccurate in the recital of his steps in the maze of these grasslands.

We drive down it.

"Check the odometer and let me know when we're about a mile away," Hollis says.

When that moment arrives, we keep our eyes open for any road on our right. The first one we skip; the second one we take. After traveling a few hundred yards along it, we stop and survey the land. The vehicle's headlights shine brightly on the ocean of grassland which makes up the majority of the Great Plains. Blindfolded and spun around twenty times, anyone might identify this as the exact place we'd hunted.

"This works for me," Hollis says.

It works for me, too.

We return to the main dirt road and eventually connect to the partially gravel one as we near the lodge. A few miles and we'll be there. In two hours Wes and Rob will arrive as well. There is something comforting in that. Maybe it's safety in numbers or something else completely. I try to pinpoint it but can't and decide to let it go because it doesn't matter. Only one thing matters: that no one ever finds out what has taken place. No one. This includes our two friends, our wives, and all of our children. Only God, Hollis, and I can know. And God help us if anyone else ever does.

As we travel through the night, which feels as dark as our new secret, we approach the lodge, where we will be treated like kings returning from our expedition. We anticipate being able to eat, drink, and revel in the splendor of Montana country as privileged guests of the Little Wing Ranch—the hunters, the fishermen, with smiles on our faces, celebrating the best of times with the best of friends. But I can barely stomach the thought of it all. I am no king. I am no hunter. I am no fisherman. I am, if anything, a disgrace.

Just before our arrival, we go over our story one last time, the words now feeling like carbon-copied documents stored within our minds. We reach the paved drive and see a figure dressed in a white apron walk into the lodge through the kitchen entrance. At the same time we smell the scent of steaks on the grill. I turn the wheel to the right, exiting the circular drive, and park the Polaris near the steps of Hollis's cabin.

He looks at me to determine if our covenant is strong.

The handshake confirms it.

Chapter Nine

She leans toward me. I want to keep my distance and continue with what I need to tell her, but I wind up meeting her halfway, allowing our foreheads to touch in support of each other like the keystone of an arch. As we sit, she holds my hands and anoints them with the teardrops that fall from her eyes.

"When I turned around, Orrin was facedown on the ground with blood gushing out of his back."

I can still see him lying there like it was yesterday, because I *did* see him yesterday, and the day before, and the day before that. I see him every day. Lisa pulls away from me. She has the same stunned look on her face that Hollis had after pulling the trigger.

"There's smoke coming out of the barrel of Hollis's gun and he's standing there completely in shock."

Lisa's lips part and her mouth opens like Orrin's wound, but no words come out.

"We raced over to him, and Hollis started performing CPR. He pumped the man's chest and tried to get him breathing again, but there was no sign of life, no breath or pulse—nothing. He kept trying, though. Over and over he kept trying to bring him back. And there was nothing I could do for him, either. We did everything we could. I swear we did."

Tears stream down Lisa's cheeks. I feel tears begin to crawl down my own. She wipes them away for me.

"He died?" she asks.

"Yes."

She cradles my head like a baby while I wrap my arms around her and hold her tight. It is the most tender of embraces—merciful, forgiving. It's been months in the making—a lifetime, in fact. I wish it would last, but it doesn't.

She sits up straight and again we are staring into each other's tear-filled eyes. "Why did you wait so long to tell me this?"

I pause for a moment before I reply. "There's more."

"There's more? Like what?"

"I promise you I fought against doing what I'm about to tell you."

"Okay, say it."

I take a deep breath and wipe my face. "We buried him and his dog there and never told anyone about it."

"You did *what?!*" She stares at me in disbelief. I pray it's just her sense of confusion.

"I didn't want to. Believe me, it's not something I would ever choose to do."

"I know you wouldn't, so tell me you didn't."

I can't tell her what she wants to hear. "I wanted to call 911." She nods in response, as though it's the obvious thing anyone would do. "But I couldn't get a signal on my phone. Then Hollis said we needed to think about things first because shooting a man in the back can have consequences."

"What kind of consequences?"

"He said he could be charged with manslaughter or involuntary manslaughter."

"How could they do that? It was an accident, right? Or self-defense?"

"I know, and I tried to convince him that he wasn't thinking straight. We went back and forth on this. I kept telling him that all we needed to do was tell the truth, and any reasonable person would understand."

"How could they not?"

"He wasn't convinced, though. He worried about it being Montana, like it was a foreign country and he'd never make it out of there if he had to stand trial."

"That's crazy, babe."

"It was, but he kept pleading with me to help him. He didn't want to chance being taken away from Helen and Aimee and Graham by being sent to prison in Montana. I remember him saying 'I saved your life, and Will's, and now I'm asking you to save mine.'"

"Hollis," she says, then repeats his name once more and looks down at the floor and covers her face with her hands.

"As hard as it was to turn him down, I still couldn't bring myself to do what he was asking. I told him I just couldn't do it. He begged me some more, then he said he had something he needed to tell me and that I had to promise to never tell anyone . . . Hollis is one step away from financial ruin."

Lisa raises her head, uncovers her face, and clasps her hands behind her head. "He's broke?" she asks. "No way."

"I couldn't believe it, either. He went on to tell me that he and a group of investors were bidding against the Sioux tribe to buy the Little Wing Ranch. It turns out the place is sitting on a sizeable amount of oil, and he desperately needed the deal to go through."

"The Little Wing is the place where you were hunting?"

"Yes."

"Okay."

"Orrin, the man he shot, was a Sioux Indian, which adds more fuel to the fire."

"This is about oil and money?"

"It's about Hollis . . . and Helen . . . and their family."

"What about that man and his family?"

"He lost his wife and son in a car accident years ago," I tell her. "Trust me. I think about him every day. But I did what I thought I had to do for Hollis."

"What about our family? Did you even think about us?" It's a question we both know the answer to, so I don't reply. She's upset. She's venting. She pulls a cigarette from the pack on the nearby table and lights it.

"Just listen to me for a minute and let me finish, then you'll know why I'm telling you this now."

CHAPTER TEN

I'm scrubbing my nails in the shower, trying to expel the dirt beneath each one in an attempt to erase the evidence brought back from the grave we dug. I am making slow but steady progress with the bar of soap, chipping away at these pesky grains of soil that found their way into my gloves, until only tiny sickle-shaped slivers of black remain. Trimmers, I decide, will rid me of what is so reluctant to leave.

Now, clean, dry, and wearing a fresh pair of jeans with a fleece, I finish the job on my fingernails and give them one final inspection. They are now as unblemished as they were upon arrival to Montana. Whatever hint of suspicion they could've drawn has been cut away and filed down to the root of innocence. And from whatever thoughts of guilt they may have represented (the remnants of Orrin's grave) I have—with zeal—purged myself.

Out of need, rather than thirst, I pour myself a drink. The Woodford is straight and on the rocks. Bourbon never tastes all that pleasant, but to swallow it in sips makes it palatable, makes you feel like you've earned it. I feel I've earned nothing, though. Another sip and I still feel the same.

With one for the road in me, I walk over to Hollis's cabin. After we inspect each other's nails, we stroll over to the main lodge for dinner. Behind a small bar to the right stands Lawton, dressed in his cowboy hat and shirt, ready to pour. It's a tiny bar with just six saddles on six stools, but it's

the most ornate, handcrafted woodwork I've ever seen—
honey-colored.

He greets us with a warm smile, and says, "How was
your day?"

"Had a few chances but came up short," Hollis tells him.

"Nothing?" he replies, mouth wide open.

"I'm not a very good shot," I explain.

"We did manage to get one," Hollis says.

"Only one, huh?" It's clear he's disappointed for us. The
expectation is for many birds. The hefty fee, a reflection of
that. His pride and reputation have been wounded. The
Little Wing is the crème de la crème and only a blind man
should have an excuse to come home empty-handed. The
place is supposed to be loaded with birds. He looks
embarrassed. "How many did you flush?"

"A fair number. The fishing was excellent, though,"
Hollis says, changing the subject.

This puts a smile back on Lawton's face. "You'll get em
tomorrow." He pulls two glasses down from the overhanging
rack. "I was wondering when Orrin was going to drop off
your birds. Guess that's why I haven't seen him." He fills the
glasses with ice. "Did you bring the one back with you?"

After I shake off the initial jolt from hearing Orrin's
name, I say, "I did. It's still in my jacket."

"Drop it off it after dinner so we can get it cleaned for
you."

"I'll do that."

"Whattaya havin?"

"Two Woodfords, please," Hollis says.

"On the rocks okay?"

"Sure."

"Hope you brought a big appetite." He fills the glasses halfway with bourbon. "Best steaks in Montana coming your way."

We'd filled out the dinner form in the morning. I'd checked the "medium rare" box for the steak, and "lobster bisque" instead of the salad, but I could've had both if I wanted. The place is a land cruise. I'll probably only be able to finish the steak if I'm force-fed like a child. I'm not hungry at all. The bourbon is all I want. That and to be lying in bed next to Lisa at home, where we and our children are safe.

"Sounds great," Hollis replies. "Any word from our friends?"

"Their flight is on time. I'll be leaving in about an hour to get em."

I would love to feel excitement for their arrival, and the added benefit of safety in numbers, but there's no room for it. Instead, I'm filled with anxiety because I know that I'll soon be playing make-believe in front of two more people for the next several days.

Home has never felt so far away. It will take more alcohol to lessen the distance. I stare at the glass on the bar counter and follow the circular course of its rim. There's something familiar about it, and when the hole in Orrin's back comes to mind, I look away. But there are circles everywhere—glasses, coasters, bottles, wedding rings.

After dinner, and after the lone bird has been given to Lawton to be cleaned, we wait outside by the fire pit for Wes and Rob while putting a bigger dent in the bottle of bourbon. Both Hollis and I are on our last legs. Too tired and too inebriated to even strike up a conversation with each other, or the two hunters sitting opposite us on the other side of the flames who occupy cabins five and six. But they don't let us off so easy.

"Where y'all from?"

I've traveled to Texas enough times to recognize his accent. "St. Louis," I say.

"Savannah," Hollis adds. "How about you guys?"

"Houston. Nice to meet you."

"Nice to meet you, too. I'm Hollis Baumgartner."

"Garrett Ingram," I call out.

As polite citizens of the Lone Star State, the Texans rise to come over and shake hands. I, however, fail to reciprocate their civil nature in earnest. Hollis, though, makes the effort and stands to greet them.

"That's okay. No need to get up," he says to me as I begin to push myself from the chair I've molded into. "Mike Sprong."

"Garret Ingram."

His friend overhears my name. "Garrett, Charlie Nettles."

"Hope y'all have a good hunt tomorrow," Mike says. "We're turning in."

Their departure is welcomed. It's nothing personal. They seem like good guys. But I'm in no mood for casual conversation—which I'm certain they picked up on—that would require the use of my rehearsed repertoire of lies.

The only person I want to talk to is Lisa, though even that orchestrated phone call will be bittersweet and, according to my watch, already past due (if my calculation of the time difference is correct).

Headlights punch through the purple tip of the blaze, announcing the arrival of our friends. Hollis and I look at each other and communicate without saying a word. I mentally review the script I've memorized—forward and backwards—one last time.

Car doors shut, and familiar voices color the night as much as the flames. As they grow louder, it's easy to distinguish Rob Henry's baritone that befits a man of his size. They approach, walking side by side, as a pair of silhouettes.

"You boys have a lot of catching up to do," Hollis calls out to them.

"Well, if it isn't the great white hunter himself," Wes replies.

They eventually step out of the darkness and into the light, each of them holding a Lawton-issued bottle of Coors in his right hand. Immediately it feels like old times. All of us—myself included—stand and greet each other.

"Rumor has it you guys are stinking up the joint," Rob says.

"Yeah, the old man is practically in tears," Wes chimes in, getting in a second dig.

"Ha! Is that so?" Hollis replies. "Then I guess we'll need to put a wager on tomorrow's festivities."

"Would that be on whether or not you guys shoot one, or none?" Rob asks. "Dogs not included."

Everyone laughs. Mine is forced, the same way I ate steak earlier. He has no idea how three words and an overindulgence in bourbon can spin a grown man's head. I need to sit back down, but I stumble before I get there. Wes grabs my arm to keep me from going in the direction of the fire pit, which allows me to grab the arms of my chair and plop myself into it.

"Looks like ol' Garrett has tied one on," Wes says.

"More than one," I reply.

"We're not talking birds, though, right?" Rob asks.

More laughter. And that's all I remember.

* * *

In the morning I awaken from my dreams. But make no mistake, I'm aware it wasn't a dream when the rabbit fled and the bird flew and the dog jumped and I pulled the trigger and Hollis pulled his. The second my eyes open—half open as they are—I know where I am and what I've done.

I rise from my bed, tossing off the blanket, and shuffle to the bathroom, realizing only then that I'm wearing the clothes I had on the night before. Along the journey, I put two and two together and surmise I must have been carried home by my friends. Once I'm standing at the toilet I smell smoke and realize it's emanating from me—due to having made the unwise choice of sitting downwind near the fire pit. I unzip my jeans and crack a smile that morphs into laughter upon discovering I'm the victim of one of Wes's notorious pranks. With bright, Cardinal-red painted fingernails, I attempt to steer my stream of urine into the bowl through the toilet seat I'm too lazy to put up. But I can't stop laughing—the good medicine that laughter is—and I'm unable to shoot straight. *Never could*, I hear Hollis tell me.

It's 7:10 a.m. and the sun's first light advances through the windows as I sit in the chair by the fireplace and put fluids back into my body. And two Tylenols. It's 8:10 back home; the time Lisa is usually driving the kids to school. I look at my cell phone and see I have a message from her. Though eager to return her call, I bide my time until I'm sure the kids will no longer be in the car. It's not that I don't want to talk to them. It's that I think I need to tell Lisa what's happened. Tell her everything and let the chips fall where they may.

At the kitchen counter I refill my cup and turn to head back to my chair. That's when I see a police cruiser approach the main lodge. I hustle to the window for a better look and crouch down to see just above the frost line at the bottom. On the white passenger side door painted in bright golden-brown letters is the word *SHERIFF* and below it, in slightly smaller font, are the words: *Richland County*, along with the signature star in deep brown next to them. It parks by the front of the Little Wing, where a uniformed officer steps out of the vehicle and enters the lodge.

My heart fires on all cylinders, fueled by my breathing which has quickened, causing the window to fog. I step back but continue my surveillance. Out of the corner of my eye I can see the Texans from last night. They've exited their cabins and are walking toward the lodge for the morning meal. In the not-so-far distance behind them a pickup, illuminated by the low sun, gains ground. Uncertain of what to do or think, I make the simple choice to grab my coat, throw on my boots, and head for Hollis's cabin.

Before I have the chance to knock, he opens the door.

"Looking for some nail polish remover?" he asks.

He has it along with other materials ready for me on the coffee table, courtesy of Dolores Mills. But it was Hollis, the friend who always has my back, who sought it out from her after Rob and Wes finished their artwork.

"Much obliged," I say, taking a seat on the couch. I open the acetone, dab some onto a wipe, and begin rubbing away the red.

Hollis sits on the raised hearth across from me in his gear—sans jacket—hunter ready, though we both know neither of us will be hunting anytime soon. We will wait around for Orrin, who will be a no-show, and when he fails to arrive after a more than reasonable amount of time, Lawton will unsuccessfully attempt to reach him by phone, after which the Little Wing will scramble to select another guide from their stable. If we're out in the fields by ten o'clock, we'll be lucky (or *un*lucky, as I see it, because I want nothing more to do with guns, or hunting, or this place).

"You're worried about the sheriff, aren't you?" he asks.

"You read my mind."

"He could be here for any number of reasons. Let's not jump to conclusions."

"What's your best guess?"

"The breakfast buffet."

"Seriously?"

"Somewhat," he replies. "But even if he is here looking for Orrin, we knew there was a good chance someone would come around asking questions. This is normal."

"None of this is normal."

"Everything is going to be fine," Hollis assures me in that calm, smooth voice of his. "All we need to do is stick to our story." He stands. "Short and simple, right?"

"Right."

"Want a cup of coffee?"

"Sure."

He begins to pour our drinks while I stare out the window watching the world outside. The lodge's front door swings open and Lawton walks out accompanied by the officer. I wait expectantly for them to say their goodbyes, for one to return to his car, and the other to his house. But they don't. Instead they start walking in the direction of Hollis's cabin.

Their approach troubles me, and without hesitation I bring it to Hollis's attention.

He carries our drinks over to the window in order to investigate for himself, then hands one to me. "Careful, it's hot," he says, without a hint of worry in what he sees headed toward us. "I think I like your nails better the other way."

I've wiped them clean, though the smell of the acetone still permeates, mixing with the scent of the black coffee. I gaze for a moment at my cup and I'm reminded of the oil which we know exists far below us. I bring it to my lips. The odor is strong, and for an instant I can't help but wonder if we dug the grave deep enough. I also can't help but wonder why my mind now works like Truck's—controlled by the nose. I picture a dog and hunters out in the fields down the road on the trail of a bird. But they're not onto a bird. It's something quite different that only the dog has picked up on. Not the smell, the difference in smells. Out of curiosity, or out of instinct, man's best friend leads his master to the bodies Hollis and I buried and begins to dig away.

"Hey, you okay?"

His question snaps me out of it, and I turn from my daydream to the morning in full bloom outside. "Yeah," I say. I sip the coffee in an attempt to imitate my friend, Cool Hand Luke, who can do it without the slightest of tremors. "They're almost here."

Out of the six, they choose Cabin #1, confirmed by the sound of their boots hammering the planks of the stairs with each step like bagpipes announcing their Old West arrival. In the same key, a loud knock echoes throughout the room. Hollis opens the door to greet them.

"Good morning, Hollis," Lawton says. "This is Deputy Trevor Maultsby of the Richland County Sheriff's office."

Hollis shakes his hand. "Nice to meet you."

"Sorry to trouble you like this, but I was hoping you could answer a few questions for me about Orrin Gall," the deputy says.

Lawton leans to his left. He sees me on the couch and waves. I return the gesture.

"No problem," Hollis says. "Come on in."

Hollis steps aside and the two men enter the cabin. "Garrett, this is Deputy Trevor Maultsby," Lawton says. I make the man's acquaintance and then return to my seat. "Garrett is my other guest I mentioned to you that hunted with Orrin yesterday."

"Oh, good. That'll make things easier," Maultsby tells us. He holds a pocket-size notepad and pen in his hands—which are a baby's compared to Lawton's, in terms of weathering. Half the age means half the sun and wind and cold. Out here, it's all about time and exposure.

"Our office got a call from the Sioux Police because one of their members reported Orrin missing," he begins. Standing as upright as the stone fireplace behind him, the muscular thirty-year-old Caucasian, wearing a baseball cap with the sheriff's insignia instead of a Stetson (so engrained in my imagination for this part of the country), represents the future of Montana Law Enforcement. That I can tell, there is no cowboy in this man. He is urban—similar to something I'd see in St. Louis, but not here. Dressed in his black shirt, pants and combat boots that match the color of his short hair and gun on his hip, he's all business and, if I had to guess, probably ex-military as well. "I'm sure it's nothing and he'll turn up soon, but I need to perform my due diligence before filing my report. This will only take a few minutes."

"Can I get either of you a cup of coffee?" Hollis asks Lawton and the deputy.

"I'm fine, thanks," Maultsby says.

Lawton passes on the offer, too.

"Have a seat," Hollis instructs them. He takes the chair by the sofa next to me.

Lawton and the deputy lower themselves onto the hearth. Trevor Maultsby looks at Hollis, then me, and says, "What time did you finish your hunt with Orrin?"

"Around three," Hollis replies, and the officer writes.

"Did he mention going anywhere afterwards?"

"No."

I confirm Hollis's reply with a nod.

"Our guides usually come back to the lodge with our guests to drop off the birds for cleaning, but they only got one—Garrett's bird—and I guess Orrin figured on letting them take it back themselves," Lawton says. "I'll make sure you boys limit out today." His pride is still crushed.

"What'd you get?" Maultsby says to me.

"Pheasant."

"Rooster or hen?"

"A rooster."

"Magnificent creatures."

"They sure are."

"When you were hunting, did Orrin mention anything about plans for later on in the day or evening?"

"Not to me."

"Me neither," I reply.

"I'm assuming he drove off in his truck?"

"He did," Hollis says just before sipping his coffee. I keep mine on the table, afraid of how my cup might shake on its way to my mouth.

"Which way did he go?"

"Toward the bridge," I answer.

"We just shook hands and he said he'd see us tomorrow morning," Hollis says.

"Probably went for a hunt himself and slept in his truck," Lawton says. "He's been known to do that."

"What time is he due here?" the deputy asks.

Lawton looks at his watch. "Thirty minutes. We like to get our hunts going by eight thirty or nine."

"Why don't I check back with you around ten, and if he hasn't shown and we still can't reach him on his cell phone, we'll go from there," Maultsby suggests to Lawton.

"Works for me. But I'm sure he'll show up," Lawton says. "He's always been a reliable fella. One of my best guides."

The deputy rises and the rest of us get back on our feet, too. He puts away his notepad and pen and thanks us for our time. Hollis leads them to the door.

"Breakfast is ready. Come and get it while it's hot," Lawton tells us. "And don't worry about your hunt. If Orrin doesn't make it for some reason, I'll have another guide at the ready for you."

As they leave and Hollis shuts the door, my cell phone rings. I pull it from my pants pocket. It's Lisa.

"I was just going to call you," I say, trying to sound normal.

"Must have been a rough night," she says.

"Very rough."

"I can hear it in your voice."

"Yeah, I'm nursing a hangover."

Hollis sits down in his chair. He mouths "Lisa?" and I nod yes.

"Take some aspirin and drink lots of water."

"I popped some Tylenol earlier, and Hollis just poured me a cup of coffee. That's where I am now."

"Tell him I said hi."

"I will."

"So, how's everything going? You having fun?"

A knock at the door interrupts our conversation. "Hang on a second."

Hollis gets up and opens it.

"Sorry to bother you again," the deputy says, "but do you remember what side of the road you hunted yesterday?" He turns and points. "The main road off the drive here that leads to the bridge."

I lean to my left on the couch and spot Lawton at the foot of the steps behind the deputy.

"We were on the right side," Hollis replies, intentionally sending Maultsby down the wrong trail.

"Sure about that?"

Hollis doesn't hesitate. "Yes."

"Okay, thanks again."

After another exchange of goodbyes, Hollis shuts the door and signals the all clear.

"Sorry," I say to Lisa as I put the phone back to my ear and pick up the cup of coffee. "Someone was at the door."

"The girls from last night forget something?"

Like her beauty, her wit and sense of humor are second to none. A one-two punch that knocked me off my feet when we met.

"That's a good one," I acknowledge, before I move on to my brief synopsis of the lodge, our accommodations, and the previous day's hunt, which in generic terms I tell her was "fun." With Hollis next to me, I think it best to leave it at that.

We say our goodbyes and I turn my attention back to Hollis.

"Why do you think he wanted to know what side of the road we hunted?"

"Probably just check-marking boxes on his report."

"Seems odd he'd come back for that."

"I wouldn't give it a second thought," he says. "Let's go get some breakfast."

CHAPTER ELEVEN

I walk the fields like a zombie. Too much bourbon the night before will do that to even the best of hunters. To the worst of them, it's child's play. But I'm plagued by more than just a distilled bloodstream. It's what's in the man's bloodstream ahead of me that's cause for even greater misery. By birthright, Sampson Sanchez is kin to the man I buried. A cousin first removed, as he explained it so dryly in his monotone voice and personality; descendants of Chief Gall, feared leader of the Sioux who was instrumental in the repulse of the Seventh Cavalry's attack at the Battle of Little Bighorn. Mildly put, he is humble in his choice of words, which he speaks without inflection.

With his two dogs—one to point and one to flush, which is an upgrade from the day before—he guides us on our hunt as a last-minute replacement summoned by Lawton Mills when Orrin failed to show, much to the surprise of the lodge owner. It's midday and we've already traveled miles. In my mind, I've gone even further, all the way to where I drop on my knees and beg for this man's forgiveness after I confess to him what Hollis and I have done.

From my coat I pull water bottles and trudge along. When needed, I aim and fire . . . and miss. But Hollis doesn't. He drops birds left and right, which turns the rear pouch of Sampson's hunting jacket into a camel's hump.

For the hunter, it's an epic day, containing no outward signs from the remnants of Kentucky's finest. For me, it's an epic physical and mental struggle, in equal parts like Big Sky and Big Land Country, and by the time the last bird falls from the former and onto the latter before ending up in the clutches of a retriever's jaws, I'm as spent as our empty shells.

I ride with Sampson, his dogs, and Hollis's birds back to the lodge. Hollis rides to the river in the Polaris, with an estimated "dark thirty" return to celebrate his conquest of both fish and game—a display of optimism as unparalleled as his stamina. In the cab of the pickup, I look out my window and into the fields we are traveling past at the speed of a pheasant in flight. Soon we will be back at the Little Wing, and soon I will be out of this man's truck that I am staring out of to avoid conversation. Sitting next to him is, at the very least, uncomfortable. The two of us go together like oil—Bakken shale oil—and water, though only I know why.

In the distance, an American flag—the beacon of the Little Wing—flutters in the north wind, with a rising wooden gabled roof below it. The wheels continue to turn and more and more of the lodge appears on the horizon, until a postcard image of it stretches across the entire windshield. But there's something else in this photo that is by no means picture perfect: a police SUV with its lights flashing.

As I straighten in my seat the lights on the SUV turn off. Then they start to flash again. Lawton steps out of the passenger side and puts on his cowboy hat. He backs away from the vehicle, as though to admire the colors that strobe like fireworks.

"See what happens when you try to run off without paying your bill at the Little Wing?" Sampson says in an attempt of humor devoid of charm or personality, which leads me to the conclusion that these bird men are not my type, or I'm not theirs. Focusing on the alarm bells going off in my head, I ignore him as we approach the circular drive and he slows down the vehicle. As we turn for the cabins, I see the officer exit his car and begin to walk with Lawton in our direction. "It was a pleasure to hunt with you."

I shake the hand he holds out, but my attention is elsewhere. "Thanks," I say. "Sorry for the bad aim."

"Just takes practice."

I unbuckle my seatbelt and reach for the door handle. "See you tomorrow."

"Unless you know something I don't, you won't."

"Not sure what you mean by that."

"Orrin's your guide, isn't he?"

"I guess I thought that since he wasn't here today, and you were, we'd have you again," I say to cover my tracks.

"He'll be here," he replies. "I'll run the birds over to the lodge and get them cleaned for you. Take care."

I get out, open the backdoor of his cab, and obtain the Berettas. He pulls away, and pauses to speak to Lawton and the officer. They have a brief conversation before they're all on the move again.

It's obvious I'm at the center of their attention, thus I wait at the bottom of the porch steps for them with the guns snug in their cases.

With high expectation, Lawton calls out: "How'd y'all do today?"

Today, I don't wound his pride. "We did well."

"Now we're talkin."

I rest the guns on the steps to free my hands in order to greet Lawton and the lawman accompanying him. A man whom I'm pray will not ask me to turn around and put those free hands behind my back.

"Hollis did most of the work," I say to confess the truth while the opportunity presents itself.

"As long as you get em. That's all that matters." It's a numbers game to Lawton. Numbers add up in dollars. I see how it works. "Garrett, I'd like you to meet Jakobe Kenton. Jakobe is a criminal investigator from the Fort Peck Reservation and proud operator of the newest set of emergency lights this side of the Missouri. He and I go way back."

"Nice to meet you, Jakobe" I say. But there's nothing nice about it.

His eyes quickly scan me from head to toe like an x-ray as he looks me over. I'm able to catch the movement of his vision and return the favor to the best of my ability. He's an American Indian—one hundred percent—in cowboy clothing. Western it's called in these parts. Boots, jeans, belt buckle, and hat. Everything but the tan long sleeve shirt that dons the insignia of the Sioux Nation and Fort Peck Police, and a badge.

"Likewise," he says. "Mind if I have a word or two with you?"

"Not at all."

"The Sheriff's office filed a missing person's report on Orrin Gall, and it states his last known whereabouts was on

Fort Peck Reservation land while guiding a bird hunt on behalf of the Little Wing Ranch."

"Okay," is all I say, with a nod for him to continue.

"Just to be sure, was it on the right side or left side of the road down-a-ways that you hunted?" He turns and points, which causes his jet-black ponytail to lift from the center of his middle-aged back.

Right, right, right. "The right side."

"Positive?"

"Yes."

He looks at Lawton and turns back to me. "Well, the strange thing is," he says, "we can't figure out why he'd take you hunting on reservation land with all that's been going on lately."

Lawton intervenes on behalf of the high-paying clientele he caters to. "Garrett, the Sioux and I came to an agreement a month ago that our guests would no longer hunt on reservation land since I'm selling the ranch to Hollis's group."

I process the information, dejected not to have Hollis at my side to help calculate my next move. *Just stick to the story.* "I don't know why he took us there, either."

"It just doesn't make sense that he'd do that." Jakobe Kenton places his right foot on the first step to the porch and looks me in the eyes as squarely as the toes on his dirt-brown cowboy boots. "And now the sheriff's office is wiping their hands clean of the matter because he was last seen on reservation land, which is out of their jurisdiction, and in mine."

"How can I be of help to you?" I say, offering my services like any man with nothing to hide would do.

"Would it be all right if you and I took a ride and you could show me the area where he took you?"

"Yeah, I can do that, but I'm not so sure I'll be able to remember how to get there."

"Even if it's not the exact place, that's fine," the lawman says. "We know it's on the right side, which should enable us to reach the general vicinity."

I don't want to go anywhere other than my cabin, but I've got to maintain the appearance of cooperation. A man is unaccounted for. At the same time, I have no idea why he wants to take me to a place where we all know Orrin isn't. Though maybe for some reason the report didn't include our last visual of Orrin as he drove toward the bridge, and if that's the case it would make sense for me to question the officer's reason for us to go there.

"I just want to let you know that we saw Orrin drive away after our hunt."

"He's aware of that," Lawton says. "Sometimes Orrin will go back and hunt on his own after guiding. This is for the tracking dogs."

The simple utterance of those animals sends my heart into a full sprint, because, in part, I'd failed to even consider them as an adversary. I'd never given man's best friend much of a thought. For birds, yes. For the sole purpose to pick up the scent of man, it never crossed my mind and I wonder if it ever even crossed Hollis's. I wonder what a bloodhound—or whatever dog they use—is capable of with a sense of smell that's superhuman. What I don't need to question, though, is the fear and disappointment—each represented by what I consider a failure at dotting the i's and crossing t's of our crime—that leverages my ability to look these men in the eye.

The three of us walk to the Dodge with the new lights on its roof.

"See you for happy hour," Lawton says, before he heads through the front door of the lodge.

I open the front passenger side door of the SUV and get in. It's my first time ever in a police vehicle and pray it's my last. Jakobe starts the engine and off we go.

A half mile down the road a pickup truck approaches, and as it passes us, I see Wes and Rob inside it next to the driver—their guide—and they see me. Before we have the chance to wave to each other in confirmation of our mutual recognition, we've gone our opposite directions; mine with guilt, theirs with confusion.

"What town are you from?"

"St. Louis."

"Nice place."

"It is."

"Born and bred there?"

"No, I grew up in Detroit."

"What brought you to St. Louis?"

"I took a job there with Boeing."

"You build planes?"

"I just sell them."

"I guess that pays the bills, too, huh?"

"I guess."

We travel a mile in silence, both of us staring straight ahead. But I know he's only keeping an eye on the road to safely drive the vehicle. Me, I'm driven by fear.

"Is this your first time out here?"

"It is."

"How do you like it?"

"I'm a bit of a bad shot, so I'm probably not a good judge of the hunting."

"No, I mean the country."

"Oh, okay. Yeah, I think it's beautiful. I've never seen land stretch on forever like this."

"Our reservation," he says, and he points out the window, "is over two-million acres. A man could easily get lost out here."

"I could see that."

"But not a hunting guide." I avoid responding, not because I'm unsure of what to say but because I'm unsure of the intent of his comment. I sense a definite coldness in his words. "We should be nearing the area. When you see what you think is the road he took you on, just holler."

A half-mile farther, I see a dirt road on the right that looks like the one I explored with Hollis. "I think this is it up here." He slows down the SUV and makes the turn. On our left and right, we pass multiple off-roads that all look the same. Everything looks the same out here—grass and blue sky. *Right, right, right,* I remind myself. He weaves the vehicle around ruts and potholes, and patiently lets me lead him deeper and deeper into no-man's-land where I exercise an equal amount of self-restraint in a delay to ensure accuracy in my description of this place.

"Hold on," he says. The right front tire dips into a rut that still holds water from whenever it last rained out here.

"I kind of remember this ditch," I say as we bounce through it and get tossed around inside the Dodge as we drive. When roughly fifty yards pass I say, "Turn here." It's as good a place as any on the right. To find another right turn, though, we travel a distance longer than expected, where upon my instruction he steers the vehicle onto a narrow dirt path lined with grass that wipes any and all dust from both sides of the Durango. "I think we parked around here somewhere."

He brings the car to a stop and turns off the engine. From the center console, he picks up a pair of plastic-framed shades before grabbing his hat that also rests between us. With both on, he opens his door and the two of us exit the vehicle and meet at the front of the car.

"Do you remember which direction you headed from here?"

I try to orient myself to lead us away from the grave. With the sun partially on my back, I think I'm able to determine north and south. "This way."

Through his tinted lenses, he combs the vast northern prairie. Unsatisfied with the results, he retrieves a pair of binoculars from the backseat. "Much better," he says as he glasses the south reservation.

I assume he hopes to spot the pickup, which he'll never do with the optical instrument he holds to his eyes. He turns his head east and west while adjusting the focus knob that rests on the bridge of his aquiline nose. After the south has been scanned, the west and northwest are given a look as well, followed by the east and southeast.

"Anything?"

"Nothing," he replies. "Odds are he never came back this way to hunt because a man in his condition wouldn't have gone too far from the road."

"His condition...is there something wrong with Orrin?"

"He's got ALS—Lou Gehrig's disease," he says.

"I never would've guessed." Not in a million years, or a hundred million, as I flashback to when he repositioned his gun the second before Hollis's went off, and a clearer picture of his possible intent for self-infliction presents itself.

"He was diagnosed a few months back when he began limping and slurring his speech at times."

"He seemed so normal."

"Seems," he corrects me. "Let's not give up on him yet."

"By all means."

He brings the binoculars up to his eyes for another glance southward, then lowers them to hang from his neck. "It makes no sense that he'd bring you hunting on reservation land. No sense at all." He looks south with the naked eye. "The impending sale of the Little Wing has caused quite a stir in my neck of the woods, with the biggest uproar coming from our hunting guides. It just doesn't add up that Orrin would take you here."

"From what you're telling me, it does seem rather odd."

"Any chance at all you could be mistaken?" he says as if to give me one last chance to change my story.

But I don't take the bait. "I can't be certain this is the exact place we began our hunt," I reply. "We definitely though took a right off the main road from the ranch if that's what you're asking."

"I am." He leans over and pulls a blade of grass from the ground. When he returns to an upright position, he gazes southward and lets the wind take it out of his fingers. "If you don't know where you're going, any path will take you there." After a brief silence, he turns and looks at me. "That's Sioux. Ever heard it before?"

"I haven't."

"Then I'll leave it open for interpretation."

"Okay."

But it's not okay. This man knows something isn't right—my story, the direction I've taken him. He sees it in me. I can tell. I can tell him lies all day long and they'll just shatter on impact. I am one big lie, and I stand there convinced he knows this as much as I know this is far from over. We are positioned face-to-face as members of two nations, adherents to a treaty signed by our ancestors over a hundred years ago. A time when mine had bullets and his had arrows. But now, it's the Sioux who has a gun strapped to his hip.

"Let's head back," he says.

"Okay."

By the time we reach the Little Wing, the sun lies as low in the grass as a sniper. Far above it, smoke rises into the twilight of dusk from the two chimneys of the main lodge and the two from the cabins occupied by the Texans. I return my visor to its upward position and unbuckle my seatbelt in preparation to exit the car that Kenton's parked in my driveway.

With a pen and pad in hand, he says, "Could I get your contact info, in case I have some more questions for you?"

"Sure."

"You've been very helpful, by the way."

"No problem."

I give him my home address, business address, phone numbers to each, including my cell phone number, before I step out of his Durango and shake his hand goodbye. As I'm about to shut the door he says, "What day and time is your flight home?"

Regardless of his objective with the question, which I'm not sure of, I smile and continue to be cooperative, with the aid of an image of myself on that plane. "Sunday at 2:00 p.m."

"Thanks. Enjoy the rest of your stay."

"I will, and I hope Orrin turns up soon."

"We'll find him, one way or another."

CHAPTER TWELVE

I stay inside the cocoon of my cabin and wait for Hollis to return from the river. Within these walls I can avoid contact with anyone—Wes and Rob included—while attempting to decompress. I look out the window into the slate of early evening and see headlights gain ground on the Little Wing. Behind the speed of light, is the speed of sound—the unmistakable whine of the Polaris's engine. By the door I linger for my friend. As he approaches the driveway to his cabin, I step outside and beckon him with a silent gesture. He parks and flashes the smile of an angler full of pride. With more of a sense of urgency than he demonstrates, I again signal for him to come to me. The absence of a smile on my face is as apparent as the one he projects.

Hollis shuts down the motor, hops out of the vehicle, and hustles over to me. He takes the steps two at a time and springs up to my porch.

"What's up?" he asks.

"Come inside," I tell him flatly.

His wet boots stain the wood floor and area rug, and when he sits down on the chair with his waders still on, the upholstery gets imprinted as well. On most occasions, I'm a better steward and would ask my guest to remove his fishing gear, or I'd obtain a towel for him to sit on, but we have business to attend to that's of far greater priority and importance than misplaced moisture.

"You look like you've seen a ghost."

"When you hear what I've got to tell you, then you'll know why."

He leans forward in his chair. "I don't like the sound of that."

"A criminal investigator from the Fort Peck Reservation paid me a visit this afternoon."

"And?"

"The Sioux police have taken over the case because the area where we claimed Orrin took us hunting is reservation property." And to express my further disappointment, I say, "You should've known that all the land on the right side of the main road out here is Sioux land."

A puzzle replaces his smile. "I don't think all of it is."

"They do."

"Well, I think they're wrong."

"Even if they are, it's irrelevant at this point because there's not much we can do about it. It's not like we can call the guy up and say 'sorry, but you have to turn the case back over to the sheriff's department because that will make things easier for us, since they're probably not going to get down on their hands and knees to scour the earth for one terminally-ill hunting guide gone missing.'"

"Terminally ill?"

"Yes, I'll fill you in. There's a lot to tell you."

He absorbs my comment and moves the conversation forward. "What did the guy say?"

"He asked me to show him where Orrin took us hunting, and when I assured him it was somewhere on the right sight of the road, he grew even more suspicious of our story."

"Why do you think that?"

"Because the Sioux are upset that you're snatching up the Little Wing out from under them and they told Lawton a month ago there will be no more hunting on reservation land. So the investigator is saying there's no way Orrin would've taken us hunting on the reservation."

"Lawton never said anything to me about that."

"Why would he?"

As a fellow businessman, he gets the picture.

"Tell me about this guy."

"His name is Jakobe Kenton and he's with the Fort Peck Police. He was waiting for me when I came back from hunting and asked if I would go with him to show him where we hunted."

"Okay," he replies, and waits for me to continue.

"I got in his car and did the right, right, right until I found a place that looked like the one we agreed on. We got out, and he looked around with his pair of binoculars, and when he didn't see anything he said, 'It's doubtful he came back here to hunt on his own because he has ALS and wouldn't stray too far away.'"

"Orrin had ALS?"

"Yep. Another 'small' detail we were unaware of."

I can see the wheels turning in Hollis's head as he glances around the room before speaking. "This may come across as cold," he says, "but if he had ALS, then he was a dead man walking, wasn't he?"

"That's beside the point."

"You know what I'm saying."

"Say what you want, but Kenton wants to bring search dogs out here." I run my hand through my hair. "This is getting really fucked up, Hollis. Maybe it's not too late to tell them the truth."

He shakes his head. "Now listen, you're getting all worked up, and probably over nothing."

"I disagree. You weren't there. He knows something isn't right."

"What could he possibly know? Think about that for a second."

"He knew I was lying."

"Okay, let's just say—hypothetically speaking—he *suspects* you're not telling the truth. Where does that leave him?"

"I don't know." And I don't.

"Nowhere. He's just a reservation cop with limited authority."

"Maybe so, but he's not incompetent by any means. That I can tell you."

"Then for all intents and purposes, let's say this guy has his shit together, and he's suspicious of us. Then what? What's he—or anyone else—going to do next?"

"Anyone else? Who might that be?"

"The feds possibly, I guess. But that's a long shot for something like this. Either way, what can they do if we just stick to our story?"

"He and Lawton were talking about bringing search dogs out here."

"To search 12,000 acres?" he replies and looks at me as though the idea alone is preposterous. "No dog could sniff out a needle buried a few feet under a haystack."

That old familiar voice of reason of his. Able to soothe me more than the drink in my hand. As logical as they come, Hollis Baumgartner. A man who can eyeball more computer screens at once than an air traffic controller. But he's a man who gambles and plays the odds. A needle in a haystack. I agree, most people would bet the farm. Me, though, I've never been willing to risk more than I can afford to lose, even if the cards are as stacked in our favor as Hollis believes them to be.

"One thing is leading to another." I pause to take a sip of my bourbon. "It's not exactly going as planned."

"As long as we stick to our story, they can't touch us."

An hour later the Texans and our party of four are all sitting in the dining room. I've explained to Rob and Wes the reason for my police escort earlier in the day. But the only explanation they will accept is the criminal offense in these parts of an aim bad enough to set a brood of pheasant free, of which I'm guilty.

The food and laughter are plentiful. Drinks flow. Judging by my exterior, it's the best of times with the best of friends. And I play along as the butt of their wing-shooting jokes. When needed, I'm their memory to set a story straight. I'm their reason for being there. And I'm there for them in so many ways; but in many others, I'm not.

"Boys," I say, "I'm calling it a night."

"No way," Wes says. He looks at his watch. "It's only nine o'clock."

"It's been a long day and I'm wiped."

"At least have one drink with us out by the fire pit," Rob adds.

Hollis sits next to me and taps my foot with his. "Okay, just one."

One becomes three; two too many. At ten thirty I enter my cabin and phone Lisa. But because I've forgotten to factor in the time zone, I'm a day late and a dollar short when I wake her from a much-needed deep sleep. We agree to catch up in the morning.

When the new day arrives, I throw logs into the fireplace and light them. This creates a glow that is twin to the rising sun outside my eastern window. Sitting on the stone hearth, I feel an unusual sense of peacefulness that I can't explain. Perhaps it's the warmth of the flame that settles me, or the light it casts. Or perhaps it's the thought of *two more days and I will be home* as I grab a pillow to lie back against. From this position I can see a light turn on in Hollis's cabin through my western window. At the dawn of the prairie, I am not alone. Life beckons, which comforts me as much as the pillow and firelight. A second light turns on, then a third. And, like a moth, I'm drawn to them. With coffee in hand, I get up to start the new day in the presence of my friend.

I pour a cup for him, throw my boots on, and head out the door. But I get no farther than the front porch before stopping dead in my tracks. Taped to one of the support posts is a white envelope bearing my name typed in black letters. I set down the coffees, pull it from the post, and open it. On the small piece of white paper contained within—typed in the same black font as my name—are the words: YOU WON'T GET AWAY WITH IT. I freeze, staring blankly at those six words, and my entire world comes to a complete halt. I can't move. I can't think. I can't do anything. I can only feel the vibrations of the runaway locomotive in my chest. Through fear, a thought comes to me: *This can't be real.* But I know it is. There's no way to deny what I hold and see in my hands. There's no way to deny the truth. Regardless, I turn the paper over and inspect its backside, which is as blank as my stare. A further inspection of the envelope, inside and out, reveals nothing as well.

I look westward. On the front post of Hollis's cabin I can see the envelope that awaits him. To view the cabins to the east, I take a step back. They are absent of anything white. At the far edge of my porch, I give them another look to make certain that Hollis and I have been singled out, and it's clear we have.

I race down the steps and across the drive and short runway of grass to his cabin. I knock repeatedly on the door until he swings it open.

"We're fucked," I say, raising my copy of the correspondence to eye level. "Yours is right there."

As water drips from his towel-wrapped body, he steps out and removes the second envelope bearing his name from the pillar. Inside the cabin we sit next to each other as he opens the message. On a small white piece of paper, matching the one that I hold, the same six words are printed. I can see them plain as day that's yet to arrive in earnest. But what troubles me even more is the look of worry on my friend's face. Until now, he's been steadfast in his belief that we have nothing to worry about "as long as we stick to our story."

He sets the paper and envelope down on the coffee table. "I'm going to put some clothes on." He returns in jeans and a gray fleece, and sits back down in the chair. "Whoever he is, he's bluffing."

"What makes you think that?"

"Because if he knew anything more, he would've taken it a step further."

"By doing what?"

"By requesting that the sheriff bring us in for questioning since we're off reservation land, which essentially means we're off-limits to him."

"You think it's the Sioux cop?"

"I think that's pretty obvious," Hollis replies, "or someone from the sheriff's department who did a favor for him."

I lean back in my chair. I've had enough. I don't want to live like this for the rest of my life. Hollis seems to have an answer for everything, but he doesn't. He only has theories, and I'm tired of them being proven wrong. "It's time to come clean."

He stares at me with the same expression I had when I first read the message. "Garrett, you can't give in like this. This is a minor bump in the road."

"Minor? Who are you kidding?"

"It's the reservation cop and he's trying to rattle us."

"If you were batting a thousand, I'd fully believe in what you're saying. But you're not."

"I never said I had all the answers," he replies. "And I don't think it's fair for you to point your finger at me like this."

"I don't feel like I'm pointing fingers as much as I'm simply pointing out that you've been wrong about more than a thing or two."

"Okay, so it's not a perfect plan. There never is or never will be any such thing in any facet of life. But I'm still as confident as ever that if we stick together, and stick to our story, we'll be fine."

"What if it's not the reservation cop or the sheriff's department on behalf of the Sioux? Then what?"

"Who else could it be?"

"Could anyone else have seen what happened?"

"There was nobody around for miles."

"How do we know that for sure?"

"If anyone saw us, we would've seen them."

"Not necessarily down by the Redwater," I say. "There are plenty of places—bushes and trees—where someone could've hidden from us."

"That's true, but we both know that's highly unlikely."

"Okay, then what's 'likely' going to happen next?"

"We're going to go hunting, just like yesterday. But I won't go fishing afterwards. We'll stay together. Maybe come back here and hang out, and shoot some skeet, or whatever you want to do."

"That's not what I mean."

"Nothing's going to happen. If the reservation cop or the sheriff stops by again, they're going to get the same story."

"Even assuming neither of them authored the letter, wouldn't it be odd for us not to report it to them?"

"Why would we report what we perceive to be some sort of prank by Wes and Rob?"

"That's a reasonable conclusion on our part, but how will they know that's what we're thinking?"

"They won't. And I think that's okay."

"I think it will make us look like we have something to hide."

"Let's just agree to disagree on this one," he says, and turns to gaze out the window. "The weather looks good for hunting. Come on, it will take your mind off things."

"I have no desire to go hunting." And I don't. The thought of a gun in my hand doesn't appeal to me at all.

Hollis detects my firm stance and avoids any attempt to try and to talk me into doing something I don't want to. "All right, what would you rather do?"

"Honestly, if getting on a plane and going home isn't an option, then a long drive over to the Little Bighorn Battlefield would be the next best thing."

"Then do that."

"Don't suppose you'd have any interest in joining me?"

"Maybe some other time."

"Do you think the Millses might have a car I could borrow?"

"For the kind of cash we're paying them, I'm sure they do."

CHAPTER THIRTEEN

Dolores loans me her Ford Explorer and a road atlas. We both look it over and agree that to and from the battlefield, with a two-hour tour of it, will allow me to be home in time for dinner. Ever the good hostess, she packs a lunch and extra drinks for me to take along for the ride.

I leave before the guides and dogs arrive, which allows me to wish my friends happy hunting over a cup of coffee in the dining room. Rob tries to convince me to switch guns with him and give it another try. He's certain I'd have better luck with a twelve-gauge than the twenty I'm using. "It's got a much denser shot pattern," he explains with the use of his hands and fingers to demonstrate coverage area. "The more pellets, the better."

"I told Hollis you shouldn't be using a twenty," Wes adds.

Hollis defends his choice of weapon for me. "A twenty is perfect for pheasant. You want there to be something left of the bird after you hit it."

Rob says, "With Garrett, everything is left of the bird, including its flight to freedom."

Smiles form.

"He'll get the hang of it one of these days," Hollis replies.

"I still say a twelve-gauge is the way to go," Wes says.

"Speaking of going, it's time for me to hit the road, boys." I stand up from the table and push in my chair. "I'll see you at happy hour."

"That's it?" Rob asks. "Just like that you're out of here?"

"I call his share of birds," Wes chimes in.

"Adios," I tell them.

With the atlas and Igloo cooler in my possession I exit the dining room while an expected onslaught of jabs and sneers are hurled my way, though none are from Hollis. For this excursion I have his blessing and, on my behalf, his defense of me. He will only let them go so far, and if or when they ever get there, I will be long gone on a Montana highway with the windows down and the radio turned up.

At the bridge over the Redwater an American Indian is sitting in a grey Toyota pickup parked on the side of the road with fishing poles poking over its tailgate. Encounters out here are few and far between, but when they occur a gesture of greeting is expected. I wave. There is no response from the fisherman, though, who appears to be dealing with lures and knots in preparation to head down to the river. On second thought, I realize I'm behind the wheel of a Mills automobile and there exists an uneasy truce between them and the Sioux. Perhaps he did see me and chose not to reply.

The atlas is spread out on the front passenger seat, and my Dolores-issued thermos of coffee rests in the cup holder. On the floor in front of the atlas, is the small Igloo cooler. With nearly a full tank of gas and my travel gear positioned within arm's reach, I'm prepared for the nonstop three-and-a-half-hour drive to the Little Bighorn Battlefield National Monument.

I search the radio dial and choose between country stations, which, for the most part, are all I can find on the FM. I crack my window to let in the mid-forties-degree air and set the heat to medium, creating a perfect mixture of temperatures. But now the volume on the radio needs to be adjusted to compete against the noise of the wind. I reach the ideal balance as I make a right on to 16 South.

At 55 mph, I pass several hunting guides traveling full bore in their pickups, loaded with crated dogs, on their way to any one of the several hunting lodges in this part of Montana. None of them is familiar to me, but I wave anyway. They wave back. The local landscape is made up of grass, farms, ranches, and lodges, and in between, every mile or so, a small wood-frame home on a lot commensurate to that of its dwelling. The road is consistent with the path of the Yellowstone River. At times I can't see it, but I know it's there. The trees give it away.

As I travel upstream I pass towns like Crane and Savage, which seem to exist solely for the Post Offices that occupy them and blow by in the blink of an eye. I can't help but wonder how anyone could call such places home. Hollis could, but I couldn't. This is not a criticism of these people or their municipalities. They are, for all appearances, quaint. I just don't have enough country in me to live in the country. I need people. I am too metropolitan to be without them. And the winters they must have here, I can't imagine.

But here I am, on my own. The "happiest" I've been in days. I'm even further away from nowhere than the Little Wing, and I look forward to going even further.

When I get there, the two-lane state route ends, and the interstate begins. I'm in the town of West Glendive, across the river from Glendive proper. In my imagination, and on a much smaller scale, they remind me of St. Louis and East St. Louis. In several blinks, I'm westward on I-94 and continue to follow the Yellowstone, though now at a higher rate of speed. On the interstate, the traffic is five-fold. People don't wave. I put the vehicle on cruise control and kick back with a Coke and a bag of Funyuns.

Twenty miles outside of Glendive, I-94 crosses over the Yellowstone and continues along its southern bank, where I discover just as much nothingness as before. But this nothingness grows on you. I'll take it, and possibly take back what I said earlier about living in the country. Maybe I could.

Past the town of Forsyth, the flat and indistinct prairie begins to change. Small rolling hills and buttes crown molded with trees come into view. Though I'm still joined at the hip by the Yellowstone just off to my right, hidden by the tree line that marks its presence the way telephone poles trace the highway.

Based on the pictures of the battlefield, and my gas gauge, I must be close, and a quick look at the atlas—now on my lap—confirms it.

With my troubles seemingly behind me, I reach the Bighorn. There are two Bighorns: the town and the river. One horn for each. At the town, the Bighorn flows into the Yellowstone. Farther south, the Little Bighorn flows into the Bighorn, and in less than thirty minutes I'm in the village of Hardin, Montana, where I fill up with gas.

Back on the highway, a sign welcomes me to "Crow Country." I check the map and it's Crow farther than the eye can see. And out here I can see like the hawk that sits on the fence post, the pilot in his Cessna overhead, and the satellites far above him that I cannot see. For it not to be Sioux or Cheyenne, I'm somewhat disappointed, since it was they, along with a few Crow scouts employed by the U.S. Army, whose blood was spilled on the battlefield with the Seventh Cavalry just up the road. I check the map again and upon closer inspection spot the Northern Cheyenne Indian Reservation tucked in behind the Crow's about twenty miles due east.

When I reach the battlefield, I take the drive to the Custer National Cemetery and find a parking space in the visitor's lot that's away from the crowd, because I want more time to myself before I venture out onto hallowed ground. From the cooler I remove another Coke and the sandwich Dolores wrapped in foil for me. I put the can into my left coat pocket and slide the sandwich into my right. For a few minutes I sit in the car and look out onto the cemetery planted with markers. All the fallen; rows and rows of them displayed in perfect domino order.

With the car locked, I walk past the cemetery and take the pathway that leads up to Last Stand Hill. As I approach, a fenced area scattered with tombstones becomes visible. Too far away to read the names, I begin to assign them in alphabetical order with each thought that comes to mind. Ambush, American, Anguish, Annihilation, Benteen, Bravery, Cadaver, Calamity, Custer, Decimation, Desperation, Eradication, Extermination, and on and on I go . . . to the point where I see my own name, Ingram, parallel with Gall's outside the fence. And there I stop and try to get the thought out of my head.

At the top of the hill a granite memorial stands sentry over the tombstones to mark the original place of burial for Custer and those who fell beside him on Last Stand Hill. In 1877, though, Custer's remains were re-interred at West Point, and many of the officers were re-interred at other various locations back East. Where the memorial was erected in 1881, a mass grave was dug, and the soldiers buried on the battlefield in shallow graves were re-interred there. It was in 1890 when the army installed the white marble tombstones I am staring at inside the fence, including Custer's—charcoaled for prominence.

Not far away, but far enough to be apart from all the other tourists, I sit down on one of the numerous grassy knolls and imagine what it must have felt like to be a member of the Seventh Cavalry on June 25 and 26, 1876, encircled by Sioux and Cheyenne. It's not the first time I've thought about it. I've read several books on Custer and the events that unfolded at the Battle of Little Bighorn. The man and the battle fascinate me, and have left me with one question I'll never be able to answer: What would I have done with my last bullet on Last Stand Hill, if I was the last man standing and all hope was lost?

For two hours I tour the battlefield. By the banks of the Little Bighorn, where the attack and subsequent retreat were initiated, there's a group of rocks on which I can sit and have my lunch. On the opposite side of the river, an Indian, familiar to me from somewhere in the back of my mind, like a novel long ago, moves upstream along the shoreline. As I watch him disappear into the timbers, I wonder if he's Sioux, Cheyenne, or Crow. I wonder if hundreds of years ago we came across each other in this exact place, would he go his way and I go mine, as we now proceed to do.

I could daydream here all day, but I have a return three-and-a-half-hour drive ahead of me that I'd like to complete before the onset of evening. Because of that I move at a good clip to cover the mile journey back to the car. By the time I reach the parking lot I'm sweaty and thirsty and looking forward to the soft drinks contained within the ice of the cooler. But I am not prepared for the parking ticket underneath the windshield wiper. With a few more steps the infraction I've been notified of is brought into focus. However, it is not a federal, state, city, or tribal-issued document. The cause for alarm is of far greater magnitude. I pull the envelope-sized white piece of paper from its mooring, and read the words printed in a similar bold font as the earlier note: YOU WON'T GET AWAY WITH IT.

Even though the wind is calm, I am now anything but; and the paper flutters in my trembling hands while I stare at the message. When I'm able to remove my eyes from it, I scan the parking lot, in search of the perpetrator. Whoever it is, though, is anyone's guess. The suspect in my mind wears the patch of the Fort Peck Police or the Richland County Sheriff. Turning this way and that, I scan the area in broad strokes, but the only uniformed personnel I find are Park Rangers. The vehicles parked in the occupied spaces reveal nothing, either. They are all empty, and civil in appearance.

If I could, I would grow wings and fly out of Montana and never come back. I want out. Out of this world. Out of this world of misery. I'm done with all of this. But I'm too upset and shake too badly to even drive, much less soar. As I fumble with my keys, I manage to unlock the door of the Explorer and get inside it. I start the car and roll down the windows at the same time to release the oven-like heat. The cool October air brings instant relief, which allows me to think in more rational terms. My literal hotheadedness declines.

After several deep breaths, I put the car in reverse and back out of my space. As I put the car in drive and turn the wheel to move forward, something pulls against the Ford up by its right front fender. A quick shift into park, and I'm out to investigate the trouble. It's the tire, and it's low on air. On second look, I realize "deflated" is a more accurate assessment, and my first thought is that it's not accidental. With my hand, I feel the tread and follow it with my eyes to look for a nail or any other object that may have punctured it. There's nothing, but I can't see the area that's in contact with the asphalt. I jump back in the car and move it forward a couple of feet. Upon returning to the tire to complete my inspection, I determine there's no puncture and all the tire needs is air, which leads me to believe this was a deliberate act of vandalism—to coincide with the note.

I could change the tire, but calling a service truck for air feels like the easier route. After several unsuccessful attempts to pick up a cellular signal, I walk to the visitor's center at the other end of the parking lot, where an employee lets me use the phone to call a tow truck.

An hour later he arrives. With his vehicle next to my Explorer, he gets out and reaches into the back of his truck for the air tank. He bends over, connects the hose to my tire, and fills it.

"Let's give it a few minutes to make sure there's not a leak," he says while he looks over the tire to see if he can locate any wounds.

"You guys busy today?" I can't think of anything else to say. I can't stop thinking.

"Swamped," he replies. "Won't slow down until tourist season is over."

"When's that?"

"Soon, I hope."

His tow truck is emblazoned with *Crow Tow & Service.* I assume he's Crow. I'm positive he's Native American.

"Probably don't see too many tourists out here during winter, do you?"

"Not at all."

I look around at the treeless landscape, which I imagine has an almost lunar feel to it when blanketed in snow. "What's winter like out here?"

"Long and cold," he replies. "Where are you from?"

"St. Louis."

He puts a pressure gauge on the tire. "Looks good."

I pay the man and thank him for the rescue.

Over an hour behind schedule, I'm back on the road, heading home, still without good cellular service, or no service at all. For the most part, it's the latter. Several times I try to reach Hollis and Lisa, but the connection fails with each attempt. Outside my windows, there's nothing to take my mind off things and ease my worry, as I'd hoped to do in conversation with my friend or wife. Instead, it's more of the same. The same old Big Sky and Land Country, infinite and relentless as my tormented soul that searches for answers.

With the long drive ahead of me, I have plenty of time for deliberations. In speculation, I lean toward the assumption that someone saw us drive the truck into the river. Even though Hollis has assured me there was nobody around for miles, it's possible for someone to have been in the tall grass or timber on the opposite bank of the Redwater. He could be there for several reasons: to fish, to camp, or to hunt. Out of curiosity, he stays low and watches us prepare to launch the pickup over the embankment and into the river. Once that occurs, he is witness to our crimes, and has followed me—as a plot for extortion—to the Little Bighorn National Monument. *No way,* Hollis refutes. *There was nobody around. If we just stick to our story, they can't touch us.*

Alone in a car on a highway in Montana, nobody can touch me as I travel the interstate while my mind wanders back to the Fort Peck Police and the Richland County Sheriff's Office. It is one of those agencies, I convince myself, or perhaps both, behaving as co-conspirators like Hollis and me, that have rattled our cages with the notes— and their clandestine ability to shadow my entire journey westward to the battlefield. Criminal conduct, I conclude, I'm not cut out for.

As a tired and worn-down tourist—and felon—who doesn't even notice the genesis of twilight's thin veil, I exit onto 16 North. At the request of a driver who flashes his high beams as he passes by me, I turn my headlights on and notice the gas gauge indicates less than a quarter tank. It's cause for some concern, but with seventy miles to go I'm confident of my return to the Little Wing, with or without the need to stop for fuel.

After ten miles, there's no trace of daylight left. No illumination on the horizon, except for the instrument panel that glows green like my daughter's bedroom lava-lamp—the one that sits on her nightstand and moths her attention while

I rub her back until she falls asleep. A sleep of angelic perfection and contentment. I'd give anything to be there with her now, to feel that last touch of her fingertips as they slide off my hand and onto her pillow.

The sudden glare of headlights in the rearview mirror extinguishes my thoughts of Jenny and almost blinds me in the process. A vehicle is closing in behind me with its high beams turned on. I slow down and edge over toward the berm in order to give it room to pass, but it doesn't race by. It continues behind me, closer than it should—bordering on dangerous. I flip the tab on the rearview to nighttime mode, wind down my window, and use my left arm to signal the motorist to jump ahead of me. Instead, he draws nearer to my tailgate. I speed up. He speeds up. I slow down. He slows down. At twenty miles per hour, I plod my way through the night on the empty county road and give the vehicle—only five feet behind me—one last chance to prove it's a drunken driver or kids pulling a prank, to prove this has nothing to do with the man I buried.

For a quarter mile, we travel well below the speed limit, until the roar of his engine coincides with his vehicle catapulting into the oncoming lane. A hundred yards ahead of me, the dark sedan crosses the broken yellow line and is now in my direct line of sight. It is brief, though. The rate of travel at which he accelerates into the black hole of nightfall devours him headfirst, with one last gulp to smother the faint smoldering of his taillights.

Relieved, I resume a normal pace for the operation of an SUV on a deserted two-lane highway in Eastern Montana. I glance at my phone. No service bars. I'm still somewhere beyond the Milky Way. However, as sure as the radio waves that I know are out there, a call home would bring me right back down to earth. Lisa, the kids, their voices, a connection to any of them and my time in solitary confinement would be over. Onward, I go it alone, on a road as black as a hearse beyond my headlights and, like the Yellowstone, I can't see but know is there. It follows the water. Long ago, people did the same with their oxen and wagons as they headed west. Not me, though. Not now. I am east by northeast as I mirror each straightaway, twist, and bend in the river.

I open the Igloo Playmate and grab a Coke as a source of caffeine. Better to stay sharp-eyed out here on the last leg home. When I feel the coldness of the ice, the road veers right and I steer the automobile with my left hand. As I search for the tab to open the can with my index finger, I remove my attention from the highway for a brief second to add sight to my sense of touch. In the moment that I return my vision from the beverage to the windshield, I'm blinded by the instantaneous fluorescence of high beams. The white flash is so bright it forces me to shut my eyes and turn my head away. From sheer panic, I slam on the brakes and grab the wheel with both hands as the Coke spills to the floor. Unable to see anything but stars from the whiteout, I hold onto the steering wheel as the Explorer helplessly skids off the pavement. It lasts only seconds, but feels like a lifetime before the friction of the field of prairie grass brings the car to a complete stop—unscathed, both driver and machine.

From such a close call, though, I have been brought to my knees. It's there I thank God for sparing me. With deep breaths I lower my heart rate and compose myself, then recollect the chain of events that sent me on a potential collision course with death. This was no accident. Those lights came out of nowhere with the express written intent to cause me bodily harm. My gut tells me the sedan had been waiting for me around that bend. At my most vulnerable, it attempted to gouge my eyes out with a flip of a switch.

I exit the vehicle and walk back to the road. Because of the bend, and the darkness, I can only see so far westbound, but it appears there's nothing to see. Homeward, the straightaway is also empty of anything but the sound of the Yellowstone where gravel beds rake its feet. Whoever it was has come and gone. Though I fear our paths may cross again before I reach the Little Wing.

After returning to the car, I grab the discarded Coke from the driver's side floor and place it in the cooler before checking the phone that sits in the cup holder. I don't want to call the police. I don't want to reach out to any law enforcement representative or vice-versa for as long as I live. But if that's what's needed to aid with my struggles, I will do it. No surprise, there is no signal. 911 is not an option.

With my seatbelt strapping me in, I manage to get the Explorer to crawl through the rugged terrain and stammer onto the asphalt. For defense, I turn on the high beams and slowly bring the vehicle's speed up to fifty—my self-imposed speed limit. In the distance, and in my rearview, there are lights. Company at last. Mixed emotions brew. Friend or foe? Real or imaginary? Is this all in my head? Am I dreaming? *Wake up, Garrett!* Twice, the oncoming car shoots its high beams at me, and because of the chip on my shoulder I return the favor and man my battle station. But a quick glance at my instrument panel alerts me to the fact I'm the one guilty of improper highway etiquette with continual usage of the high beams, which I'd forgotten were still on, and the oncoming driver had done nothing other than attempt to make me aware of this faux pas.

We zoom past each other. I watch him diminish in the reflection of my side mirror. In the rearview I see the other one. For some reason the latter is of more concern. Maybe it's my guilt, and it has determined some form of punishment is in order. I am Catholic, and for us sinners there is always torment on the road to redemption, if that's the one I'm on. However, it feels like even more of an uphill climb than that. And when a road sign appears, informing me that Savage will arrive in the not-so-distant future, there's an interpretation of Calvary in its letters. I'd like to take another look. I'd like to find out if I'm seeing straight. I'd like to know if I've lost my mind or how much of it is lost with each mile traveled at fifty miles per hour. God, get me out of here. Get me home. I can't do this anymore. I'm done. Sorry, Hollis, I'm not as strong as you. This isn't for me.

The lights behind me get bigger and bigger, and yet the phone remains unlit. To increase the separation between us, I step on the gas. The needle moves past 60, 65 . . . 80, and continues to crawl toward three o'clock like the floor indicator of an old elevator going to the top. I'm going way too fast. In daylight it would be considered dangerous; at night, it's borderline felonious, especially when an oncoming car from around a bend lays on its horn and flashes its high beams into mine. And so once more, I'm guilty of another crime as I choose to flee at a reckless pace from what I perceive to be another threat. As far as I can tell, I am not hallucinating. Either way, though, provoked or not, with or without criminal intent, there is a strange connection between this action of mine and those to whom I am responsible for with regard to Orrin Gall. To break the law is to break the law, and with this connection comes the added guilt, which becomes so formidable that when I reach the town of Savage and a bar appears on my cell phone I see it as a second chance for absolution and take it.

But before I can push the final digit of my 911 call, the signal is lost. I slow down to pick it up once more before I'm out of range again. But even at this reduced speed, I am through Savage in a fraction of a second and back into the deep sea of the Montana plains, where the only form of communication available is prayer. I pray for guidance, almost as an excuse to continue to head North instead of a U-turn to make a confession in Savage, which I know is the right thing to do. I pray for the strength to do it.

Talk is cheap. When all is said and done, much more is usually said than done. I've been in business long enough to know the cold hard truth of that. And, for the moment, I talk a big game. Hollis talks even bigger. He has my right ear. I have my left, because God is speechless, and He never saved my life, or my son's. That was Hollis. Now my friend has both of my ears as I get closer and closer to the Little Wing, and the lights that were once behind me, were vanquished miles ago. After Crane comes Sidney, and the road for the Little Wing—the last leg—is in between. I'm almost there. I'm the ridden horse, and the ranch is the barn that I see at the end of the trail. Giddy up.

One last check of my cell phone—still deaf, dumb, and blind—causes me to send it back to the cup holder for the duration of the ride.

When I reach the bridge, my high beams allow me to cross the Redwater in virtual daylight, and it is through this perception that I make my way from there to the Little Wing.

At the ranch, there are no lights on in Hollis's or Wes's cabins, and only the bedroom light is on in Rob's, which means they are bellied-up to the bar. I take the circle drive and park by the front door of the ranch. Inside, Lawton sees me from the dining room where he and Dolores are preparing the tables with two members of the staff. He comes out to greet me.

"I was starting to worry about you," he says. "Can I get you a drink?"

"A glass of water would be great." I'm dehydrated, and my mouth is completely dry. The semi-arid steppe climate has finally caught up to me.

"Coming right up."

I follow him down the hall and to the right toward the bar, where I'm surprised to see the saddles sit empty.

"Where is everyone?"

"Oh, I thought they got ahold of you."

"No, I haven't talked to anybody."

He grabs a glass, adds some ice, and fills the remaining space with bottled water. As the liquid spreads into each frozen crevasse, he says, "They all went into Sidney for happy hour."

"The Texans, too?"

"Yep, you've got the whole place to yourself."

I take a seat and set the car keys and a twenty-dollar bill on the bar and slide them toward him. "Thanks for the loaner. Sorry I didn't have a chance to refill the tank or clean up the Coke I spilled on the floor."

"Happy to oblige, and don't worry about the mess. I'll take care of it." He lays a cocktail napkin down in front of me, followed by the glass of water, and pushes the twenty back in my direction. "Gas is on the house. How was your tour?"

"Thought provoking, to say the least," I reply, before downing my drink.

He reaches for the bottle to refill my glass. "One of the things most people don't know about the battle is the tremendous suffering from thirst the soldiers endured all day and night up on that ridge without water. Especially the wounded ones. Drink up."

I follow his orders and shoot the chilled H_2O down my throat again, then look at my watch. "What time did my friends say they'd be back?"

"By eight."

"Any word from Orrin yet?" I ask, in an attempt to sound appropriate and continue playing the part.

"Nothing."

I leave it at that. "One more, please." I push my empty glass toward him.

He honors my request and refills my glass before sliding a pewter bowl of honey-roasted peanuts my way. "I can get you some smoked salmon and crackers, if you'd like."

"No, the peanuts are plenty. Don't want to spoil my appetite for dinner."

"It's a good one, that's for sure."

"There's something I was wondering if you could help me out with." I excavate a handful of nuts and wait for his reply as he begins slicing a lemon.

"Sure. What is it?"

"Might you know of anyone who, for whatever reason, might be holding a grudge against Hollis and me?"

He pulls the knife out of the lemon and looks at me, but not as if the question is odd or out of the ordinary (though it should be) for a high-paying guest of the Little Wing to ask its owner.

"Why do you ask?"

"I had a run-in today at the Battlefield, and possibly another on my way home."

"What kind of run-in?" He lays the knife next to the lemon and spreads his arms, placing both hands on the bar counter to give me his full, unbridled attention.

I lean forward and place my elbows on the same piece of ornate wood and look at the man twenty years my senior in his turquoise-embroidered black cowboy shirt and white Stetson. I look him in the eyes and say, "During my trip today someone put a note on the windshield of your Explorer that said, 'You won't get away with it.' It was the same note that Hollis and I found this morning taped to the porch beams of our cabins."

Lawton hesitates to reply. The pause tells me he knows something I don't. "I'm sorry to hear that," he finally says.

"Not as sorry as I am."

"You said something else happened on the way home?"

"I had some headlights shining in my eyes that made it very hard to drive. Long day is probably all it was."

He picks the knife up and makes quick work of the lemon. With me, he's not as fast. "Let's have a drink together and a little talk—man to man, okay?"

"Okay."

He grabs a glass, shovels ice into it, and fills it halfway with Maker's Mark. A citrus wedge straddles the rim of the highball. "Don't know why I like lemon with my bourbon. Old habit, I guess."

"They don't die easy."

"I reckon they don't," he replies, prior to his sip. "I got a fella here named Arapaho Sanchez. He's one of my ranch hands who, among various other duties, cleans all the birds. He's Sampson's cousin."

"Okay," I say, and nod for him to continue.

"When he cleaned the bird you and Hollis brought back from your first day's hunt, he comes to me and says, 'I gotta show you something, Boss Man.' That's what he calls me."

"Got it."

"I go with him to his cleaning table in the room behind the kitchen. When we get there, he picks up two items by the dressed bird and says, 'I found these matted to the pheasant.'"

As though in reenactment, Lawton opens his own empty hand. "In his palm are a canine tooth and half a dog's nose."

I'm stunned. Red-faced stunned. "I guess you don't typically find those types of things on a pheasant," I say.

"No, you don't," he replies and takes another sip. "I suppose a dog with a loose tooth could leave one behind when biting into a bird to retrieve it, but not his nose."

"I wouldn't think so."

"I didn't know what to make of it, and neither did Rap. That's his nickname," he adds. "But I know he told a few people about it on the reservation because Jakobe Kenton mentioned it to me when he came out here and rooted through the trash, hoping to find one or the other, but never did."

"The reservation cop?"

"Yes, the guy you went with to look for Orrin."

"Got you."

"Anyway, where I'm going with this is that there's talk among the Sioux Police that you and Hollis know more about Orrin's disappearance than what you're letting on."

"What?" I say, feigning an expression of disbelief.

"Now, I'm just telling you what I've been hearing. I ain't pointin fingers, Garrett."

He's not, but I am, and mine are aimed at Hollis. He should've known to check the bird. He should've known what side of the road is Sioux land. To have things unravel this way is egregious, and I wonder what else we should've done but didn't.

"Well, tell me what they're saying."

"They just don't believe Orrin would've taken you hunting on reservation land like you said, and that there's just no explanation for a dog's tooth and nose to be in a bird like that."

I sit back in the saddle. Elbows off the table and in my lap. "That's what the Sioux are thinking, huh?"

"Yes." He again tastes the Maker's, then puts his hands back on the counter to form a tripod with his body.

"What are you thinking, Lawton?"

"Honestly, I'm just doing my best to stay neutral in all of this."

"Neutral? What do you mean by that?"

"I mean," he begins, then stops to quench his thirst before saying, "hell, all these fields and roads out here look the same. You could've easily gotten it mixed up about taking a right or a left. I told Jakobe that." He pauses, grabs the Maker's Mark and says, "But, you know . . . sorry about that." He puts the bottle down. "Guests first," and he turns for the Woodford. "You ready for one?"

"Sure," I reply. He pours a drink for me. "But what?"

"Because I'm selling the ranch to Hollis, and Orrin was last seen with you and him, a few eyebrows have been raised."

"Did you stop to think that maybe that's exactly why they've raised them and are making a fuss?"

"Yes, I know the Sioux are unhappy about the sale. And yes, the thought did cross my mind."

"You've got a beautiful place here, Lawton, but I didn't come to Montana to be hassled like this."

"I'm truly sorry for the trouble you've encountered. As a guest of the Little Wing, I want nothing but the best for you, and a lifetime of good memories for you to take home when you leave. Me and my staff really do pride ourselves on our ninety-five percent return rate."

"I don't think I'll be back."

"I'm sorry to hear that," he replies. "I hope you understand we're good people out here. We are. And one of our own has gone missing."

"I understand."

"And I hope you can see—with the dog tooth and nose and all—why some feathers have been ruffled. You're my guest and I'm here to do everything I can to make your stay a pleasant one. But in equal respect, I'm also a citizen of Richland County."

"I hear you." I do hear him loud and clear but choose to focus on the benefit of the nose and tooth getting thrown away with the trash. The less evidence, the better.

"I'm doing what I can to keep the peace."

We both drink up. "I appreciate that. I hope they find him soon."

He swirls his glass, and the cubes and bourbon whirlpool counterclockwise. "He'll turn up."

To show empathy, and continue with the illusion, I say, "Hollis told me about how he lost his wife and son in an accident."

"Tragic. A sad day for all of us."

"How long ago was it?"

"Gosh, I'm gonna say coming up on about fifteen years now."

"Can't imagine."

"Me neither," he says. "They were all he had, besides his dog at the time."

"Sounds awful."

"It was." He takes a sip and points to my glass to offer me more, but I signal with my hands like a blackjack player that I'm good. "Anyhow, Orrin got even further involved with his community service work on the reservation and I think that's what got him through it. Damn shame to weather a storm like that, and then come down with ALS."

"Sounds like he was a good man."

"*Is* a good man, who'll turn up any minute now."

He takes the bowl of peanuts, and with his back to me, fills it up on the counter behind the bar then returns it to my domain.

"I'm a good man, too, Lawton."

"Garrett, I take you at your word. I take every man for his word until he begins to talk out of both sides of his mouth. For the Sioux, though, they've been lied to for so long they see things a little differently," he says. "And to them, there's just no explainin how the tooth and nose got where they were."

Not knowing what else to say, I'm thankful for the voices and footsteps that echo in the hall. I turn my seat in their direction. "They're back," I tell Lawton, who pulls glasses down from the rack in preparation for their arrival.

Chapter Fourteen

To the pitter-patter of my fingertips on her back and the intermittent drops of rain on the roof, Lisa cries herself to sleep. Like the clouds, she has shed nearly all her tears and drifts off. I remove my hand from under her sweater and stand next to our bed. Toward the children's hallway night-light that penetrates our room with its brightness—and a rising sun that will soon do the same—I tread. By design, the lead-paned windows on the east side of that long corridor are always first to circulate the break of day on the second floor of our home.

On the first floor I take a seat on the antique wooden bench against the wall in the foyer. The old piece of furniture is hard and uncomfortable, which is why I choose it: to stay awake. I could not remain vigilant otherwise. With two more hours of darkness to endure, I sit up straight and rigid in the shape of the handgun I hold and gaze across the room, looking out through the windows on either side of the front door. Off in the distance, lightning flashes. I count the seconds that follow: *one Mississippi, two Mississippi, three Mississippi, four Mississippi*—the thunder reaches me. It is powerful but elusive because you can't see it coming. Like the thunder, holding my own form of lightning in my hand, I am an invisible force sitting here in the darkness of my home. Whether outside looking in, or inside looking out, the playing field is level for anyone who wishes to challenge me.

As the flashes in the sky resume, I continue to count. For me, counting the seconds that follow the lightning has the opposite effect of counting sheep. I become more alert the more I count. When I'm able to reach as high as "twelve Mississippi," I know the storm has moved on and I will soon need something else to try and occupy my mind. It turns out I get more than what I bargained for when the security light above the garage on the left side of our house kicks on and illuminates the driveway and a portion of our front lawn. I rise and rush to our living room. I stand there by the radiator and inch open the curtain which hangs above it. There's no one (that I can see) standing where the light shines brightest. Advancing my line of sight toward the shadows yields nothing as well. But I know something had to have triggered the motion sensor on the floodlights, so I zero in on the ground to search for anything with four legs instead of two. After a thorough scan for deer or a raccoon and coming up empty, I'm back to square one. At that point I remind myself that downdrafts can provoke the sensor.

I conclude it to be a false alarm, exit the living room, and return to the bench. But just as I'm about to sit down, the security light at the other end of our house activates. This time, I race to the window in the dining room—a second too late—and see part of a shadow out on the lawn disappear into the even darker contour of night. I lean closer to the glass. In this position, I'm able to get a visual of the landscaped area of boxwood and yew that abut our Tudor, where someone or something could hide. I can't see all of it, though. Even with my cheek to the window pane a portion remains hidden, and that bothers me. Anything that might threaten the safety of my family, upstairs asleep, bothers me, and I know I won't be able to let it go until I'm certain there's nothing to worry about.

But there's no way to accomplish this without going outside. *At least the rain has stopped,* I tell myself, as though in some way—because of that—I will be less inconvenienced. It's not a matter of wet versus dry, though. That's just a game I'm having of casual conversation between my ears. Beyond the walls of my home, I'm vulnerable—even armed as I am—and my instinct nips at my heels to try and prevent me from doing what I feel compelled to do.

Next to the front door, I flip the alarm cover and type in the deactivation code. The dead bolt—apt in name—is next. As I turn and pull the handle, the gateway to my home swings open. But midway, I stop and reverse course due to a combination of gut instinct and second-guessing myself. My decision is confirmed by the security light that turns off a moment later and turns the night back on. It's the right call. As quietly as I can, I close the oak door and lock it.

With even less volume, I retreat to the bench to contemplate my options, none of which sounds better than to call the police for a second time in the same night. It's what they get paid to do by the taxpaying citizens—I reason—of which group I am a member who contributes his fair share. *There's no reason to hesitate. Call them!* But I'm also a grown man with a nine-millimeter semi-automatic firearm. I'm capable of a late-night walk out my front door to check on a disturbance, without the need for anyone's assistance, aren't I?

What kind of a man are you? What kind of a father? What kind of a husband? Are you going to continue to live on your knees? Wouldn't you rather die on your feet instead?

It feels good to stand and I sense blood circulating through me. I slink down the hallway, through the breakfast room and into the kitchen, where I open the drawer containing our flashlights. I grab one and press the switch to make sure it works. It does. With the flashlight in one hand and my gun in the other, I head for the front door. This time, there is no hesitation to open it and turn my world inside out.

Either the air has chilled dramatically, or I've suddenly become less warm-blooded. Maybe it's a combination of the two as I witness my breath rise like smoke into the upper bands of the Maglite's beam. Whichever it is, it's most acute in my fingers that grip the steel objects in my hands.

I turn to my right and take a few steps onto the spongy lawn and shine the light along the side of the house. I give each of the bushes bordering the stone up to the height of the windowsills a thorough inspection, if such a thing can be done from a distance. At the far end, though, where the now dormant security light is positioned, the shrubs are too thick for the beam to penetrate. With a twist of the flashlight's handle, I concentrate the light into a narrower beam. But the boxwoods and yews that fortify my home resist. Another step closer, another slosh from the soggy earth under the impact of my shoe, and I still can't see a thing in that hedgerow.

With the use of sound judgement, I know I've gone far enough—on my own, at least—and turn back for the house. Once inside, I slip off my wet shoes and climb the stairs up to Jenny's room to get Friday. He's on her bed when I enter, and the white hair on his neck and chest catches my eye as he raises himself to make certain it's just me.

Friday is an Australian Shepherd, and the best dog I've ever had. The only one that Jenny and Will have ever known. Just above a whisper, I call for him and he springs onto the floor.

"Good boy."

Side by side, the two of us take the rear steps down to the kitchen. A small room off that doubles as a mud room and a place for Friday's crate, toys, and his bowls for food and water. On the wall hangs his collar and leash. I attach the two together and secure them onto our dog. With the gun in my right hand and the leash and Maglite in my left, I'm now much more prepared to explore my property.

As an added precaution, I take one last look through the dining room windows before I put my shoes on, unbolt the front door, and step out into the pre-dawn darkness once again. With his first steps, Friday pulls hard on the leash, as though excited to begin his morning walk—hours ahead of schedule. At the end of the walkway, the maple tree appears to be his beacon, and when we reach it, he hoists his leg to mark his territory.

"Good boy, Friday. Good boy."

For his proper sanitation, I reward him with a pat on the back and more praise. He thanks me with a smile and tugs for the house. Now that he's relieved himself, perhaps he wants to go back to bed. But he veers off the walkway and onto the yard. Attached at the wrist, I veer off with him as I shine the flashlight ahead of us to see where we're going. He pays no attention to it, though, because his nose leads him along the ground like a blind man's cane.

He's caught wind of something, which becomes more evident as he lowers himself to dig in and pull with more power. Straight ahead, he lurches for the boxwoods and yews; the ones I declined to investigate earlier. Within ten yards of the shrubs, I wrench him to a stop and let him off his leash. In his master's spotlight, he sniffs his way into the bushes, where I lose sight of him. When he trips the floodlights, they are so bright I'm forced to turn away, like that night on the highway in Montana nearly five months ago. The chime of the dog tags on Friday's collar, though, alerts me to his presence behind the bushes. Even louder is the sound of his teeth clamping down on a solid object.

To shield my eyes, I bring my hand—the one holding the Maglite—up to my forehead and call to him. "Friday, come."

He doesn't.

"Friday, come here."

The grinding and chomping continues.

"Friday, come now!"

He emerges from the bushes—dog bone in mouth. "Good boy." I attach the leash. "Drop it." With reluctance, he rattles it around in his jaws. "Drop it now!" After one last chomp, he sets the bone free and I pick it up from the grass. Confident the threat has been assessed, and found absent, I'm ready to head indoors. But Friday wants the opposite and struggles to pull me away from the bushes and out into the yard. He is on to something again. *What's a few more feet?*

Fifteen yards later, he pounces on another bone, where I repeat the command to drop it; a command he disobeys twice before his eventual obedience earns my praise. This one I throw deep into the thicket far to my right toward the back of our house. He wants to give chase, but I'm not in the mood to play games. In preparation for the return trip home, I shorten the leash and tighten my grip. He counters this with a heave of his neck. It's powerful—thought-provokingly powerful—and the goosebumps daisy-chain themselves up my sleeve resulting in the image of bones in my mind; bones that I've never seen Lisa or the kids give to Friday. In fact, I recall Lisa's lecture to all of us on the danger of dog bones—something about fragments that can poke holes in Friday's stomach. So, it's odd that they would be in our yard.

Based on Friday's insistence, there must be another one up ahead. He can probably smell it. I'm certain that's what it is. We head in that direction. It's the direction of the wooded area that divides our property from the Bartholomews', which turns a light on in my head at the same time the one attached to my house turns off: their Labrador is responsible for the bones in our yard. Bingo! That's it. That's what this is about. But now it's about Friday's health, and I'm as determined to rid our yard of bones as he is to find them. Off we go, and another fifteen yards, another bone. Another fifteen, and so on and so on . . . until we're in the woods . . . and we've gone far enough. Maybe too far. And in a straight line . . . as if being lured away from our home.

Chapter Fifteen

All six of us sit on the saddles of the Little Wing's cowboy bar. I'm three seats away from Hollis and four drinks behind everyone else, already three sheets to the wind. At this point, though, I have no intention of catching up, and from the looks of it, they have no intention of slowing down, either. Even as Lawton prompts us on several occasions by saying, "If you boys are hungry, they're ready for you in the dining room."

They have injected the ranch with the revelry they brought back from Sidney. It turns out Hollis was skillfully able to kill two birds with one shot. Rob, Wes, and the Texans propose a toast with (what else) a round of shots. From what I learn, it's not the first time this gesture was made. The same proposal with the same result also took place at the bar in Sidney—twice. Everyone's in but me.

"He'll do one with us," Rob says to Lawton, who's placed only five glasses on the bar at my request. "Won't you, Garrett?"

"I'm not drinking to something I didn't see," I reply.

"Hey, I was there," Wes says. "I can vouch for him. Fucking amazing shot."

"I thought you were hunting with Rob?" I ask.

Rob replies, "Wes ended up going with Hollis, and I took your spot and had the guide and dogs all to myself. It was awesome." He lifts his glass. "I've never seen so many birds."

"He's in," Hollis tells Lawton.

"What's it gonna be?" Lawton asks, in reference to their choice of liquor rather than my final decision. He's already made it for me, reaching for a sixth glass.

"B-52's!" Charlie shouts.

"B-52's?" Wes replies. "What the fuck—while you're at it, how about some Duran Duran to go with that, Charlie?"

Laughter erupts amongst them, followed by horizontal movement in their saddles. Squeezed in the middle like ballast, I take it from both sides and manage to keep everyone upright. Lawton shakes his head and patiently waits.

"I'm going to 'shoot' down your suggestion, Charlie Brown. Get it?" Hollis asks all of us.

"Yeah, we get it," Rob replies.

"Then, Kamikazes it is, Lawton. Pour us a round."

To avoid capsizing, I act fast and throw my arm around Wes's shoulder and lean the opposite way. Even Lawton reaches from behind the bar to do what he can. But it's not enough, and Mike, sitting at the end, goes overboard. It is damn funny, and though I'm in no mood to frolic, I join in with the others as Mike climbs his way back into the boat, in time to be met there with an ounce and a half of glacial-colored alcohol.

A short while later Lawton regains control after removing the snacks and cleaning up the bar counter. He announces that dinner is served. We all take the hint and remove ourselves from our saddles. As Lawton escorts everyone toward the dining room I pull Hollis aside and speak to him privately.

"Listen to me," I whisper, gripping him by the arm to get his undivided attention. "They found Truck's tooth and part of his nose in the bird we had them clean."

"What did you say?"

"Let's go outside for a second." It's obvious I need to raise my voice, and I think the fresh air will do him good.

Unnoticed by the others, we leave the lodge through the front door and step out into the chilly air. For me, it's the equivalent of a splash of water on the face. For Hollis, I hope it feels like a slap. The vehicles belonging to Dolores and Lawton are parked at the end of the short walkway. I lead Hollis around them to ensure we're alone and nobody is within earshot to hear us.

He leans back against Lawton's Jeep. "What's so important it can't wait until after dinner?"

"On day one, remember the bird we dropped off after dinner to be cleaned?"

"Yeah."

"Well, they found Truck's tooth and part of his nose in it."

"What? That doesn't make any sense."

"Yes, it does, if you think about it." Hollis is quiet for a moment as he contemplates what I'm telling him. "The shotgun blast blew pieces of the dog into the pheasant. We should've checked the bird."

"How do they know it's Truck?"

"What other dog could it have been?"

"It doesn't matter," he says. "As long as they can't prove it's Truck, which they can't and won't ever be able to, we've got nothing to worry about."

"What if they're able to prove it?"

"You think they've got the dog's DNA in storage somewhere? No way," he says. "And a bit of dog hair they might be able to scrape off Orrin's bedspread isn't enough for them to work with, or even a trace of saliva from one of his toys. We're good."

Hollow leg or not, his wealth of scientific knowledge and cognitive function is impressive for someone so heavily under the influence of alcohol. And even though my judgement is somewhat impaired, I still recognize his unusual ability to keep his wits about him under circumstances most others would not, myself included.

"There's more," I say.

"Of course, there is." He smiles and tilts his head back to look up at the sky.

"I'm being serious."

"Of course you are."

"I think I know who left us the notes."

"Is it Sherlock Holmes?"

"You need to sober up."

"I'm fine," he replies, and he brings his attention back down to earth. "I'm just fucking with you."

"There's somebody else fucking with me, too—the Fort Peck Police or the Richland County Sheriff's Office."

"Tell me something I don't already know."

"Listen to me, Hollis, and knock off the bullshit."

He runs his hand through his hair, pushes himself off the Jeep, and stands up straight. "Sorry for being a dick."

"It's okay," I say, accepting his apology; though I appreciate the change in his tone even more.

"No, really, I'm sorry."

"I know you are. I get it."

"Okay . . . promise."

"Yes," I say. "Now just shut up for a second. When I returned to the Millses' Explorer after touring the battlefield, there was a note under the windshield wiper. It was identical to the ones taped to our porch beams."

"You won't get away with it?"

"Word for word."

"Did you see any deputies or Sioux police?"

"I scanned the entire parking lot. There weren't any cop cars, and I looked for someone maybe sitting in an unmarked car but didn't see anything."

"They must have followed you there."

"I know. And that's a long way to tail someone."

"You didn't notice anyone behind you?"

"No, but I wasn't really looking, either."

"Even if you weren't, can't believe you wouldn't spot a cop car at some point during your four-hour drive."

"I agree, but then again maybe they were in an unmarked car."

"Or maybe you weren't followed. Maybe they knew where you were going and had someone there waiting for you."

"Which would mean the Millses had to have told them, because they were the only ones who knew about my trip."

"It's possible that Lawton could've mentioned something to the reservation cop or the Sheriff," he says.

"But Lawton sounded like he'd rather not get involved."

"I wouldn't think he'd want to, either, and so I'm pretty sure Lawton hasn't gone out of his way to stir the pot," he says. "This deal is important to him, too. Maybe one of them stopped by the ranch this morning and it came up somehow."

"Okay, I'll go with that." I cross my arms in a defensive measure to fight the cold, before I continue with my story. "After I settled down a bit and was ready to hit the road, I got in the car and started to back out of my parking space, but the front right tire was flat."

"Coincidence?"

"I don't think so," I reply. "I got a tow truck to come and put air in it, and after we waited to make sure it wasn't leaking, I got on the highway. Then, about an hour before I reached the ranch, a car started tailgating me. I slowed down and moved to the side to let it pass, but he just stayed on my ass with his high beams on. Eventually he blew by me. And I figured it was probably just some drunk, or high schoolers getting their jollies."

"Highest alcohol-related fatality rate in the nation, right here in Montana."

Hollis has all the facts and figures. Always has. "Well, I'm not so sure it was either one because not much farther down the road there was a bend, and just as I began to veer to my right, out of the complete darkness, somebody flipped on their brights and I couldn't see a thing. I slammed the brakes and the next thing I knew I was skidding off the road."

"Fuck."

"Yeah, fuck is right. And I saw my life flash before me until I finally came to a stop in a field."

With interlaced fingers, he clasps his hands together on the crown of his head. "Are you convinced it was intentional? I mean, could it have been someone who thought his lights weren't on and you happened to be at the wrong place at the wrong time on the highway? Or maybe you nodded off for a second and dreamt it."

"I don't know what to think anymore. I'm still hoping this is *all* just a bad dream and I'll wake up soon."

Hollis steps away from the Jeep and turns his attention toward the Siamese twins of Big Sky and Big Land at evening's horizon. When his eyes return to mine, he says, "We just need to stick together, and stick to our story. Okay?"

"Yeah."

"We'll get through this. Almost home."

CHAPTER SIXTEEN

The next sound I hear is unmistakable, even from this distance where Friday and I are standing in the woods. I've come to recognize it like my children's faces, memorize it like their birthdays, and cringe when it's louder than it should be. The massive front door of our home is solid oak. When it shuts, its thunder can penetrate deaf ears. And now, hearing it shut penetrates my own hearing tenfold.

To have left it open and be led away from my family could not have been more unwise or foolish. *He has double-backed and is now in my house—and locked me out of it.* I drop the leash and begin to sprint for the house, the image of me traveling faster than the speed of light fills my mind. That is, until I see the actual light inside my home turn on. In panic mode, I consider firing my gun into the air, but my arms are moving back and forth too wildly to do that. I'd have to slow down to fire, and I'm not going to slow down.

With each foot I pull out of the rain-soaked sod, Friday nips at my heels in playfulness and disrupts my stride; a stride he's trained me to shorten over the years to avoid a kick in the jaw when he does this. Tonight, I kick him, and he backs off.

Midway there, I begin to tire from the extra weight of the wet and muddy shoes and the metal objects in my hands. Or maybe seventy yards is as far as I can sprint. On legs of rubber, I labor for air. I gasp for it. I need to stop. *But you can't stop! Your family needs you. You need them.* I keep going and going, while Friday bounds ahead of me, his leash trailing behind him; a leash I'm tempted to dive for in order to have him drag me across the finish line.

In desperation, I fight to move my arms and legs in the motion of a runner. Even if it's in slow motion, it's still forward progress, and I'll reach the house in a shorter amount of time than I would if I stopped to catch my breath. *Don't stop! Don't stop! Almost there! God, don't let anything happen to my family. Please!*

Friday reaches the front door before I do and waits for me there. Ten strides later, we're together and I lunge for the latch. But it's locked, just as I knew it would be. With the flashlight and my fist, I begin to pound on the oak to awaken my family. At the same time, I use my gun hand to ring the doorbell over and over.

Out of nowhere, Lisa's face appears in the window by the door, and the door opens.

"Are you okay?" I say as I jump inside.

"Yes, of course. What's going on?"

"Are the kids okay?"

"They're in their beds sleeping, unless you've awakened them."

"Were you the one who shut the door and turned the family room light on?"

"Calm down and please put the gun away."

I slide it into my back pocket. "Did you?"

"Yes. Who else would've done that?" She reaches up to my forehead and feels the sweat. "Let's go sit down and I'll get you a towel."

She heads for the kitchen and I take off my dirty shoes. When she returns with several towels, Lisa hands me one, then lets the dog in. After she wipes Friday's paws clean, she escorts him to his crate. The two of us head toward the couch in the family room, where I place my gun on the coffee table in front of us and sit down next to her.

"Sorry."

"It's okay," she replies.

I take one end of the towel draped around my neck and wipe off the left side of my sweaty face. Lisa touches up a spot I missed and swings her legs up onto the couch. After she tucks them underneath herself, she faces me in her white Terry robe as my heartbeat slows and I regain my composure.

"I'm tired of all this," I say out of breath.

"It's going to be all right," she says. "We'll get through it."

"I actually thought someone had gotten into our house."

"Is that what this is all about?"

"Yes." I wipe myself once more with the towel. "After you fell asleep, I went downstairs and while I was sitting on the bench in the front hallway, the security light above the garage came on, and then the one at the other end of the house." Lisa removes the Maglite I'm holding like a security blanket and places it on the coffee table next to the gun. "I went up to Jenny's room and took Friday outside to have a look around."

"You're borrowing trouble, babe."

"Maybe so, but I'm not going to let anything happen to our family," I say, as she stares into my eyes, which I know must be bloodshot. "We walked toward the light—it's off now because of the timer—where the boxwoods and yews are thick, and Friday started tugging really hard. He picked up a scent of something."

"We see rabbits and deer around the house all the time."

"It wasn't a deer. I would've seen it."

"Okay."

"When we got near the bushes, I let Friday off the leash and he found a bone back there behind them," I say. "You or the kids haven't been giving him bones, have you?"

"No, we never give him bones."

"Well, he found three in our yard."

"Three?"

"Yes, and we were in the woods between our house and the Bartholomews' when Friday came across the last one. That's when I guess I kind of just freaked out thinking that maybe it was all a ploy to draw me away from you and the kids."

"That's crazy. Think about it. It's just the Bartholomews' dog burying bones or whatever."

"You're probably right. But when I heard the front door shut and saw the light turn on, I thought back to the alarm going off earlier—that it was a break-in—and that someone was still out there and now he'd gotten in the house and locked me out of it . . .because of what I'd done in Montana."

She knows the story. I'd told her about it. In the kitchen, we had stayed up very late until there was nothing left to be said, other than me insisting on putting her to bed, which I did. She was drained. We both were. But as soon as her head hit the pillow she began to cry again, even harder than before. And there was nothing I could do other than rub her back and hope that sleep would come to her soon.

It did come, though it didn't stay long. I'd been downstairs and outside only a short while before she awoke and came looking for me.

"You've got to change your way of thinking."

"Trust me, I've been trying."

"Well, you've got to try harder because whatever you're doing isn't working. For you to be running around outside in the middle of the night with a gun isn't the least bit healthy, and borderline dangerous."

"Agreed. But I don't know what else to do. I mean, I feel like I'm losing my mind."

"Maybe you should talk to someone."

"I'm doing that now."

"You know what I'm saying."

"A shrink?"

She pauses and wraps her hands around her exposed ankle. "Not necessarily. What about Father Seb? Maybe both of us need to go see him."

"So that's why you're up."

"Yes," she replies. "I think we need to talk to someone who can help us because I don't think we're going to be able to keep this inside us for the rest of our lives. It's just too dark of a secret."

Sebastian "Father Seb" Gonzales, S.J. is a Jesuit priest from our old parish in Savannah whom we befriended upon arrival and whom we've stayed in touch with ever since our departure. He baptized our kids, administered their First Communions, and never lost a game of ping-pong to me those times he joined us for dinner at our house. We hold him in high esteem, and the idea of going to see him has merit. But I've also made a pact with Hollis to carry our secret to the grave, which I've broken with my confession to Lisa, and an additional one—in my rationale—potentially borders on betrayal.

"I already feel like I've said too much."

"To me? Are you kidding me?"

"You don't understand. Hollis and I swore that we'd never tell a soul."

"And where's that gotten you? Where's that gotten us?"

"At least I'm not in jail."

"Physically, you aren't."

She's a brilliant woman. I love her. I will always love her. She looks at me with her big blue eyes and I see the pain in them I've caused. But there's sympathy there too, which, I'm sad to say, I can also take credit for. As I stretch out my legs to rest them on the coffee table, she nestles against me and extends hers on the couch. In this position, it would be easy for us to fall asleep, in which case I give in to temptation and reach for the switch on the lamp beside us.

Out the window, the first hint of daylight softens the sky like the cotton of her robe in my hand. With tenderness, I move it over the smooth curve of her shoulder and ease her into pleasant dreams that often stem from affection. For me, though, nothing comes except doubt. Because the reality of exposing ourselves to anyone, even to a priest, is tough to fathom. I'd almost rather endure the pain than chance the consequences of informing one more person of where Orrin Gall lies buried, all for the sake of some peace and harmony that will be temporary at best. In the long run, my thought is things would still be unresolved, and we'll be back to where we started. To ask for help, for forgiveness, for mercy, and for peace of mind, Lisa means well, but to do this puts faith in a course of action she's only had a few hours to contemplate. After five months of my prayers for peace of mind going unanswered, I'm at the point where action needs to be taken—whatever that may be—to change what I believe can be changed. As I've said before, talk is cheap.

Lisa is asleep. I can hear it in the slight movement of air between the sliver of her parted lips. I can feel it in the rhythm of her ribcage as it expands and contracts—as I felt my children's when they'd shut their eyes and drift away while cradled on my torso. And just as I did back then, I remain motionless—except for the hand I caress her shoulder with—to keep her undisturbed. In the candlelight of dawn, she's beautiful—inside and out. I can't stop staring at her. In this light, she's my harvest moon, with the same primitive effects. Subliminal or not, I reconsider her suggestion to contact Father Seb. I will give serious thought to anything that will make her happy. Perhaps, though, it would be more prudent for her to sleep on it some more.

Time passes, and the sun—now a full circle above the horizon—has its own celestial tug on Friday. He whimpers to be let out of his crate. As I slide out from under Lisa, I replace my body with a pillow to fill the void before I leave the room to set him free.

As always, he's excited to see me. To him, a hundred years have passed since we last said hello. Maybe more. Back and forth, his tail polishes the aluminum side rails that contain him, while I fumble with the latch, until out he springs. He stands up on his hind legs and wraps his two front ones around my thigh and holds onto me. It's Friday's unconditional hug of joy and love. He does this with all of us when hours have passed without each other's company. I stroke his back and chest and remind him over and over what a good boy he is, until he tires and lets himself down.

From the mud room, I grab a spare jacket and doggie bag, and head out the back door with him. For some reason—even with my coat on—it feels even cooler than it did just hours ago. While Friday pulls on his leash toward the ivy, I button up. "Good boy, good boy," I say to encourage him to remain on course so that I won't have to pick up what he drops off. The grass I keep clean, the ivy we don't.

He reaches the unkempt ground cover and I unhook him. With sniffs and circles of travel, he singles out his commode of choice. When he finds just the right place, he drops trowel and looks back at me to make sure I keep an eye on him while in such a vulnerable position. Upon completion, he bursts out onto the lawn and dashes for the silver maple. It's one of his favorites to piss on. To mark his territory, he hoists his leg and continues down the row of trees that line our backyard.

My hope is he finds more bones, not only so I can remove them from our property and keep him safe, but also to discredit the negative thoughts that linger on the ones we found earlier and how they might have gotten there. With his tail rudder, he tacks his way toward the wooded area over by the Bartholomews' property. That appears to be the path he's chosen. Out in front of him, I scan the yard in search of bones but see nothing other than some scattered leaves and grass. I quicken my steps, though, just in case he latches onto one that is hidden from my line of sight. When I catch up to his zigzagging forward progress, I attach the leash to him. At the edge of the woods, he lowers his nose to the ground and slows his pace. There's something on his radar, which prompts me to try and find it before he does. It will be white, off-white, or pale with mocha streaks.

But white of any shade isn't what catches my eye, or Friday's nose. It's steel. Blackened in the middle with a slice of nickel on each end that flickers in the sunshine, and he's on it at the same time I am. As he pulls, I tug and wrap my hand around the leash to shorten it—all the way down to the scruff of his neck. He stops. Below him on the ground is the head of a club hammer in the partial cover of a maple leaf. I wrench Friday back and reach down to pick it up by its rubber-gripped handle.

To find a tool like this is odd, and for a better examination of it I back out of the woods and into the direct sunlight. Without question, it's not a possession of mine or anyone else in my family. The only other possibility is that it belongs to the Bartholomews. But since Bill and Margot are in their seventies and seldom venture into the depths of their yard, much less with a handheld sledgehammer to prune honeysuckle, I can almost with the same certainty rule them out as well. In my most logical and rational frame of mind, which Lisa would encourage my use of now, I think about every time I've ever seen a landscaping company tend my neighbor's property. They mow and mulch, that's it. Not once have I ever seen a worker—of any type—in this wooded area. And I know my neighbors well enough to know that if there was ever something they wanted to do on behalf of our common border, they would discuss it with Lisa or myself. They are kind and considerate people.

Thus, I begin to look at things the way I've done it for the last five or six months and let my imagination run wild, as though someone has fled our home after the alarm was tripped during a break-in. The police arrive. Through the backyard he goes on a mad dash, and into the woods where a branch he doesn't see knocks the club hammer—that he used to pound his way into my house—out of his hand.

It's no challenge to continue in this direction with my mind—the road of torment and agony I've come to know all too well, like a familiar place. The glass is half empty. The pessimist. The faithless. The man who runs around his yard in the middle of the night with a gun in his hand. The chicken with its head cut off. To be more appropriate, make that a pheasant. No, I'm not insane. I haven't lost my mind. I'm of sound mind and body. I found the evidence. The tool used by the criminal—perhaps plural—bent on revenge. But I can't wrap my head around the fact that the Fort Peck Police and/or the Richland County Sheriff's Office would do something like this. They wouldn't. *Would they* . . . rattle my cage like this? Or is it someone else? Or something else unrelated. *Is this just all in my head?*

I need to know. I need to know more. With Friday in tow, we travel deeper into the woods, into its nebula beyond the sunrise. We are headed west, over fallen limbs and in between the heavy growth of honeysuckle and maples. Near the backside, which is the front side of the Bartholomew property, a patch of euonymus draws Friday's attention. I let him sniff and hoist a leg.

We exit the woods and enter our neighbors' manicured grounds. As uninvited guests, we stand there in view of their home, from which they've probably already spotted us. The drapes are open on the second floor, which leaves little doubt they've begun their day and won't be too bothered by a knock on their door. Along the edge of the backyard, we cover its entire length and flank the east side of the Tudor to gain access to the front yard. There, the sun warms our backs as we cross the grass to the stone walkway that leads to their door. With the options of the brass knocker or the doorbell, I extend my index finger and make my choice. The chime is followed by an eruption of their dog. At attention, Friday stands by my side—on a short leash—to say hello to his friend.

The deadbolt turns, and the door opens, but only about twelve inches. A magenta-robed Margot Bartholomew, all sixty inches of her from slipper to the crown of her grey hair, looks up at me with a smile as she uses her knee to keep Baxter from squeezing through the gap. She is no match for the animal whose bark and strength combine to overwhelm her. While she deals with her pet, she asks to be excused for a moment. When the door opens for me the second time, Baxter is nowhere to be seen and Margot is much more composed.

"Sorry to bother you, Margot, but I was out walking Friday and found this club hammer in the woods between our properties." I produce the tool for her to examine. "Does this belong to you or Bill?"

"I've never seen it."

"Any possibility one of the grandkids might have been back there playing with it on one of their visits?"

"I wouldn't think so."

"Think any of the guys who take care of your yard might have dropped it?"

"That I can't say," she replies. "Let me get Bill and see if he might know something. Come on in."

"Oh, thanks, but that's okay. Friday's paws are wet. I'll just wait here."

When Bill comes to the door, Friday tugs hard toward him—the good buddies they've become. As always, the old man is never without treats, and Friday can smell the one he has for him in his hand. They make each other's acquaintance, after which, Bill, all sixty-seven inches of him, extends his Friday-licked hand and says, "Beautiful morning, isn't it?"

"Sure is," I reply, and we shake. "Hope I'm not intruding at such an early hour, but I wanted to see if this club hammer I found in the woods between our yards might belong to you."

He takes it from me and eyeballs it. "Little bit of rust on this edge here, but all in all it's in decent shape," he says. "Can't claim it as mine, though."

"Any idea whom it might belong to?"

"I don't."

"I thought maybe one of your landscapers accidentally left it behind."

"Don't think they'd be carrying something like that around to cut the grass."

"Okay, point well taken." I turn for home. "Just thought I'd check with you before adding it to my toolbox."

"I appreciate that. How are Lisa and the kids?"

"They're great. Thanks for asking," I say. "Sorry to bother you."

We take the long way home. It will give me time to think, time to question my own questions, of which I have many. At the intersection of the stone walkway and asphalt drive, I turn left on the patibulum the two paths form. To the cul-de-sac that is the artery for my home and seven neighbors, there's a gentle rise in the pavement. One hundred fifty yards long, it runs parallel to my own for part of the way on the other side of the split-rail fence well hidden by the pines on that border property, until we reach the street and make a hairpin turn. Down our driveway, we step in synchronization—left, right, left, right, left, right. I'm right. I'm wrong. Lisa's right. She's wrong. *Go see Father Seb. No, there's no reason to. You know what's going on. The club hammer is no accident. Maybe it is.*

Lisa is still asleep on the couch when we return. With her head on the pillow, I wedge myself back underneath—without waking her—so that her cushioned head rests in my lap. On the Oriental rug a few feet away Friday parks himself and stares up at me. Though it won't be long before his eyes are closed like Lisa's.

How wrong I can be. When the home phone rings, he lifts his head. At the same time Lisa lifts hers as I try to remove myself from the sofa with as little fanfare as possible. But I need to hurry or else the children will be awakened too. I grab the phone in the study.

"Hello?"

"Hi, Garrett. Bill Bartholomew here."

"Hey, Bill."

"After you left, Margot remembered that a guy from Invisible Fence came out to give us an estimate," he says. "Maybe he left that hammer behind when he walked around the yard."

"I guess that could've happened. How long ago was this?"

"A few weeks," he answers. "Did you see any stakes back there? He was going to mark our property line with them."

"I didn't, but that brush is thick."

When I return to the living room, Lisa is sitting upright in the middle of the couch. Friday has taken the open seat to her right. I claim the one on her left.

"Who was that?" she asks, as she takes her cell phone out of the pocket in her robe and places it next to the gun on the coffee table.

"Bill Bartholomew."

"Little early for him to be calling, don't you think?"

"Kind of."

"What did he want?"

"I found a club hammer in the border property and he thinks it might belong to the Invisible Fence guy who stopped by their house to give them an estimate."

"Hope they go with it. No more bones for Friday." She settles back onto the couch and strokes Friday's left flank.

"The thing is, I'm not so sure Bill is right."

"Why would you even think twice about it?"

"Because I'm worried."

"About what?"

"That maybe it has something to do with our alarm going off last night."

She senses the change in my tone and straightens once again. She removes her hand from Friday and places it on her knee. "What are you trying to say?"

"That maybe I'm not so crazy after all and that someone broke into our house."

"There's more to this, isn't there?" she says. I don't want to frighten her the way I have already. But at the same time, I feel compelled to put everything on the table. "I want you to be perfectly honest with me."

"Okay," I say.

"Do you think someone tried to break into our house to hurt us?"

"I just don't know. But yes, that could be true."

"With the hammer?"

"Do you mean to break in the door with, or to use to harm us?"

"Both."

"It's possible. But again, this could all be in my head. And if it isn't, it could be to scare us, to get me to confess." I don't know what to tell her. Unfiltered, my next thought comes out of my mouth: "Or maybe someone did see us drive the truck into the river."

She turns red, the color of anger; then maroon, the color of hatred. "How could you do this to us?" She tries to strike me with her right hand, but I deflect the blow. Her left hand follows suit. "How could you do this to our family?!"

She breaks down and sobs. I draw her to my chest to comfort her, but she resists.

CHAPTER SEVENTEEN

The morning is slow to arrive. In my bed, saturated with sheets and blankets, I wait for it. For over an hour I've waited for it. I'm content to stay where I am, lying on my side facing away from the window I left open overnight to let the cool air seep in, and let the entire day pass me by. That would allow me to rise, pack my things, and head to the airport for my flight home. But I have one more day to endure before that will happen. Thus, I lie in wait, in the darkness of my cabin—cocooned in flannel, down, and wool, as though fortified against the world.

For our final day I've agreed to shoulder a gun and walk the fields one last time. Hollis convinced me doing anything else would add fuel to the fire of suspicion, and that the two of us should remain together from here on out, which I fully endorsed. "United we stand, divided we fall," he said when we made our way home from the fire pit just before midnight.

As the room lightens I pull the sheet and blankets further over my head to remain in the dark. But it doesn't last long. While the covers may shield me from light and air traveling through the open window, they do very little to prevent sound from reaching my ears. The sound of engines, exhaust, brakes, tires. Car doors that open and shut. Voices that overpower the songbirds. For the staff of the Little Wing, the workday has begun.

Without choice, I begin mine, too. I'm a good ant, a good bee. I'd like to think it's the Protestant work ethic in me, but I'm Roman Catholic, an ancestor of aqueducts, concrete, sewage systems, roads, and arches, the Colosseum, and forums. In this mindset, I throw back the covers and head for the shower, determined to work my way through this last day of "vacation."

After cleansing my body, I hear the motorcade outside and begin dressing for the morning hunt. As soon as I lace up my boots, I head for the door to look for our guide, which will prompt me to hurry things up if he's arrived, to hurry with the coffee I've yet to brew. Without it, I cannot function.

As I swing the door open and step outside I'm jolted by the amount of law enforcement vehicles lined up in front of the lodge, with Lawton and the posse huddled beside them. Three police SUV's, two sedans, and a heavy-duty trailer; enough men and machines to momentarily divert my attention from the white envelope attached to the post. Out of the corner of my eye, though, it seems to bellow for me to step forward and yank it loose from its moorings.

With my index finger, I slice it open and remove the white piece of paper. In black type, like the previous letters, is printed: THE GLOVES HAVE COME OFF. Over and over, I read it as though in search of some hidden meaning between the words. But the message is loud and clear, like the crowd that's gathered, and I can't help but wonder if the two are somehow related. I put the paper back into the envelope and slide its folded body into my jean's pocket. Out of sight, out of mind—where trepidation condenses to form a drop of sweat on my forehead.

To my left and right there are no signs of any other envelopes taped to support beams. No stirring in the cabins. And I could retreat to mine and pretend the same, but I choose the opposite path: down my porch steps and onto the drive. As I approach the men, Lawton sees me and steps out of their circle, as I'd hoped he would. We meet at the end of the walkway by the front door of the lodge.

"Thought I'd grab some coffee and a hot breakfast," I say.

"It's all waiting for you inside," he replies. "I want to let you know a Fish & Game warden found Orrin's truck at first light this morning."

The blow is swift and powerful, but I manage to stay on my feet. "Is that good or bad?"

"It's in the Redwater."

"Oh, geez!" I feign. "What about Orrin?"

"Don't know yet. They're going to try and pull it out now with my tractor and we'll see what they come up with, I guess. Sounds like he drove it off the road."

"Where?"

"Down a ways from the bridge. There's a few sharp bends and if you're not paying attention you can find yourself in trouble right quick," he says, and puts his thumbs into his jean's pockets. "I own that stretch of land along the west side of the river there and used to post signs, but kids would just shoot em up for target practice."

"The news isn't promising, is it?"

"No, but I'm still keeping the faith."

"Me too."

"Thanks," he replies, then turns and walks back to the group.

Inside the lodge I pour myself a cup of coffee, a task made more difficult by hands that shake. As a prop, I pick up a newspaper and take a seat at an empty four-top. Across from me, the buffet line starts with an assortment of fruit followed by numerous stainless-steel domes that cover the hot foods I'm downwind of.

They'll search for his body downstream. How far they'll go is anyone's guess. Mine is several miles that they'll scour the shorelines and drag the bottom. I look at the paper and sip my coffee with both hands to steady the cup. I'm not reading a single word. I just stare and pretend—pretend to be someone and somewhere I'm not.

The thud of car doors shutting and revved engines break the silence as well as my train of thought. It's obvious the detachment has mounted their horses in preparation for a departure to the river. To avoid them, I stay put until I know they are long gone, before I make my way to Hollis's cabin, which becomes unnecessary as soon as I see Rob and him stroll into the dining room.

"Well, if it isn't Elmer Fudd himself," Rob says to me.

"Good morning, boys," I reply.

They are dressed in their hunting apparel like me and pull their chairs out to take a seat. Rob moves slower than Hollis, which is the price he pays for his attempt last night to keep up with a man with a hollow leg. They unzip their jackets and lay them over the backs of their chairs.

Rob leans forward, places his elbows on the table, and says, "Any idea what the armada heading down the road is all about?"

"They're going to the river to pull Orrin Gall's truck out of it." I glance at Hollis and see the startled look on his face.

"Wow, that's a shame," Rob replies. "I guess he's dead, huh?"

"Lawton said they wouldn't know until they pulled out the truck."

"Did Lawton say anything else?" Hollis asks.

"He said it was the Fish & Game warden that spotted the truck this morning."

"Was it sticking out of the water?" he asks.

"He didn't say."

"The river does seem to be running low and clear," Rob says.

"Is it?" I say to Hollis.

"I don't think it is," he replies.

"Thinking and knowing are two different things," I say.

"Couldn't agree with you more."

"They'll find his body in the cab, won't they?" Rob says.

"Not necessarily," Hollis replies.

"How's that?"

Hollis says, "If his windows were down, he could easily have been sucked out and carried far downstream if he wasn't buckled in."

"All the way to the Mississippi," I add.

"Well, for his family's sake, I hope they find him one way or another," Rob says, unaware of Orrin's lost bloodline.

When Rob gets up to head for the buffet, I take the envelope out of my pocket and slide it across the table to Hollis. He opens it, reads it, and sends it back my way.

"Fuck them."

"Easier said than done."

"Maybe not."

Brushing his bravado aside, I say, "The shit's hit the fan, Hollis."

"I don't think so," he replies. "I'll admit I'm surprised they found the truck so soon, but there's no need to panic."

"I'm not panicking. I'm just tired of nothing going right."

"You're looking at the glass half empty."

"No, I'm looking through the looking glass and there we are checked in to the Montana State Penitentiary for an extended stay."

"You're letting your mind run away with things again. Remember, they aren't going to find his body, and without his body, they can't charge us with anything," he says. "Tomorrow we'll literally be home free. Just think of that."

It's remarkable how well he handles stress and pressure. I wish I could do the same. For me, the uncertainty is more of an equation that, if I'm unable to calculate correctly, I have no business attempting to solve it. In over his head, the commodities trader is much more at home than the aviation salesman trying to keep his feet on the ground.

Rob comes back to the table with enough food to feed all three of us, but it's just for himself.

"Craving grease, Big Guy?" Hollis says, then steals a piece of bacon before Rob's able to slap his hand.

"Get your own," he replies, and he wraps his big arms around his dish to ward off future attacks.

"Can I get anyone anything while I'm up?" Hollis scoots his chair back and rises to his feet.

"O.J., please," Rob requests.

"Anything for you?"

"I'm good, thanks."

Wes enters the dining room and walks right past Hollis, who is filling two tall glasses with a pitcher of orange juice. One for him, one for Rob. Or two for Rob. Not one to let his friend's impoliteness go without notice, he says, "Good morning to you too, Mr. Reardon."

"Hola," Wes replies as he carries his haggard body to our table and takes the last remaining seat. "I'm hurting big time."

"You look like it," Rob says.

"Why did you guys let me do that last shot?"

"You need to start pounding a lot of water, my friend," Rob advises. "The bacon and sausage will help, too."

"I'm not the least bit hungry."

He's not the least bit ready to go hunting, either. Sockless in his Birkenstocks and sweatpants, a long-sleeve T-shirt under a black down vest, and topped off with his disheveled hair, I can see how easy it would be for him to make the decision to crawl back into his bed after a cup of coffee or two.

Hollis returns with the O.J. and puts one of the glasses in front of Wes, and says, "You look like you could use this. Drink up."

He obeys his friend, drinks half of it, and sets the glass back down. "Thanks."

"Do you remember hitting on Dolores Lawton?" Rob asks him.

"What?" Wes replies. We all laugh, although mine is fake.

"Yeah, you tried to get her to come back to your cabin after Lawton shut down the bar and told us he was 'retirin' for the evening, but if we needed anything else, Dolores would 'take care of us.'"

"Funny."

"I'm serious," Rob says, though there's not a hint of seriousness on his face or anyone else's. On Wes's, there's only agony.

"Not buying it."

"Well, you certainly tried when you whipped out a hundred-dollar bill and offered it to Dolores for her services."

The group begins to laugh. Wes included, who then replies, "Now I know you're fucking with me because I only carry fifties. Who wants to go up and get me another glass of O.J.?"

Hollis volunteers. As he gets up, Rob joins him and heads to the buffet for seconds. I'm content with my coffee and remain seated next to Wes.

"I'm glad I left early and went to bed," I say.

"You were smart."

"What time did you guys call it quits?"

"I think it was around two when we left the fire pit. Hollis kept pouring shots. Never again."

"Did you pop any aspirin?"

"I didn't bring any."

"I've got some. Want me to go get you a couple?"

"That would be great."

"They're only fifty dollars each."

"I feel so shitty, I'd pay fifty thousand."

"I'll be right back."

As I walk out the dining room and into the cool air of the morning, two pickup trucks approach the lodge. One of them I recognize. As I stride to my cabin, Sampson Sanchez reaches out the driver's window and waves to me. I wave back.

With two leaps, I summit the steps and enter the sanctuary of my world behind closed doors, where I pull out my phone and dial Lisa.

"Good morning," I say.

"Hey, babe."

With just two words, she knocks my socks off. Always has, always will.

"I'm coming home," I tell her.

"Today?" she replies. "I thought it was tomorrow that I was supposed to pick you up at the airport."

"It was, but I've decided to cut the trip short."

"Why?"

"Because I've been away too long and I miss my family."

"Someone's homesick," she says. "But we're fine. We really are. Stay and enjoy your time off."

"I'm just not into hunting, and I don't think I can eat or drink one more thing."

"Aw, that's too bad, because I talked to Helen last night and she said Hollis is having a blast with you, Rob, and Wes. It's only one more day."

"I love you."

"I love you, too." We know each other too well to know when something's wrong with either of us, which she hears in my voice as much as she does in the silence that's now between us, which she breaks. "What's bothering you?"

"If you call me Babe, I'll tell you."

"Babe."

"Last night I dreamed I lost you."

"In what way?"

"Forever."

"That's never going to happen."

"It was so real. I was being taken away and you were crying, and I was fighting to get to you, but they dragged me away down this long corridor and then a door opened, and they threw me into a small windowless room where everything was black, and then they shut the door and locked it. And I never got out, until I woke up."

"It was just a dream."

"I miss you and the kids."

"We miss you, too," she replies. "I think you're just a little homesick is all."

I wish it were, but I know there's much more to the hasty decision and impetuous call home than meets the eye. I walk to the bedroom and look in the side pouch of my duffle bag for the aspirin. "You want me to tough it out, don't you?"

"Yes." She hears the rattling of the pills in their container. "Don't tell me you're self-medicating."

"Just getting some Tylenol for Wes. He's in rough shape from last night."

"Well, go take care of him and make the best of it. You're not missing anything here, and I'm sure it's beautiful out there."

Dream or no dream, I would be lost without her. In my wallet, I keep a picture of Lisa from our trip down Pacific Coast Highway. It was before we had kids. I pull it out and give it a look long enough to take my mind all the way back there—to that grove of Bishop Pines just north of Big Sur where we camped for the night. As the sun was about to set, its last rays streaked through the branches and caught the side of her face at the same time as my camera lens, and I captured the image for posterity.

In the dining room, the Texans have seated themselves at the table next to ours. The chatter between our two groups is light as all the guests of the Little Wing occupy themselves with food and drink. Talk is secondary.

"Here you go," I say, handing Wes the aspirin.

"Thanks." He pops them into his mouth and downs them with some orange juice.

"The guides are here," I inform everyone. "At least two of them are. They just pulled up in their trucks."

"They're going to have to wait," Wes replies. "I need to let these aspirin kick in."

"The true breakfast of champions," Rob remarks.

Hollis prods everyone to hurry up and finish their meal (while the dogs are still happy) before he excuses himself to make some final preparations for the day's hunt. To seize the opportunity to speak to him alone, I claim the need to do the same, and follow him out.

On our way to the cabins the third guide arrives and parks his pickup next to the others in front of the lodge.

Hollis senses my nerves have steadied. "Feeling better?"

"Not sure I'd call it that," I reply. "What are we going to do if they come back later to question us some more?"

"We just stick together today and stick to our story."

"Do you think the reservation cop or the sheriff will want to talk to us again?"

"Let's assume they will, and that way we won't be surprised if they do."

We stop at the steps to his cabin.

"How do you think they found his pickup so quickly?" I ask.

"I'm kind of puzzled by that myself," he replies. "That hole looked deep."

"Is Rob right about the water being low and clear?"

He runs my question around his head before spitting out his answer. "October is usually pretty dry out here. But in the last couple days I can't see the Redwater dropping enough to expose any part of the pickup."

"Maybe it's not sticking out but can be seen below the water."

"You'd have to be looking for it, I guess."

"Or be at the right place at the right time and have it catch your eye."

"Or be there when it happened," he replies. "Is that what you're trying to say?"

"No, but now that you mention it."

"Nobody saw us."

Hollis places a hand on the railing and his boot on the first step. His body language tells me I'm beating a dead horse. I get what he's trying to say, so I move on to the other pressing matter at hand as I place my foot next to his on the step.

"What do you think about the letter?"

"Not much, and we're leaving tomorrow. Besides, I think it's more bark than bite."

"What makes you think that?"

"It's just a gut feeling I have."

I want to trust his gut. Now more than ever. But I've lost confidence in my friend. Too many swings and misses will do that. Therefore, I take his gut instinct with a grain of salt. Still, I value his opinion enough to continue with another question. "Do you think it has anything to do with finding Orrin's pickup?"

"Perhaps, but perhaps it's coincidence," he says, which is the direction I'd like to lean. "Let's get ready to shoot some birds. How about if I meet you back out here in ten minutes?"

"Okay. See you then."

"Do you want the twelve- or twenty-gauge?"

"Doesn't matter. Whatever you think I should use."

"Probably both."

I almost smile, which my face could now use more than ever. "Am I really that bad?"

"I'm not going to answer that." He turns and heads up the steps.

Chapter Eighteen

The terrain looks familiar. Not that one patch of prairie is distinguishable from another, but the one we're in feels trodden. Maybe it's the ridge or slope of the field that jogs my memory. Hard to say as I walk with gun in hand on full alert, much like the dogs out in front of us.

Hollis seems to be in his own little world, if such a thing is possible in Big Sky and Land Country. With his game face on—from direct hits on the first two pheasants—he stalks the Montana fields, ready for more. More of anything that comes our way. Me, I blow smoke, shoot blanks, and set birds free—with precision.

I'm as good at what I do as Hollis is at what he does, who at that moment raises his gun and pops the hen that bursts into the sky.

"Nice shot," Sampson says, as his retriever runs to the fallen bird. "Excellent. Excellent shot."

Either the man is in good spirits or he can't contain his appreciation for Hollis's marksmanship, because I'm under the impression all Sioux have us under investigation. And because of that I find it odd that our guide treats us in such a professional manner. I expected worse. Much worse. But perhaps the discovery of Orrin's truck in the Redwater, and the first impression of an accident that it gives, has removed the shadow of doubt cast upon us by the tribe.

As we move east below the late morning sun that rises to its zenith, another wave of déjà vu strikes me when a tree appears in my peripheral vision. To keep up with the dogs that are getting "birdy" (as Sampson calls it whenever one of them appears to have caught wind of a pheasant) I move with purpose and angle my way toward Hollis on the far left.

"Garrett," he calls, "I need you to stay on my right flank, please." But I ignore his command and continue the approach toward my friend. With my gun broken open, I pose no threat to man or beast, which should allow for me to maintain the course I'm on. "Garrett, I need you over here," Sampson calls again.

"It's okay, I won't shoot." He relents and allows me to reach Hollis's side. "Do you recognize this place?"

Hollis's eyes are on the dogs, not me. "No, should I?" he replies, and closes the breech of his gun.

"I think this is where we buried Orrin," I whisper.

"What makes you think that?"

"That tree," I say, subtly nodding to my right. "And that's where we pulled the grass from the ground to plant over the grave."

"Where?"

"Straight ahead, eleven o'clock."

In that area, the dogs go back and forth like vacuum cleaners. "They're getting birdy," Sampson says.

"I don't see anything," Hollis says.

I begin to second-guess myself, to question my eyes, my paranoia. The odds are as low as the dogs' noses to the ground that with thousands of acres to hunt we'd hunt one of them twice. One in twelve thousand at best. Then, to come within yards of Orrin's grave, one in a million. I'm not a man who gambles, but I like those odds. I take off my sunglasses, and with the naked eye, give things another look.

The English Pointer freezes. "Get ready," Sampson says. I step back behind Hollis so that he can shoot left or right unobstructed. Sampson nods in approval and gives the command for his springer spaniel to flush the bird. The black-and-white canine charges into the thick grass, and a rooster shoots up into the air like an answered prayer. It's just a bird the dogs have sniffed out and nothing more.

It chooses a flight path straight into the barrel of Hollis's gun. To give it a fair chance, he waits for it to fly overhead and westward toward the horizon, as I drop to the ground. On the balls of my feet, I watch the pheasant gain steam after it levels off at an altitude of thirty feet. For their size, they are jet-plane fast. Though not faster than lead pellets that travel 1,200 feet per second, which I expect to hit the bird any moment.

But that moment never comes. Instead the rooster sprints to freedom two hundred or so yards away where it lands in the grass, the pointer and flusher in hot pursuit.

"Let's try that again," Sampson says, then hustles to keep up with his dogs, and we hustle to keep up with him.

On a swift pace by his side, I watch Hollis break open his gun and shoulder it. "Why didn't you shoot?"

"I saw it as a good opportunity to get the dogs out of this area, just in case you're right," he replies.

Only Hollis could think on his feet like that. "I don't think I'm right," I tell him, "but, either way, that was smart of you."

"Better safe than sorry," he says.

We catch up to the dogs and Sampson. When one of them points, Hollis does the same at the bird that flies, and this time pulls the trigger. I pull mine, too, because the pheasant is fair game on the center line between us—same as Sampson—at twelve o'clock. Westward ho it dashes. But it doesn't get far before the window of opportunity closes and the bird slams into the pane. Hollis has blasted the pheasant in the tail. I know it's his kill because I aimed too far to the right, making sure I have nothing to do with the death of any animal—with or without wings. At this point, from my perspective, it's all make-believe. It's all repetitive. Track, point, shoot, repeat. As we follow the sun I can't help but feel time is on my side because there's less and less of it left for me to spend in Big Sky and Land Country.

Like I told Lawton, I will never set foot in Montana again, unlike Hollis who will be back for his business dealings with him. Me, I'm leaving in the morning—on a jet plane. Funny how a song can get stuck in your head and play over and over. All afternoon it plays. That, and the cannonade hurled at birds that take flight, which I'll admit, don't seem like the proper accompaniments for each other. Guns shooting things from the sky and aircraft homeward bound go together like oil and water. Hollis being oil, the Redwater being . . . well, water.

At the end of our hunt, Sampson drives us back to the lodge. We are the last group of hunters to arrive. I know this because the boots belonging to the others sit empty on the stoops of their cabins. Though tips are discouraged, we grease the palm of our guide as a true gesture of gratitude. Mine is out of pity and guilt. In terms of wealth, I have so much more than this man, which means I have so much more to give. "From everyone who has been given much, much will be demanded; and from the one who has been entrusted with much, much more will be asked." I can't tell you where in the bible that can be found, because I've never read it. But I know it's there. Just as I cannot see but know what's buried a few miles away. The quote is one of Father Seb's favorites. He knew which of the parishioners could afford to donate more, and he singled me out to spearhead this objective of his. Over ping-pong, I termed it "peer pressure." He termed it "winner takes all," and he won each and every time.

Getting a chance to unwind inside my cabin before Hollis's mandatory roll call for happy hour, I feel home free. Crossing over the threshold of the cabin door, I feel as though I've crossed the finish line. But I still have nineteen hours and thirty minutes until I'm wheels-up.

In my hunting clothes, I collapse spread eagle onto the bed. After a six-mile walk weighted down with shotgun shells and the twenty-gauge that fires them, I'm exhausted. To take the last bit of weight off, I shut my eyes, and dream of the airplane—with me inside it—on its climb to 30,000 feet. I wait for sleep to wash over me as I hold that thought and the breeze flutters the drapes on each side of the opened window.

Sleep doesn't come, but night does. Our final stay at the ranch. At the bar, we gather—Texans, Georgians, a Michigander, and Lawton. He appears to be as worn out as we are. Empty might be the better word, same as he used to describe the cab of Orrin's pickup. With just a glance, all of us can see his forgone conclusion that the Redwater has laid claim to his friend.

Aware of his loss, it's agreed upon by the group to close the bar down much earlier than usual to relieve Lawton of his duties. In consideration of Dolores and her staff, who are sullen members of the Sioux tribe, our dinner meal is eaten in short order and we exit the dining room without delay.

Around 10:00 p.m. we have our final drinks around the fire pit and say our last goodbyes to the Texans. They are ticketed for the 6:55 a.m. flight. My friends have the 10:30 a.m. that connects into Atlanta, and I'm on the 12:10 p.m. to Minneapolis, then St. Louis. As the ranch's chauffeur, Lawton will need to make several trips to and from the airport in Sidney to drop off his departing guests and pick up his arriving ones. And he's informed us of the times we need to be ready: "Bags packed and curbside would be much appreciated."

With bells on, I will be there. Come hell or high water, I will be there.

* * *

And, in the blink of an eye, I am. A long blink. Grouped on the drive by Hollis's cabin, the four of us wait for Lawton to swing his Jeep around. The fit will be tight, so we decide to draw straws to see who will be crammed into the back-middle seat. Because of his size, Rob is eliminated. The three of us pick, and it's Wes who ends up with the low card.

As forecasted, a chrome bumper of clouds gathers near the horizon, with much cooler air from Canada behind it to push the storm our way. It's a good day to leave. It will rain most of the afternoon, which only die-hard hunters like Hollis would tolerate.

Instead of the Jeep, the Explorer comes from around the side of the ranch, with Dolores Mills at the wheel. I'm surprised to see her, and so are the others.

"Hey, Wes. Looks like you're going to get one last chance with ol' Dolores," Rob says.

The laughter awakens our sluggish ensemble. But it's just temporary, as the Explorer pulls up and we compose ourselves for the ride with the sweet and genuine woman.

"Lawton had to attend an early morning meeting with the Bureau of Indian Affairs, which means I'm your taxi driver," she says. "He wanted me to tell you how much he enjoyed meeting all of you, and that we hope you'll come back and see us soon."

We thank her for the hunting and hospitality and sit quiet for most of the ride.

At the airport, she drops us off in front of the terminal where her next set of guests stands waiting. We trade places with them, and roll our duffels and guns inside to check in for our flights.

When the time comes to say goodbye to my friends, I shake their hands and hug them. "See you on Daufuskie," each of them says to me in one form or another, and to each I promise to be there soon. But we all know it's an empty promise. It's October, and Daufuskie lies dormant this time of year. It will be summer before Lisa heads southeast with the kids, and I'll join them every other weekend.

I watch my friends head for their plane. When they exit my line of sight, I pull out my laptop and begin to review company reports that were downloaded before I left St. Louis. I'm far behind and need to catch up to avoid the onslaught when I return to the office, which, after a trip—business or pleasure—can take several days to get my head back above water.

Out of the corner of my eye, I notice someone. A man. He's easy to spot in an airport where travelers are as few and far between as the flights, because he looks like me—like he doesn't belong here. Even dressed in jeans, hiking boots, and a canvas jacket that is common wear out West, there's little doubt his origins do not spring from this soil. And with the same unmistakable assertion, there's little doubt—based on the speed at which he approaches—that he has an interest in me.

Without any movement of my neck or head, I watch him hold a small photograph up to his eyes and return it to his coat pocket. Within a few steps of me he says, "Garrett Ingram?"

From my roost in the row of airport chairs, I look up and reply, "Yes, and you are?"

"Special Agent Curtis Vaughn of the Federal Bureau of Investigation." He displays his leather-bound badge. "Mind if I take a seat?"

It's clear he's taking one no matter what my answer is, as he turns and descends into the chair next to my laptop shoulder bag.

"Not at all," I say.

I close my computer to respectfully give him my full attention, which is what an FBI badge placed in front of your eyes for the first time does to you, in addition to causing an elevated heartbeat.

He crosses his legs, and clasps his hands together atop his knee to make himself at home. For me, I couldn't be further away.

"How was the hunting?"

"I didn't do so well. But everyone else did."

"Those birds sure do get up and go, don't they?"

"They do."

"This your first time shooting wild pheasants?"

"First time shooting, period."

He turns his broad shoulders and shifts in his chair to square up to me. "This is a tough place to learn. You'd be better off getting your feet wet with farm-raised game birds."

"I take it you hunt."

"Mostly criminals . . . and birds when I get the chance," he says, then smiles.

It's a good-looking smile on a good-looking man. If I had to guess, he rowed his way through college twenty-five years ago on his six-foot, three-inch frame, or swam it. Yes, that's it, because his short ash-blond hair has a hint of chlorine in it. If he wasn't a swimmer, he is one now, though where you'd find an indoor pool in this part of Montana is beyond me.

To end the small talk, I say, "What brings you here?"

"I was transferred two years ago from Rhode Island," he replies, in avoidance of the true intent of my question.

I play along. "As punishment?"

His smile returns. "That's what I thought at first."

"I was only kidding, you know."

"Yes, I know," he says. "Surprisingly, it's turned out to be a great experience for me and my family. These are wonderful people out here."

"Do you live here in Sidney?"

"No, we live in Glasgow, where my satellite office is. It's about a hundred miles west of here just outside of the Fort Peck Reservation."

"Satellite of what?"

"Salt Lake City. All of the resident agencies—satellite offices—in Montana, Idaho, and Utah report to the Salt Lake field office."

"I see."

"Out here we're the jack of all trades," he says. "Child porn, fraud, terrorism, Indian affairs, you name it."

"Terrorism?"

"Malmstrom Air Force Base and the Tenth Missile Squadron aren't too far from here. There are more ICBM's in Montana than IBM's."

"That's interesting."

"It is. And you know what else is interesting?"

"What?"

"The Native Americans I've come to know." He uncrosses his leg and now has both feet on the floor. "You talk about getting the short end of the stick. Man, they sure did get it."

"I would agree with you there."

"When I first got out here, I met this old Sioux, and one day he says to me, 'How come the Confederates got to stay in all their states when they lost, but we had to give up every one of ours and move to reservations?'"

There's insight in this man; I can see it in those hazel eyes of his. I think he sees it in me, along with a few other things someone in his position looks for. "Sounds like a wise old man."

"He is, and there are many other Sioux like him that I've had the good fortune to meet in my two years on the job out here," he replies. "You've had the opportunity to spend a few mornings and afternoons with a couple of them. What's your take?"

He's smooth. He could sell planes. Lots of them. "I enjoyed their company."

"I'll bet Orrin Gall enjoyed yours, too."

"Should I take that as a compliment?"

"Why wouldn't you?"

"Because of the way you said it."

He turns in his chair away from me and faces forward. Across from us is a row of windows. Through them we can see a CRJ100 that's just landed. It's my plane—built by a competitor—come to take me home. Vaughn continues speaking to me.

"We had a chance to analyze Orrin Gall's truck yesterday."

The plane taxis toward the terminal—toward us.

"Lawton Mills said they didn't find Orrin's body in it," I say.

"We didn't," he says. "Nor did we find the dog's, which is strange because the divers retrieved the dog's crate from the riverbed and the door on it was latched shut."

"That is strange." We continue to watch the plane as it pulls up to the gate. "Could the dog have been in the cab with Orrin?"

"You tell me." He turns in his chair. Once again, we're face-to-face.

"What do you mean by that?"

"You saw him drive away after your hunt, didn't you?"

"I did."

"Then where was the dog—in his crate or the cab?"

"That's a good question," I reply, in full regret of the ones I volunteered. As though in deep thought to recollect that day, I look beyond the windows in search of a response that doesn't back myself further into the corner. "I can't be sure, but maybe I do remember seeing him up front."

An odd silence comes between us, and he leaves it there to further make me uncomfortable, until I shift in my chair.

"We considered the possibility of the dog being in the cab, but there are two things we looked at closely to determine that wasn't the case." He pauses. But this time I don't take the bait to supply him with more questions he can use against me. "If the dog was sitting on the passenger seat, his weight would've activated the airbag, which didn't activate. If he wasn't heavy enough to activate the airbag, then we would've found impact marks on the dash or windshield, but there weren't any. Not even a scratch."

I let a few seconds go by while the passengers disembark the plane. "Don't know what to tell you."

He looks at me as though I might change my mind and tell him something he'd like to hear. But I don't, so he continues. "The other strange part of this equation is a dog's tooth and partial nose found lodged in the bird you gave to the Little Wing to be cleaned. You have to admit, that's not something you see too often."

I won't admit to anything. *Stick to the story. He can't prove anything without Orrin's body, or the dog's, and he's not going to find either of them.* "I'm a beginner, so you would know that better than I would."

"If you had to take a wild stab at it, what would be your best guess as to how they got there?"

"I have no idea."

"None whatsoever?"

"I don't."

"Would you like to hear my theory?"

"Sure." I look at my watch to signal to him that I have a plane to catch.

"I think a dog got hit with birdshot when the bird was in its jaws," he says. "That's what the Sioux think, too."

"Okay."

"We also think that dog was Orrin's."

I look at my watch again. "I'd better start heading over to my gate."

"Mind if I walk with you?"

"Be my guest."

We stand, and I slide my laptop into the shoulder bag. As I carry it by the handle, the two of us begin the short walk to the other side of the terminal.

"Did you know that Orrin Gall is an ancestor of Chief Gall, one of the Sioux's greatest war chiefs?"

"I think I did hear something about that."

"What you probably haven't heard, though, is how upsetting Orrin Gall's disappearance is to the tribe," he says. As he walks next to me his stride matches mine. "He's 'big medicine' and because of that there's a very heavy weight on my shoulders to find him."

"I hope you do."

"One way or another, I will." He reaches into the chest pocket of his coat and pulls out a small notepad and pen. "Could I get your contact information in case I have more questions?"

When he's through writing, he thanks me for my time and wishes me a safe flight home. But he doesn't leave the terminal. While I wait in line to board the plane, he walks over to where we'd been seated and stands by the row of empty seats. With his back to me, he pulls out his cell phone and makes a call.

I want to be on the plane so badly I can taste the jet fuel. The line inches its way forward. But Curtis Vaughn does too. In mid-conversation, he starts heading towards me. *Come on, come on, line, keep moving.* Just beyond the ticket agent, the doorway leads out to the plane . . . to freedom . . . to my home. And I'm almost there. Only five people are ahead of me. That's when I feel a tap on my shoulder.

"Could you step out of line for a second so that I can have another word with you?" Vaughn asks.

"I can't miss this flight."

"I'll make sure they don't leave without you."

With that, I have no choice but to accommodate his request. Any man with the authority to delay an airline's departure isn't going to take no for an answer. We walk over toward the windows where it's quiet, until my cell phone rings. It's Lisa.

"Excuse me," I tell the FBI agent. To keep our exchange brief, I let Lisa know that I'm just about to board the plane and will call her back when I reach my connecting flight in Minneapolis. "Sorry about that."

"No problem," he replies. "I read the Sioux police report and noticed a lack of clarity involving a few of the basics and I'm hoping you can set the record straight."

"I'll do my best."

He pulls out his pen and pad again. "What time did your morning hunt begin with Orrin?"

"Around nine o'clock."

"What time did you break for lunch?"

"Noon."

"What time did your afternoon hunt begin?"

"An hour later."

"Did you hunt in the same general area, or did you take your vehicles and move to another location?"

"We stayed there."

"When did your hunt end?"

"Three or three thirty."

"Only got one bird all day, right?"

"Right."

"Was that during the morning or afternoon?"

"Afternoon."

"And later in the evening you dropped off that bird to have it cleaned?"

"Yes."

"That's all I have for now. Thanks for your cooperation."

"Anytime."

CHAPTER NINETEEN

With my duffel in tow, I see my family and quicken my pace. Lisa has double-parked in the passenger pickup lane and an airport policeman is headed her way. Sitting in the backseat, Jenny sees me and waves—with both hands—and the smile on her face seems wider than the Mississippi. Jenny, my treasured little girl who's still the proud benefactress of a run-and-jump-in-my-arms welcome whenever I return home from a trip. She'll have to wait until I get there, though; it's too busy and crowded for Lisa to let her out to greet me.

I throw my bags in the trunk, hop in, and off we go. I give Lisa a kiss on the cheek as she maneuvers through traffic. Buckled in the back, the kids settle for my outstretched left arm for our reunion. Jenny leans forward and presses my hand against the side of her face.

In the five days I've been gone, Will appears to have grown several more inches—outward not upward. The kid needed meat on his bones. I welcome the change.

"How's my boy?"

"Good, Pops. Welcome home."

"Welcome home, Dad," Jenny says. "I missed you."

"I missed you guys more than every hair on Friday's tail."

"We were going to bring him, but Mom wouldn't let us," Will says.

"Hey, don't make me look like the bad guy," Lisa replies. "I just said that if he threw up, then you'd be cleaning the car."

"Is he sick?" I ask her.

"He threw up twice today."

"Probably just found something out in the yard that he shouldn't have eaten," I tell them.

I wish they would've brought him. He's family. The best dog ever. But now it's impossible for me to think of him without thinking about Truck, and what he meant to Orrin. I hear Lisa and the kids talking to me and each other, but it all seems to go in one ear and out the other like the breeze on the Montana plains. It's just background, as though I'm back on that same ground of hunters, dog, and guide.

"Dad...Hello, Dad."

"Hey, Pops, where are we going to eat?"

On the way home, we grab a bite at The Crossing, where my mind continues to drift back to the Little Wing. The kids are without the need of conversation as they devour their food, but Lisa would like more engagement from me.

"I'm just tired. It's been a long week." I say to her.

In time, Lisa gets us all back to the house. The Tudor is another welcome sight, that and Friday whom the kids race to and let out of his crate. After our reunion with him, the kids go up to get their showers while Lisa and I unwind in the family room with an eye on the dog in his bed over by the corner.

"I really, really missed you."

"Aw, you're sweet," she replies.

We're next to each other on the couch. In the basement right below us, the main line enters the house, and we can hear water run through it (it's louder than it should be) whenever the kids take showers in their bathrooms, which alerts us to where they are and what they're doing. Lisa looks at me with bedroom eyes and slides her hand down to my groin. She moves it clockwise in a circular motion as the diamond on her engagement ring sparkles in the dimmed light of the table lamp across the room. She slides off the couch and kneels in front of me. When it feels right to her, she unzips my jeans.

Though, for the first time ever, it doesn't feel right to me. "How about a rain check?" I ask.

She looks up at me from between my legs. "What's wrong?"

"The kids might come down."

"That's never stopped you before."

"I know, but what if they do?"

"As long as we hear the water running, we're fine."

She crosses her arms and grabs the bottom of her black cotton sweater. With one quick motion, Lisa pulls it up over her head and off her body—and is just as fluid in the removal of her white lace bra. The invitation to massage her breasts is irresistible. She's stunning, gorgeous, and looks the same as she did to me that first night together twenty-one years ago. With her pride intact, Lisa is eager to resume my welcome home. After two minutes of give and take, though, I'm back to where I was when she started; all the way back to Montana.

That's where I am. This feeling, or lack thereof, has nothing to do with Lisa. It's all in my mind and my mind won't let me stop thinking about what I've done and what I need to do to keep it hidden. The water turns off—for which I'm grateful—and I use that as my excuse to end our rendezvous, rather than endure more of Lisa's questions and the lies I was prepared to respond with.

But this is just the beginning. I know there will be more to come—questions and lies—in time. They say time heals all wounds. I say only time will tell. Who knows? For now, all I know it's time to try and get a good night's sleep.

After she puts her clothes back on, I follow my wife up the stairs.

* * *

As agreed, Hollis and I send each other overnight letters on the first day home from our trip; letters that contain a telephone number to a pay phone each of us can access within a fifteen-minute drive from our homes. If there's something urgent we need to discuss, we're to call each other from our cell phones and use the code word "weather" in a sentence and be ready for the next call at the pay phone sixty minutes later. This, we feel, is the most thorough way to prevent our private communications from being compromised. Excessive, maybe, but we've decided not to take any chances with the possibility of our landlines or cell phones being tapped. We're done making mistakes.

It's not easy to locate a pay phone, much less one I feel comfortable to use. With the widespread use of cellular, they've fast become dinosaurs. But I find one at a 7-Eleven. Hollis finds his at a Parker's.

Two days after our goodbye in Montana—two long days and sleepless nights—I call him. After a short superficial conversation, I ask how the weather is in Savannah. An hour later, the pay phone rings and I pick it up.

"Hollis?" I ask.

"It's me."

"The goddam FBI has gotten involved."

"Take it easy," he says, "we knew this might happen."

"We did, but it wasn't supposed to. That was one of your main reasons for burying him in the first place, remember?"

He ignores my jab. "Tell me what's going on."

"While I was waiting for my flight out of Sidney, an FBI agent comes up to me, flashes his badge, and sits down and starts asking me all kinds of questions."

"Okay, just take a deep breath and walk me through it."

I take several and then look over my shoulder to scan the parking lot once again to make sure I wasn't followed. "We fucked up."

"It's not the first time you've said that," he replies. "What did he say?"

"They found the dog's crate at the bottom of the river and the door to it was locked shut with no dog inside."

"Which means he was riding up front with Orrin."

"I suggested that as a possibility, but the agent said the airbag didn't deploy, and if the weight of the dog wasn't enough to deploy it then there would've been impact marks on the dash or windshield. There were none. 'Not even a scratch,' quote unquote."

"What if the dog was on Orrin's lap?"

"Maybe you should call him and mention that."

"Hey, we're on the same team, okay?"

"I know we are, but we're fucked, Hollis, because this guy knows we're lying, and he's not going to just turn a blind eye and walk away."

"He will eventually."

"I don't think so, not with Orrin Gall being Sioux royalty. And the agent is convinced that the tooth and nose found in the pheasant are Truck's after being hit by birdshot. Sooner or later he's going to put two and two together."

"Even if he does, he can't prove shit without the bodies."

"And if he finds the bodies?"

"He won't. But if he does, I will take full responsibility."

Other than his intent of well meaning, there's little comfort in his willingness to step forward if that time should ever come. No judge, jury, or prosecutor is going to allow me to get off scot-free on charges of obstruction of justice, making false statements, and the litany of other crimes I'm guilty of that involve the "self-defense" shooting and illegal burial of Orrin Gall. If anything, they will throw the book at me.

Me, why me, I say to myself, though not as a plea for help, but to answer the question that's been in the back of my mind: Why have I been singled out by the long arm of the law, or whoever else it might be?

"Let me ask you something."

"Go ahead," he replies.

"It sure seems like I'm the one they're leaning on, doesn't it?"

"I guess I can see why you feel that way, but I bet I'll be hearing from that same agent soon," he says. "What's the guy's name?"

"Curtis Vaughn."

Without an admission to each other, we both know I've been marked as the weaker of the two links, for which I feel isolation, but not shame. I know as well as anyone—through the years, through friends, associates, and all those I've hired and held accountable—that all men are not created equal. If I've been designated the "lesser" of the two evils, then so be it because I know as well as Hollis—or anyone—that when going through hell, you keep going. But Hell and Hell on Earth are two different places.

By the end of our phone call, I've recollected every detail of my conversation with Special Agent Vaughn, which enables Hollis and me to close the gaps in our story and corroborate the timeline of events with more accuracy. "Things happen for a reason," he says in faith of our tightened defenses. "The stronger the wind, the stronger the tree. And our roots go deep."

CHAPTER TWENTY

With the arrival of the New Year, there is hope. Even with trees stripped to the bone and icy talons hung from gutters, I'm optimistic my troubles are behind me. January, of all months, when the holidays have been boxed up and sent to the attic, and there's nothing on the horizon but muted daylight, cabin fever, and the coldness of drafty old lead-paned windows and out-of-tune piano keys.

On a rare day when I'm not on a plane or with a customer or in a meeting at corporate, I look out my office window and think of Hollis. My window faces northwest—the direction of Montana, where he is. As the new proprietor of the Little Wing—that Lawton and staff continue to operate for him—he devotes his workweek to the oil fields up there and flies home out of nearby Williston, North Dakota every Friday night to spend weekends with Helen and the kids in Savannah. Three weeks have gone by without a word from him, which I take to heart as no news is good news. When we last did speak things seemed to be going satisfactorily for him and his group of investors. But talk of business was kept to a minimum. I got the impression he wanted to focus more on the two of us and our families, which was more appropriate since the conversation took place on our unsecured office phones. With that being the case, his mention of his third interview with Special Agent Curtis Vaughn was brief and to the point, which I knew meant nothing of significance had occurred, otherwise he would've inquired about the "weather" in St. Louis.

January does offer one bright spot, however, which is why I've arranged to be in town this Tuesday: today is Jenny's birthday—number twelve. Born on the same day— different year—as Hollis and Helen's daughter, Aimee. As I lean back in my chair while staring out the window, I can't help but think of my friends, with the bulk of my thoughts centered on Hollis and all the good times he and I have had. The cup half full, as he would like me to see things.

On a Post-It note I jot down a few gifts to pick up for Jenny. These are in addition to the ones Lisa has already bought and wrapped and will give to her at dinner. Ill-advised or not, I never hesitate to spoil my baby girl when the opportunity arises. The smiles and hugs she gives in return are my addiction. Building blocks are at the top of the list. They are my daughter's indoor passion. If she doesn't turn out to be an architect, I will be surprised. She will sit on the playroom floor in the basement for hours and construct intricate structures, some of them as tall as she is. I'm always amazed when she calls me down ("Eyes closed, Dad . . . okay, now you can open them!") to look at her next wonder of the world. There is a talent there—I see it—and she will see more blocks on this birthday than all the other birthdays put together. (Along with a giraffe or two; those are her favorite stuffed animal to collect.)

I look at my watch and make the decision to put my thoughts into action without delay. Today, I will leave work an hour early—which is rare for me—to stop by the toy store on the way home. Out the door I go, my satchel in one hand, my wool overcoat draped over the other.

"I'll be in first thing in the morning," I say to my assistant, Carol, as I pass by her desk on my way to the elevators.

"Have a good evening," she says, "and say happy birthday to Jenny for me."

In the parking garage I throw my coat on as I hustle toward my car. The cold mixed with the concrete bites hard. Maybe even harder if you throw in the soiled light.

A midwestern-grey winter skyline towers over me as I pull onto the downtown streets of St. Louis. Traffic is bumper to bumper until I reach the stop-and-go "freedom" of I-64. After thirty minutes, I'm not too far from home or from Jenny's favorite store, Imagination Toys. At the Clayton Road exit, I turn off the highway and arrive at the retailer's doorstep in no time.

"Building blocks and giraffes," I say to the woman who offers her assistance to me.

When a city block of blocks and two giraffes are loaded into my company-issued Mercedes, I begin the short drive to the other side of Ladue, where my birthday girl awaits. With the radio up and my eyes on the road, I almost miss the call. But the bloom of the cell phone's screen catches my attention and I'm able to grab the phone from the cup holder before the call goes to voicemail.

"Garrett?"

"Yes?"

I turn down the stereo.

"This is Special Agent Curtis Vaughn of the FBI."

Three miles from home, three months since I last heard from him, and on a day as special as my daughter's twelfth, I am severely disappointed to receive his call. To give him my complete attention—for my benefit, not his—I find a place to pull over and put the car in park.

"From the airport in Sidney," I say, "Yes, I remember."

"I know it's been a while, and I apologize for not following up with you sooner, but I'm juggling many things and the workload here at the Bureau keeps piling up," he says. "I'm sure that running a large division for Boeing, you're no stranger to this sort of thing."

"I'm not."

"Hope I didn't catch you at a bad time?"

"Well, to be perfectly honest, I'm in my car and just about to reach home to celebrate my daughter's birthday with the family."

"Congratulations. How old is she?"

"Twelve."

"It goes quick, doesn't it?"

"Sure does."

"I'll try to be just as quick."

"Okay."

"There have been some recent developments in our ongoing investigation of the disappearance of Orrin Gall," he begins. "When my team and I analyzed these, along with the other statements, evidence, and documentation we've collected, we couldn't conclusively rule out criminal activity. To do that, which I hope for everyone's sake we can, I could use your help."

"Like I said at the airport, I'm happy to assist in any way possible."

"Good, that's what I was hoping you'd say," he replies. "Then what I'd like to do next is come down to St. Louis and administer a polygraph test for you to take at our field office there."

"A polygraph?"

"Yes. Are you familiar with them?"

"I wouldn't say I'm familiar with them, but I do know what they're used for."

"At the Bureau we sometimes use the polygraph to determine whether or not to intensify an investigation of a suspect or drop it all together."

"Are you saying I'm a suspect?"

"Let me put it to you this way: I'm getting lots of pressure from the Sioux to make progress. If I've got to go down dead-end roads to do this, then that's what I'll do. Will you help?"

He's as smooth as a perfect landing. One of the best I've ever had the unfortunate pleasure to make an acquaintance with. Into the corner, where he's boxed me, I'm damned if I do and damned if I don't. Though in that same corner, which just so happens to be on my side of the ring, I have Hollis, and he shouts at me to fight my way off the ropes. "*Stick to the story. Without the bodies, he can't do squat.*"

"I hope this doesn't come across the wrong way, but it's probably in my best interest to discuss this with an attorney. Wouldn't you agree?"

"Unfortunately, that's not a question I can answer. Since this is an ongoing investigation, I can't talk specifics of what you should or shouldn't do. I can say though that whichever course of action you choose to take will affect what the Bureau chooses to do next."

"Again, I'm not 'familiar' with polygraphs but what limited knowledge I do have of them is that their results are not admissible in a court of law."

"You're correct."

"And I believe a polygraph is only by consent?"

"That's right, which is why I'm simply asking for your help in this matter."

He's not asking shit. If he could subpoena me to take a polygraph, he would. He's "simply" playing the best hand he has, and it's not good enough.

"I'd like to help you, Agent Vaughn, but I'm not so certain you have my best interest, or that of my family's, at heart."

"I have the interest of justice—first, and foremost—for the Sioux Nation and its member who has gone missing, Mr. Ingram. As a sworn agent of the Federal Bureau of Investigation it's my duty to uphold the commitment the United States Government has pledged to them," he replies. "Unlike you and me, they don't have much, and when what little they do have is taken away, it's grossly unfair and sometimes criminal, in my humble opinion."

With the conversation going south, I put my car in drive and head north on Barnes Road for home. There my family waits. A birthday girl sits by the living room window and watches for her dad's car to pull in the driveway. For her, this day is everything, and that is what I intend to give her in love, gifts, and happiness.

"Agent Vaughn, I'm going to decline your offer to take a polygraph and will be contacting my attorney to seek legal guidance."

"I'm disappointed to hear that."

"Well, I'm sorry to disappoint you."

"Is this your decision final?"

"Yes, unless my attorney advises me otherwise."

"That will be too late because this offer goes off the table when this phone conversation ends."

"If it's now or never, then it's never."

"Very well," he replies. "But be advised, I intend to throw the full weight of my agency and all its resources behind this investigation."

"I understand."

"And you should also be aware that your refusal to fully cooperate will only further antagonize the Fort Peck Police, the Richland County Sheriff's Office, and all their affiliates who hold you in suspicion and contempt."

"That almost sounds like a threat."

"Not at all. It's a warning."

"Then what are you warning me of?"

"Law enforcement officials who don't believe your story, and two hundred years of a tribe's pent-up frustration."

"Okay, thanks for letting me know."

"No problem."

"Best of luck to you, Special Agent Vaughn."

"You as well," he says. "Enjoy your daughter's birthday. It may be the last one for a long time to come where the two of you aren't separated by security glass and steel."

"Goodbye."

Jenny sees me through the window and smiles. Dressed in a red sweater and black velvet dress, she waves Friday's paw. He's next to her, up on the chair that he uses to keep an eye out on his front-yard territory. Through my windshield, I wave and smile back, which excites her even more. With Friday's other paw, she doubles the welcome.

I park in the driveway and walk toward them across the lawn. As I make my approach, Lisa, in a sequined dress, and Will, in a blue blazer and tie, emerge from the rear shadow of the room and stand behind Jenny and Friday in the glow of the fireplace.

When I reach them, I put my hands on the outside of the window. They put theirs on the inside. We appear to touch, but don't. To each one of them I give a peck on the lips through the glass. After I kiss Lisa, though, she jets away into a ceiling of clouds and is nowhere to be found. The kids, aware of my concern, hold up their hands to let me know she'll be right back. In moments—up in those same clouds—light appears, as though the fire from the fireplace has risen with the smoke. When the smoke clears, Lisa comes toward us with sixteen lit candles on a birthday cake. As they sparkle in the presence of my family, Jenny looks at me and I nod to let her know it's time for her to make her wish, because my time with them burns with the candles. She turns from me and extinguishes the flames in the exhale of one long breath.

"I love you, Dad," she says.

"Happy birthday, Jenny. I love you, too. I love you all."

In unison they reply, "See you next year."

As the curtain begins to close, they pull their hands away from the window and everything fades to black; a darkness black enough to hide my own hands in front of my face. But I feel them and the tears they wipe from my cheeks.

A car horn startles me. The light has turned green. I push down on the gas pedal and turn right at the intersection to reverse my course. I get back onto Clayton toward the highway. The rush-hour traffic has filled the roads, but I manage to weave my way around the slower vehicles and make steady progress. After several miles, several turns, and even more second-guesses, I see the store sign up ahead.

I pull into the parking lot and take the open space by the store's front entrance. For a moment, I just sit there and second-guess myself again. In a car filled with stuffed animals and building blocks, it makes no sense to me that I'm at a firearms dealer. But these past few months, nothing has made much sense. As much as I will do anything for my daughter on her birthday, I will do an equal amount and more to protect her and the rest of my family if the threat of impending danger exists. Thus, I get out of the car and walk inside.

It's the complete opposite of the toy store. I'm surrounded by weapons and what I presume are men who know how to use them. For me, it's an uncomfortable environment. I know blocks, giraffes . . . my little girl. But guns . . . this is Hollis's department, not mine.

"Can I help you, sir?" the brawny man behind the glass counter asks.

"I'm interested in buying a handgun."

In a blue button-down with an embroidered NRA logo, he spreads his arms and leans forward to rest them on top of the glass. "Is there any particular type you're interested in?"

I look down at the huge assortment of them that stretch the length of the store in the display case. "I'm not sure."

"Would this be your first gun?"

It's obvious my apprehension is on display, too. "Yes."

He slides the door open and brings out two firearms. He lays them onto a thin rubber mat atop the counter.

"This one's a semi-automatic." He picks it up and hands it to me. "How does that feel to you?"

I extend my arm and point—like Truck. But I should know better than to point a gun in a store with so many people around. "Sorry about that."

"It's okay. The clip's out." He takes the gun from me, slides open the top part, then shows me the cavity inside the handle to prove the gun is unloaded. He sets it down and hands me the other gun. "This one's a revolver."

Other than the rubber grip, the heavier weight of the gun is the first thing I notice. There's no way Lisa would ever feel comfortable holding a cannon. Not that the gun is for her, though—it isn't. It's for me. But if ever she had to use it in an emergency, a lighter gun would be easier for her to aim and shoot. I set it back down.

"I like the semi-auto better. The revolver is too heavy."

"We have plenty of lighter ones, but you can't go wrong with either one."

"Not to get all technical or anything, but what's the main difference between the two types?"

"The revolver holds six rounds and the semi-automatic—on average—holds thirteen, that's probably the biggest difference," he replies. "Still, it's just a matter of preference and what feels comfortable to you."

I settle on the nine-millimeter semi-automatic, and we travel the length of the display case to look at the various models. He puts several into my hand and explains the features as well as the pros and cons of each. Amongst the black pistols, the stainless steel Beretta catches my eye, and so does the name.

He hands me the gun. "Nice choice."

It's small but not too compact. Adequate for both me and Lisa. Right away, I know it's the one.

"It feels good."

"It should, it's the Cadillac of my inventory."

"I'll take it."

"Great."

He reviews the gun with me and demonstrates its features and how to care for it. After answering all my questions he hands me a form that I need to fill out to purchase the gun. It's a background check, which he'll call in to the ATF so that I can get immediate approval and walk out with my new firearm. A gun for me, a sale for him.

At number eleven on the form, the yes-or-no question asks if I'm under indictment for a felony or any other crime that a judge could imprison me for more than one year. I hesitate and read the question over. Four times, in fact. Reluctant to ask the clerk for clarity on it, I mark the "No" box and continue because to the best of my knowledge I'm not under indictment, just suspicion.

I complete the form and hand it to the clerk. He heads down to the other end of the counter where the phone is and begins the background check approval process. In suspense, I wait. But in just a few minutes he returns to let me know all went well. Spared from the embarrassment of being rejected, I agree to buy ammo, a cleaning kit, and a small safe for the gun that has an electronic keypad for quick access.

"I keep mine loaded in the safe by my bed," he says, and we begin our discussion on where the best places at home are to store a handgun. The thought of a loaded firearm being inches from Lisa's head and mine, however, is a tough sell. "It won't do you any good if you can't get to it quickly when you need it."

"Does it ever worry you that it might go off by accident?"

"You mean while I'm in bed sleeping?"

"Yeah."

He chuckles. "A gun doesn't just fire on its own."

"See what little I know."

"It's all right. You gotta start somewhere."

I start my car and back out of the parking space, out of the parking lot, and onto the road home in less than forty-five minutes from entry to exit of the gun shop. And since I left work early, Jenny won't even consider me late when I arrive, which lessens the guilt of the purchase.

Unloaded, the gun sits in the safe along with the ammo on the passenger seat next to me. In the back are the blocks and stuffed animals. It's a strange combination, like the one

I came up with for the safe. One that I know my kids would never figure out. As I drive, I think. I plan. I will call Hollis in the morning. It's the first call I will make. Tempted as I am to dial him now and rendezvous for a second call at the pay phone, it can wait. Everything can wait. I have a birthday party to get to. Maybe afterwards when I put Jenny to bed, but even then, I'd rather not spoil the evening with an "errand to run" lie to Lisa.

CHAPTER TWENTY-ONE

At noon on the sidewalks of downtown St. Louis, I pass by hundreds of people on an ordinary day. In my suit and tie and overcoat, I return smiles to the few who recognize me. To the sax player at Seventh and Washington I return the favor by throwing a dollar into the open case at his feet. But I'm anything but ordinary or normal as I walk to the coffee shop that I've begun to visit almost hourly (it seems) since my conversation with Special Agent Curtis Vaughn three days ago on Jenny's twelfth. Because, in an odd way, the caffeine seems to level out the adrenaline in my body that refuses to sleep. I mean that both ways—the adrenaline and my body. Neither stops. That's why I walk when I get the chance, or the need arises . . . to the coffee shop, to the deli to pick up a sandwich for Carol, and back to my office where I'm too restless to accomplish anything, too stressed to even gain an appetite to fuel a man fourteen pounds less in weight than he was in October.

"I'll be back by two," I say to Carol when I pass by her desk on my way out of the office for the third time today. As far down as I can go, I ride the mineshaft and exit in the garage where my car waits, with its straightjacket of a seatbelt to strap myself into and remain in one place for an extended period.

In the constant grey of everything my life has become, I drive the highway west, while I worry about my friend. These days if I'm not worrying about something, then something's wrong. Yesterday, when I spoke with Hollis—after a day and a half of phone tag—I could sense a disappointment in his voice when we began to speak of his progress in the oil field of the Bakken. Without going into detail of it all, he made it known that perhaps the most eastern edge of the ranch property was just west of the gold mine. That perhaps, even after all their due diligence, all their t's crossed and i's dotted, they erred somewhere in the process, or just happened to be unlucky, as is often the case in the oil exploration business. And since he paid more for the Little Wing than what it's worth—to make sure he got it—he would be even further under water if he sold it. Therefore, that was not an option. "We'll push on," he said. "The glass is always half full." When I told him of my refusal of the polygraph and Agent Vaughn's subsequent promise of the screws to be tightened, he replied in his usual stiff upper lip manner. "Good for you for letting him know you won't be pushed around." And twice during the conversation, he said with confidence, "The guy's grasping for straws." He also seemed impressed when I told him I purchased a 9mm handgun.

After twenty minutes of travel, I reach the shooting range—a long narrow building in an industrial park. Except for the glass front door, the concrete block structure is as windowless as a gun safe. With my tie pulled from my neck, I grab the black canvass bag for transport of my gun and ammo, and head inside.

Unlike my office tower, the place feels dark and cold, which makes me even more uncomfortable than I already am with a firearm in my possession. In the background, gunshots filter through the conversations between sales clerks and customers as I follow the signs that point the way to the registration counter for the range. From the crowded sidewalk-look of the place, business is good.

At the counter, I fill out the form to be issued a shooting card and inquire on the services and availability of a private instructor. Being short on instructors, the owner volunteers to show me the ropes. In appreciation, I purchase ammo. The safety glasses and ear plugs added to the tab are requirements.

With the paper target in his possession, Randy Butler leads the way through the door to the shooting range. Down a hallway we go, and through another door where we enter a room with live fire. Even with my plugs in, it's loud. Randy, muted by headphones, which looks to be the better choice, guides me to an open bay.

"Let's talk about safety first." With each shot fired to the left and right of me, I flinch, which he takes note of. "You'll get used to it."

With my empty gun in his hand, he reviews the laws of the shooting range that are to be followed to the letter. To me, it's basic common sense, which just happens to be the same words he uses upon conclusion. After the rules and regulations, he moves on to the gun. He reviews the safety, the proper grip, how to stand, and how to aim and fire. Without any questions from his student on this portion of the lesson, he attaches the paper target to the target carrier and pushes a button to send it out twenty feet. A push of a button on the gun releases the empty magazine, which he loads with nine-millimeter ammo and returns to the cavity inside the handle after pulling the slide to its rearmost position.

"Stand behind me and I'll shoot a few rounds," he says.

As instructed, I stand behind the sixty-year-old man in jeans and a white polo, legs spread shoulder width apart. He clicks the lever to release the slide and a round is chambered. With military-like precision, he fires off three shots in quick succession, engages the safety, and sets the gun down with the barrel pointed away from us toward the target. Summoned to his side, he retrieves the target that showcases three shots in the chest of the black outline of the man.

"Think center mass instead of head and limbs," he says. "Ready to give it a try?"

We trade places, and he sends the target back to where it was. I pick up the gun, then imitate him as best I can. On the first shot, the power of the gun and the explosive noise it generates indoors almost overwhelms me. But there's also a death-defying attraction to it as well. It's so much different than a twenty-gauge shotgun on a skeet course or an upland field. The way it feels in my hands, the way I stand when I fire it, like it's an extension of me. The second, third, and fourth shot I fire as fast as I can pull the trigger, before I engage the safety and put the gun down.

"That was good," he says. "Try to pull the trigger more smoothly, though, and slow it down a little."

He steps back and lets me deplete the rounds still left in the magazine—lets me get more and more comfortable with each shot. We retrieve the target and assess my skill by the number of holes in the would-be adversary. There are ten.

"How'd I do?"

"Not bad. Not bad at all," he replies. "You're a good student."

CHAPTER TWENTY-TWO

Like all businessmen, I must go where the business is. Like Hollis, mine is also tied to oil. Not all of it, but a hefty chunk, which requires me to visit the Middle East when necessary. Today—late February—it's necessary.

It's necessary to say goodbye to my wife and kids, to board a plane for the unadorned fourteen-hour flight to Abu Dhabi of the United Arab Emirates, to help my regional representative close a deal there. A big deal, as the sale of two customized 737s would be considered in just about anyone's book—Boeing's included.

Over the years, I've become acclimated to travel. In time, and with the incorporation of a daily routine that revolves around our kids, Lisa's friends, Friday, and what I consider to be a far too ambitious schedule of volunteer work, Lisa has adjusted to my life on the road, too, with a preferred type of busy where she almost doesn't even know I'm gone.

For three nights, though, I will be, and because of where I'm to venture on the globe, she will notice the empty space next to her in our bed. Of my overseas travels, she's apprehensive; an anxiety that's compounded when my trips involve the Arabian Peninsula and the Persian Gulf, which she considers hazardous to Americans. But I've assured her that's not the case, and that Abu Dhabi, in fact, is quite beautiful and safe—an island city much like Hong Kong, less the mountainous backdrop.

Prior to bon voyage, I pull up pictures (same as I did two years ago) for her on the internet to show her how modern and westernized of a metropolis Abu Dhabi is. I show her the turquoise waters and the white sand beaches that moat the skyscrapers. "And look," I say as I pull up the Hilton—a spitting image of resorts we've traveled to with the kids—"just like the Caribbean, isn't it? And like always, I'll be home in three days."

My time on the road was never something she asked me to limit. I established the no-longer-than-three-nights policy on my own. It was either four for the company and three for my family per week, or the other way around, which is how I chose to tip the scales to my household's benefit. To the company's benefit, my division has delivered beyond expectations.

We touch down in Abu Dhabi at noon. Maybe, just maybe, I've managed to get two hours of in-flight sleep. But I've gotten used to the lack of it for some time now and can function well enough to evade detection as the victim of insomnia that I've become. Through Customs, I rush for the men's room to relieve myself in a stall that's palatial in comparison to what Boeing or any of my competitors offer on any of our planes. This happens to be my biggest pet peeve with airline travel—bathrooms the size of phone booths.

When I'm through, I head for the sink and mirror to make myself look more reputable. Some Visine for the eyes, a razor for the face, a comb for the hair, and a tie for the money.

I hustle out to the curb and find the driver who holds the coded sign only a select few are aware of. I'm one of them, and make my identity known to the man. He puts my bag in the trunk and speeds off for the office tower where I'm scheduled to meet with two other Boeing team members prior to our appointment with our customers there.

As to be expected in that arid region the world, the sun shines and the temperature is a pleasant eighty-five degrees, an almost perfect Arabian late-February day. Compared to the grey skies of the Midwest, the Middle East is a respite from the gloom that's had its grip on me longer than I'd care to admit. I roll down my window and soak it in, oblivious to the wind and its effect on my well-groomed appearance.

We cross the bridge and motor onto the island that the city of Abu Dhabi is. In the shadows of the high-rises we pass in the congested urban core of the city, I crane my neck to see the changes that have taken shape to the skyline. It's been two years since my last visit, and in those two years, it's as though the number of buildings on the island has doubled. The growth is remarkable, almost as impressive as the wealth I've come to tap into.

Up ahead I see Tom Hildestadt as he waits for me outside the office tower where he's rented a conference room for today's meeting. In the masses of Arabic men and women, he is the tree in a desert with his red hair and fair skin. A two-hour drive from here, he works out of our Dubai office and uses this building whenever he has a presentation for clients who prefer to meet in Abu Dhabi. I've known Tom for years and brought him over with me from Gulfstream when I made the switch to Boeing. He's a solid performer, and as equal in importance, an ex-patriot with a desire to live and work overseas—for handsome compensation.

On foreign soil, I shake hands with the pleasant and good-natured man, and because we are more than just business associates, we wrap our arms around each other in representation of home away from home. He leads me inside as we talk of our families on the way up to the eighteenth-floor conference room, where two other members of our Middle East team greet us: Nils Billeaud from finance and Harris Burch from engineering.

"Good to see you, Nils. Good to see you, Harris," I say.

If ever there was an A-Team, these three would be it. Nils is Swiss and speaks five languages, Arabic included. Harris, who's British, has the faculty to go in depth on the technical side of things with the charm of a salesman, which is a unique trait for an engineer. And Tom is our regional manager in charge of all business development. He runs the show. I'm there to represent corporate to our clients, to show respect. A bit dog and pony, yes, but I also have the authority to negotiate a final sale price that Tom cannot. He always needs my approval.

Our 3:00 p.m. meeting with an Emirati billionaire and his entourage ends with the sale of a 737. It was what we'd expected would happen, but there's always the possibility things could go south at the last minute. In my industry, I consider all deals to be up in the air until the client is up there, too—in his new Boeing. With a celebration in order, we agree to meet at the restaurant in our hotel at seven o'clock for dinner, which gives each of us an hour and a half of free time to do whatever we want.

At the hotel, I head down to the pool for a swim. *When in Rome.* But when I arrive there, I change my mind and walk down to the beach instead. For the most part, it's empty except for the few who've ventured out to enjoy the sunset. To test the water, I dip my toe into the calm surf. It's cooler than expected. Mid-to-low seventies, give or take. As a Michigander, though, it's a temperature I should be able to tolerate, so I dive right in and begin to swim freestyle.

With my legs, I kick hard, and pull even harder with my arms in my attempt to generate enough body heat to insulate myself from the frigid Persian Gulf's rude and ungracious welcome. Head down, I swim and swim and swim, and by the time I lift it out of the water to take a deep breath, I'm beyond the hotel's buoy—beyond what is deemed safe for its guests. Unimpressed, I cold-shoulder the advice and continue out into the darker blue colors of the sea.

When I tire, I turn over to float on my back—fetal by nature, spread-eagle in design, weightless as my thoughts and stars and planets that begin to hatch. Nine hours ahead of Lisa, Will, and Jenny, I drift in the slack tide and imagine where they are and what they're doing. My kids are in a classroom. As for Lisa, perhaps she's with Friday on her mid-morning loop around the St. Louis Country Club.

But in the cold water there isn't much time to think. Soon I will be chilled to the bone, so it's time to swim again. To do that, I flip over onto my belly and head for shore. At the buoy, I stop to get my bearings. It's more mental than physical, though, because for some odd reason I want to swim back out and see how far I can go. Maybe even swim home, or someplace else. *But that's crazy, right?* I pull my head out of the sand and put it back into the water, and in compromise, swim parallel to shore until I tire and switch from freestyle to breaststroke, the easier of the two. *I could swim for miles like this.*

Without a care in the world, which has been months in the making, I glide through the Persian Gulf. Head down, head up to breathe. Easy pull, easy kick, I ease my way into the shallow water where the last rays of the sun kiss the nape of my neck goodbye.

I touch bottom, and wade to shore—renewed and invigorated beyond the reach of jetlag. But it will come. It always does.

After dinner, it arrives at the same time I arrive back at my room, which is good timing now that my business day is done. Within an hour, it will put me to sleep, of which I hope to get five hours tonight (or more if I'm lucky) and the sleeping pill I'm about to take works its magic.

At the desk with my laptop, I follow up on emails and send one to Lisa and the kids, with the hope I hear back from them before I climb into bed. Next in line is the mail that Lisa packed for me, along with all the bills that need to be paid. On the road like I am, I try to take care of as much family business as possible so that I can spend as much time with my family when I'm home with them.

Checkbook and pen at the ready, I sift through the pile to weed out the junk mail, and what remains I divide between bills and correspondence deemed worthy enough to be opened and read. Midway, a letter marked for my attention, without a return address and postmarked Savage, Montana; February 16, catches my eye.

I open it. Inside is an oh-too-familiar piece of paper cut to the same size as the envelope, identical to the ones at the

Little Wing. In typed print, it reads: MONDAY, TUESDAY, WEDNESDAY, THURSDAY . . . ?

To give it more thought—which is nothing more than self-inflicted torture at this point—I set it down on the table in front of me and focus on it there, oblivious to the steeple my hands have constructed at my lips. But I'm altogether aware of the meaning behind the words, and the one that isn't there: Friday. Unchained, I pick up my cell phone and dial Lisa's number using my international calling plan. It's noon in St. Louis and she could be anywhere. By now, Friday could be too, and by now, I begin to pray that he isn't; that he's at home where he should be, safe and happy.

Her phone begins to ring. A fourth, a fifth, a sixth ring—voicemail. I hang up, dial again, and wait for the connection from my side of the world to hers. After a brief delay, the call goes through. But I don't get through to her. Next, I try the house phone. *Pick up the phone, pick up the phone, Lisa.* The line gets dropped. *Fuck!* Once more I type away on my cell phone's keypad and wait . . . and wait some more. A connection is made, and this one seems much stronger, like a grip with two hands instead of one. *Come on, pick it up. Come on, come on, come on. Answer!* She doesn't.

With my index fingers, I tap my lips and debate whether, or not to call the Ladue Police. But what do I tell them? What *can* I tell them? That my dog may be in imminent danger and to please send a patrolman to our house right away to prevent any harm that might come to Friday, if it hasn't already. I mean, it's such an odd request that without an explanation of all that's occurred and why I think this could happen, it may sound borderline psychotic, which is the last thing our family needs. We've only been in the neighborhood for ten months, and if something like this gets around there could be so much whispering behind our backs the breeze would be felt more than the words.

Think clearly. I try but can't. In my irrational state, I pick up the phone and dial Lisa a fourth time. Maybe it's the fifth. I don't know. I've lost count. I've lost my mind. She doesn't pick up. *Where are you, Lisa? Answer your goddam phone.*

Calm down. Take some deep breaths and calm down. Whoever it is, they're just toying with you again. Think about it. If something had happened to Friday, Lisa would've called. Deep breaths, deep breaths.

In a more reasonable frame of mind, I make the decision to call Bill Bartholomew and ask him to check on Friday if I'm unable to contact Lisa within the next thirty minutes. Bill will sometimes lend a hand and let him out of the house to go to the bathroom when I'm traveling, and Lisa is gone for the day and the kids are at school. He has a key to the house, and the alarm code. He would do it in a heartbeat, as he has done for us several times, and wouldn't think twice about the nature of the call.

Ten long minutes pass before I dial Lisa's cell, which I promise myself will be the last, because too many attempts will raise possibly unnecessary suspicion and worry on her end. At the prompt, I record my message.

"Hi, it's me. I'm at the hotel. The flight and the meeting went well. Give me a call when you get this. Would love to hear your voice."

I put on an act, the same one I've worn for months. Not that I wouldn't love to hear her voice, the kids' voices, Friday's bark. In fact, I'd give back today's sale for those sounds right now. But I do what I need to do, say what I need to say to make it through each day in the hope that someday all of this will end.

At the thirty-minute mark, and still no word from Lisa, I honor my self-imposed contract and make the call to Bill Bartholomew. On the other end, Margot picks up.

"Hi, Margot, it's Garrett."

"Hello, Garrett."

"Is Bill around?"

"He is. He's just sat down for lunch. I'll hand him the phone."

In the background, I hear her travel across the floor and inform Bill that it's me on the phone.

"Hi, Garrett."

"Hey, Bill. Sorry to bother you, but I was wondering if you might be able to walk over to the house and let Friday do his business in the backyard? I'm out of town and I think Lisa is gone for the afternoon."

"No problem," he says. "Is it okay if I do it after lunch, or does he need to be let out now?"

"After lunch is fine." But it isn't fine. It's just too rude to ask him to do it now.

"Okay, I'll take care of him then."

"I really appreciate it."

"Happy to help," he replies. "What part of the world are you in now?"

"Abu Dhabi."

"Trying to think where that is."

"In the United Arab Emirates, just south of Saudi Arabia on the Persian Gulf."

"Amazing, sounds like you're next door. This modern technology is something else."

"It is."

"Well, have a good trip and a safe flight home."

"Thanks, Bill. Thanks for everything."

In sixty minutes, I will call him back to make sure all is okay with the dog. I note the time on my watch and return to the chore at hand, which not only involves unpaid expenses, but also the struggle to remain awake—now that the pill and jetlag have joined forces. Minutes into the fight, I look at my watch again in expectation of significant advancement, but it too shows signs of jetlag.

When the torturous hour-long wait ends, I call the Bartholomews. Margot answers. Bill is down in the basement, but she volunteers to go and get him for me. I volunteer to wait. They're in their seventies, which requires patience on my end while she descends two flights of stairs.

"Take your time," I say, from guilt for the inconvenience.

After another protracted delay, Bill picks up.

"Hey, Bill. I hope I'm not causing too much trouble by calling you back, but I wanted to make sure all was well with Friday and that you didn't have any issues getting in or out of the house."

"No trouble at all, Garrett," he replies. "I took care of him. He told me to tell you to hurry home."

"I'll do that."

"Safe travels."

"Thanks again for being such great neighbors. We couldn't have picked two better people to move next door to."

"We feel the same."

I am quick to praise, to give thanks, and exude appreciation in the euphoria of good news. For my victory lap, I strip down to my underwear, brush my teeth, and climb into bed to take advantage of the peacefulness of the moment—the heaven-sent sleep it will bring. Before I turn to my left to turn off the light though, I lie on my back and stare at the ceiling, because maybe I miss the pain. *Maybe they're just playing games. Yeah, that's all they're doing. It's been nothing but games all along. See? And you got yourself all worked up over nothing. But whoever it is, how did they find out Friday's name?* Maybe through our registration of his rabies vaccination or license? Or maybe some other way. It wouldn't be too difficult a thing of someone to accomplish; a someone who possibly saw us drive Orrin's truck into the Redwater, and much easier for the Fort Peck Police or Richland County Sheriff. Mere child's play for the FBI. As I reach for the light switch to turn the pain off, I hear Hollis's ever-optimistic words of encouragement, my kids' voices, Lisa's voice, Friday's pant after he retrieves the tennis ball, the faint sound of the elevator doors as they open and close in the hallway . . . and my cell phone.

In the dark, I reach for its glow on the nightstand and see Lisa's number on its screen.

In Arabic, I greet her. "Marhaba."

"Hey, babe."

"I miss you."

"Miss you more," she replies, "Sounds like someone's ready for bed."

"Not ready, I'm in it."

"Did I wake you?"

"No. Perfect timing."

"Good, I was hoping you'd still be up. How did everything go today?"

"It went really well."

"How's Tom doing?"

"He's great. He and Becky say hello."

"Tell them the same."

"I will. How are the kids?"

"I'm on my way to pick up Jenny from school and take her to dance, and Will has basketball at five."

"What time is his game this weekend?"

"At four on Saturday. It's a home game."

It kills me to miss any of my kid's sporting events or performances. It's the worst part of my job. Being away from them is tough enough, but it fills me with regret when I miss their athletic competitions.

"Maybe there's some way I can get on an earlier flight to be there."

"I'm sure he would love that, but do what you need to do there first."

"I will. How's Friday?"

"I took him for a long walk this morning and gave him two treats for you."

I don't see the need to tell her that Bill let him out. Could be days until they even see each other and by then it will be long forgotten by Bill. "Give him a hug for me."

"I will."

"Well, I better get some sleep. I've got another busy day tomorrow."

"I bet you're exhausted."

"I am."

"Okay, sweet dreams."

"You too."

She laughs. "It's only three."

"Oh yeah, I forgot." Bleary-eyed, I say, "I'll call you in a day or so."

At 4:00 a.m. I awaken in the dark, disappointed with the five-hour sleep. I'd hoped to get more. But I'll take it because it's more than the four I've been averaging. I turn onto my side, away from the digital clock, and stretch out my arm under the pillow and shut my eyes with a false pretense of an eventual loss of consciousness. It won't happen, though. Not after ten, twenty, or thirty-five minutes. Hence I flip on the light and start my day, like all the other days before it when I rise before the sun in the loneliness of some hotel room thousands of miles away from home. And sometimes I'm not even away from home. I'm there in that most comfortable of places surrounded by those I love most, and yet, still a tranquil night's sleep eludes me.

My mind brightens from the light. I get out of bed and take a seat over at the desk containing the laptop, the mail, the bills—I look over the menu. On the far right of the desktop, is the letter from Savage, Montana. With no desire to ever see it again, I crumble it up, along with the envelope, and throw it away.

To be productive, I open my laptop, because I know all too well these days that idle hands are tools of the devil. While it powers up, the stack of remaining bills grabs my attention and I switch my priority from business to family. With diligence, I tackle the load to ensure all my attention will be given to Will and Jenny and Lisa when I return home. But when the mundane predawn monotony of the task fails to hold my attention for long, I grow restless and head back to the sanctuary of my bed and turn out the light.

There's no sanctuary there, though. And who was I kidding to think there would be? I know what I'm doing. I know where this is going, and right away I'm there. Toss and turn. Toss and turn. A mind on tumble dry. The cup is half-empty.

Friday isn't going to be harmed. Yes, he is. No, I think it might mean something else. Like what? I don't know yet. Let me think about it some more. And that's what I do—lots of it—because I can't find a way to put this whole thing behind me. Because it's not going away. Not now, not ever. *Why can't you just accept that?*

In my head, the switch is flipped, and the light turns on. *Friday is going to be hurt this Friday.* I fight the thought. I fight hard. I try to push it out of my head, out through my ears and onto the pillow where it can be hidden underneath. But even if I could get it out of my head, which I can't, you can't hide the truth, and a further read between the lines reveals just that: *Friday is going to be wounded or killed on Friday.* Convinced of this, I begin to formulate an early departure from the United Arab Emirates to make it home in time to stop what I think is going to happen.

Hold on! You're acting all crazy again. Can't you see what you're doing? You're just torturing yourself. And that's exactly what whoever it is wants. Don't let them win like this. Be a man!

A man, though, protects his family, and if I need to leave a day earlier than planned to do that, so be it. Because every man's first priority is his family. Without question, it's mine. But I'm also a businessman who understands how important my job is to my family and the importance of doing my job well. It provides us with almost everything. In fair compromise, I make the decision to stay today and help Tom close on the sale of the second 737, which is the main reason for my travels here. And when the dust clears, I will jump on a red-eye tonight or leave first thing Friday morning, provided there's an open seat.

* * *

There is an open seat, and twenty-four hours later I'm on it—after a record sale of two planes in two days, after I satisfy my obligations to Boeing, as well as Tom, Nils, and Harris.

As a father and husband, I travel fourteen hours to New York City on a bumpy, and brutal-in-duration flight. On American soil, I touch down at JFK, clear customs, and search for an area where the cell signal is strong, and the terminal is quiet for my call to Lisa. Near an empty gate, I find one and dial.

"Surprise, surprise."

"Surprise, surprise? What are you surprising me with?"

"I'm back in the States."

"You are?"

"Yeah."

"That *is* a nice surprise. Where are you?"

"I just got into New York City where I'm laying over until the 2:50 flight to St. Louis."

"Then you'll be home tonight."

"Which means I won't miss Will's game tomorrow."

"You didn't need to do that."

"I know, but I wanted to."

"You're a good dad."

But I'm not. A liar is what I am, and so I ignore the praise. "How's everyone?" *Come on, tell me everything's fine, and Friday is asleep on the living room chair by the window.*

"Busy as always."

"How's my little buddy?"

"Playing with his new toy here in the kitchen."

"Love that dog."

"We all do."

"Have you made any plans for dinner or anything else tonight?"

"I haven't, but I was thinking about asking the Elliott's over with their kids."

"Sounds perfect," I say, because a plan like that would enable me to keep an eye on Friday throughout the night. "If you want me to, I can pick up some pizzas on my way home from the airport."

"That would be great. I'll call Lynn and see if they're available."

"Okay, let me know what they say."

"I will, and if you're in the air I'll leave you a message on your voicemail."

Chapter Twenty-Three

There was nothing to worry about after all, because Friday comes and goes without incident. And on the Tuesday that follows, I do the same and spend two days and nights in Seattle for company meetings, before I return home Thursday night. The next morning, fresh from a miraculous six hours of sleep, I'm in the office to work on budgets when Carol buzzes me.

"Do you want to take a call from a man by the name of Curtis Vaughn who says he's an agent with the FBI?"

Using pretense to mask any knowledge of who the man is or what he may want, I reply, "Sounds interesting. Go ahead and put him through."

My phone rings and I pick it up. "This is Garrett Ingram."

"Good morning, Garrett. Special Agent Curtis Vaughn of the FBI."

"Hello, Agent Vaughn. Could you hold a second?"

"Sure."

I take my headset off and get up to shut my office door. Back at my desk, I continue the conversation. "How can I help you?"

"I'd like to meet with you in St. Louis next week."

"Why?"

"I have something I'd like to show you."

"Mind telling me what it is first?"

"It's something I think you'll find interesting, and probably better left unsaid until we're face-to-face."

"What day were you thinking of?"

"How does Tuesday work?"

"I'll be in Los Angeles."

"I'd be happy to meet you there, especially this time of year. It'd be nice to get out of the snow and cold of Montana."

"I won't have time in L.A."

"When do you get back?"

"After L.A., I'm heading to Dallas."

"Any place in the South is good with me."

If he isn't going to take no for an answer, then—to keep things as quiet as possible—meeting somewhere out of town is better than anywhere in St. Louis.

I pull up my schedule on the computer. "On Wednesday afternoon I arrive at DFW at 3:02 p.m. I could meet there or at the Hyatt Regency in downtown Dallas."

"Let's meet at the Hyatt. What time?"

"Five o'clock. There's a bar on the second floor of the atrium. I'll save you a seat."

I open the door to my office and walk around the bend to Carol's desk, where I'm sure curiosity has gotten the better of her. "I've got some good news."

"Let's hear it," she replies.

"I've been taken off the FBI's Most Wanted list."

"That is good news."

"Did the fax from GE Aviation come through yet?"

She looks through the pile and pulls it out. "Here you go."

"Thanks. And by the way—in case you're wondering—that was just some fed looking for a hunting guide my buddies and I met when we went to Montana back in October."

"It's good to know you're off the list."

"It'll be nice to be able to step inside a post office again."

My corner office has two windows. The one that faces east offers a view of the Gateway Arch and the Mississippi River. But you need to look out of the top-left side of it to see them, and to do that you need to stand. That's where I am, a foot from the glass, wondering if the proverbial glass is half empty or half full while I gaze at those Midwestern icons.

I know Hollis's answer to the question, and so I see no reason to call him for a shot in the arm or to get his take on what it is that Agent Vaughn wants to show me. It could be anything. Though no matter what it is, unless its's a dead body he plans to transport to Texas for identification, "*He doesn't have shit. If we stick to our story, he can't touch us.*" Up and down like barges on the Mississippi I run that through my head, until Hollis's indelible mark is carved into my brain. Because I think he's right. No, not "think." He is right. *Right?* I'm tired, though. That's where I am with all this, more so than the space I occupy. The insomnia, the anxiety and stress, the roller coaster of a ride; it's a brink-of-exhaustion marathon. The lies, the masquerade, the veneer of a human being I've become.

For no particular reason I lean forward to try and fog the glass with my breath. It's childish, but I don't care, and I do it again to make another faint cloud just below it, to make more clouds in an attempt to mimic the ones in the sky that block out the sun. The sun that hasn't been out for days— days that are so much shorter than the nights. I lie awake in bed during the night to await the arrival of the day. And on and on it goes, out the window, past the arch, over the Mississippi, and into the dark and light grey of my world.

* * *

Five days later I awaken, like always, in the dark. Also, like always, in a different bed, in a different city, a different time zone. Five hours after that I give a presentation to a wealthy real estate developer interested in an upgrade from his Dassault Falcon to a 737. Then once again I'm up in the air, over the Pacific, where we bank left out of LAX on our ascent to 15,000 feet. As we climb, we burn fuel like sweat, and the plane reaches an eventual cruising altitude of 33,000 feet for the flight to Dallas. In comparison to an international flight, California to Texas is a hop, skip, and a jump, and before I even have the chance to finish a follow-up proposal on my laptop for the client I pitched in the City of Angels, we're wheels down at DFW.

I grab my rental car, and soon find myself amidst a sea of Ford F-150 pickups on the highway as I head for the downtown Dallas Hyatt Regency. Surrounded by them, I almost fail to notice the sun. But it's there, along with the blue sky and the majestic rhinestone cowboy skyline that sprouts up from the edge of the prairie. On I-30, I travel east, a stretch of interstate I've trodden many times. Most of them from my days with Gulfstream, when the market for corporate and private jet ownership seemed almost limitless from Fort Worth to Dallas—in the boom years of the oil industry, though, not the bust. Make no mistake about it, oil drives a large sector of the Texas economy. And under a different set of circumstances, I'm driven there, too.

At the front entrance to the Hyatt, I hand my keys to the valet and wheel my carry-on into the hotel, where it's eye-popping seventeen-story atrium screams, "Everything *is* bigger in Texas." After I check in and get my room key, I ride the glass elevator up to the tenth floor, all the while searching for Special Agent Vaughn down at the bar. But he doesn't appear to have made an early arrival.

In my room, I change out of my suit and tie into jeans, a button down, and running shoes that these days walk far more than they run. With an hour to kill, I will walk them some more. The fresh air will do me good, in theory.

From the hotel, the road leads north under an overpass up to Houston Street, which I take past Dealey Plaza to Elm to Market Street. Amongst the many restaurants of the West End is a retailer in an old red brick building that I typically stop in to buy Texas souvenirs for Will and Jenny whenever I'm in Dallas. Its distance from the hotel makes for the perfect walk.

By the time I step through its doors, I've produced a light perspiration from the fast pace in upper fifty-degree weather. One of the clerks assists me in purchasing a bracelet for Jenny and a Texas-image baseball for Will. Afterwards I head back to the hotel on the streets of Dallas.

At Houston and Wood, a block from the Hyatt, I stop. I should've stopped an hour ago, days ago. Instead, from place to place, hotel to hotel, city to city I go. All with the hope that time will go by unnoticed, to bring me here to this moment as soon as possible, and have it fly by me without episode. And I've gotten this far, and so far so good. But now with the hotel in sight, I can't help but wonder if I might be making a huge mistake walking in and sitting down with an FBI agent who seeks justice for the Sioux Nation. I wonder if I should call Hollis. I wonder if I should call an attorney.

As cars race home in the rush-hour traffic, I give serious thought to doing the same. In my pockets are my phone, wallet, and keys to the rental car. They're all I need. I could just walk to the car, drive to the airport, and get on a flight and be home in an hour and a half. Or if I wanted to, I could just skip the airport and drive home. Yes, I like that. I like the sound of that. The open road. The freedom of it. Yes, freedom. Maybe that's what this is all about. I could get in the car, drive home, pack a few things, get the family and take off for Alaska or Maine or cross into Mexico and go as far south as the roads will take us. I've seen pictures of Tierra del Fuego. It looks remote.

"Excuse me, sir."

I pull my eyes away from the Hyatt and turn toward the voice. "Yes?"

"Is Dealey Plaza this way?" He extends his index finger and points.

"It is. Only a block or two. You can't miss it."

"Thanks."

He walks away. I walk away too. But not from Special Agent Vaughn. Right or wrong, wise or foolish, without counsel, I proceed to the Hyatt—down Reunion Boulevard and under the overpass where the sun sets and rises in the time it takes to travel sixty feet. Beyond there, a drive on the left leads up a short incline to the hotel.

For safe passage, a porter opens the door and I enter the Hyatt, where the escalator carries me to the second floor of the atrium. In the northwest territory of the bar just beyond, Vaughn sits at a table in his charcoal suit and navy-blue tie, and upon my approach, gives me a slight wave.

I cross a small terrace, take two steps up to the bar level, and follow the mahogany crafted woodwork from one end to the other. A few feet farther, is the table Agent Vaughn occupies. Out of professional courtesy, he stands to greet me, and in the faded daylight that shines through the four-stories of glass behind the bar, we shake hands.

"Thanks for meeting with me," he says.

"No problem."

I take the empty seat across from him and set my gift bag down on the table as the waitress arrives with two glasses of water and places one in front of each of us.

"Could I get you fellas something to drink?"

He and I look at each other before answering. Vaughn orders a Coke. I ask for an iced tea. The waitress smiles and says she'll be right back. She turns and leaves—leaves us alone.

"How was your flight?" he asks.

"Smooth and on time. On a Boeing, of course. And yours?"

"Bumpy and late. And come to think of it, it was an Airbus."

"That's what you get."

"I'll make a note to try and fly only Boeing aircraft from now on."

"I'd appreciate that."

He leans back in his chair and crosses his legs, as though in expectation of our drinks to arrive with the same impeccable service as the waters. But behind him, four women seat themselves at the last empty table in the bar area and begin a jovial conversation that puts his ears closer to their words than mine. Because of this, he sits up and scoots nearer to me, and we're back where we began.

"Let's talk business, okay?"

"Okay," I reply, and join him at the fifty-yard line with my elbows on the table too.

"When we last met at the airport in Sidney, you stated that the day you went hunting with Orrin Gall, that your vehicles, a Polaris ATV that was leant to you by the Little Wing Ranch, and a 1999 model year Blue Chevy Silverado 1500, owned and operated by Orrin Gall, remained where they were parked during the entirety of your hunt, which began around 9:00 a.m. and ended at approximately 3:00 p.m., with a lunch break from noon to one o'clock. Is this an accurate statement?"

"Why are you asking me this?"

"I want to make sure I have an accurate account of the day's events."

"I thought we were meeting because you had something to show me."

"I do, and I will be happy to put it in front of your eyes. But first, let me know if what I just said is correct. That is what you told me, right? The vehicles stayed put."

He knows what I told him, and I know what I told him. "Yes."

"Thank you for answering."

The waitress returns with our drinks and sets them down along with a bowl of cashews and pretzels. While she does her job, he does his and reaches into the satchel on the floor by his chair. He pulls out a large manila envelope, which he places onto the table. As the waitress leaves, I pick up my drink. Just before taking a sip, I ask, "What's that?"

"It's what I brought to show you." But he doesn't show me anything, yet. "Going back to our conversation in Sidney, do you recall me telling you about the Tenth Missile Squadron at Malmstrom Air Force Base and all the Intercontinental Ballistic Missiles that Montana is home to?"

"Yes."

"Well, funny thing is, I completely forgot about it myself . . . for a while, until a few days after I called you to see if you'd be willing to take a polygraph—which you refused—and I'm sitting in the waiting room at the dentist's office, and I see a National Geographic magazine." He takes his elbows off the table, and with one hand straightens his tie, and takes a drink of his Coke with the other before he resumes. "I drink more of this stuff than I should, but I need the caffeine and hate the taste of coffee."

"I'm just the opposite."

"To each his own," he replies. "Anyway, I pick it up and start looking through it and I come to this article about the joint NASA/USGS Landsat program and the agricultural benefits from the use of satellite imaging, and it gets me thinking—"

"Are we eating?" the waitress interrupts, with menus at the ready.

"I'm good," he says.

"Me too."

She leaves and he picks up where he left off. "It gets me thinking about those ICBM's and the satellites used by the Department of Defense to keep a close eye on them and the ones in the hands of our adversaries. And it gives me an idea." He stops, leans forward, and clasps his hands together on the table. "Any idea what that idea is?"

"No."

"What if one of those satellites, or one operated by the USGS has pictures of you and Mr. Baumgartner hunting with Orrin Gall while it's mapping the earth in that same neck of the woods? A long shot maybe, but what if?"

If he could see through me, he'd see the knot in my stomach, as it twists and turns and moves upward to become the lump in my throat that, from fear of exposure, I can't let out. But because of it, I can't let words out, either, so I say nothing and wait for him to break the silence. He waits, too. It feels like forever. I pick up my drink to try and clear my throat with tea. Two sips, then a third, and it feels like I've washed it all down. "To answer your own question for you, there'd be photos of one of those hunters missing lots of birds."

"Maybe so." He slides the envelope in front of him, turns it over and straightens the metal clasps. He opens the flap, removes a photograph, and positions it for me to view. "Take a look." In color, there are two blurred objects surrounded by indistinguishable browns and greens. Browns more than the others. "See anything there?"

"I don't."

"Let's try another one." The second photo is higher resolution and gives shape to the dark objects. From my hesitation though to determine what they are, he pulls out a third to eliminate any doubt.

"That's the Polaris and Orrin's pickup."

"Yes, it is," he replies. "We confirmed it." He takes another drink of his Coke. "Now here's where it gets interesting. The picture was taken at 11:03 a.m. Traveling at about 18,000 miles per hour, the satellite orbits earth every ninety minutes." He pulls another picture from the envelope, but he leaves it facedown on the table. When he turns it over, he says, "This photo of the exact same location taken at 12:33 p.m. tells a different story."

Because the story is non-fiction, the Polaris and Chevy are absent. "I don't see the vehicles in this one," I say, as though ignorant of where Hollis and I moved them.

"They aren't there, which means the satellite is lying about those vehicles remaining in place for the duration of your hunt, or you are. Which is it, Garrett?"

"I don't think I like where this conversation is going."

"Of course, you don't, because it's going to be continued in Federal Court if you continue to be uncooperative."

"If you have nothing further to show me, I've got to get going."

"This envelope contains many photographs. And they tell a story. Either you tell me the truth about what happened to Orrin Gall—and this is the last time I'm going to give you the opportunity to do this and gain goodwill—or believe you me when that day comes and you plead for leniency from the court, I will vehemently object and use all of my resources to prevent anything other than the maximum penalty under law from being handed down." He pauses, stares at me and says, "And let me tell you this, Mr. Ingram, that courtroom will be packed with the citizens of Richland County and more Sioux than Custer's Last Stand."

He's bluffing. Ask him to show you the rest of the photographs. How can you be so sure, though? What if he has pictures of us digging the grave? What if he has pictures of Orrin's dead body? He doesn't. If he did, he wouldn't be here with photographs; he'd be here with a warrant.

"I have nothing further to say to you." I push my chair back and stand with a firm hold of the plastic bag that contains the gifts for my children.

He remains seated. "How do you live with yourself?"

"I don't. I have a family."

"Then, if I were you, I'd start practicing because you won't have one for long."

With that, I turn and walk—out of the bar and down the escalator, where I exit the hotel for the streets of Dallas once again. When I'm a good distance from the Hyatt—and Agent Vaughn—I pull out my cell phone and dial Hollis. He doesn't pick up, though, and the call goes to voicemail. After traveling two more city blocks, I try again, and again he doesn't answer.

Without an answer myself, I continue to walk in search of one at the next street corner. And the next one. And the next. But nothing is found except the tired remnants of a day's work—on the sidewalks that whittle away high-heeled and hard-soled pedestrians.

In the maze of the high-rises, I have no idea where I'm going, other than in an eastward direction. And I only know this because of the long shadow the setting sun casts in front of me when it has the brief chance to catch me in the openness of a crosswalk.

As darkness falls on the city, I pop out like a newborn on the other side of it, into Deep Ellum. That's what they call this part of Dallas; an old warehouse district converted to arts and entertainment. But I don't need either of the two. I just need a drink. Or two. Or three. Because I've been here before—though never on foot—it's recognizable in many ways. And in many ways, like me, it isn't. Unsure of which way to go, I just keep going, and after I pass a row of eclectic retail shops and two restaurants, I find an uncrowded drinking establishment with "Live Music 9:00 p.m." according to the advertisement on display.

At the bar, I find a stool two seats away from the closest guy and pull out my phone while I wait for the bartender to notice me. It doesn't take very long.

"What can I get for you?" he asks.

"Bourbon on the rocks, please."

"Maker's?"

"Sure."

He goes away and I dial Hollis, with the promise to myself that this will be my last attempt. When the call is sent to voicemail, I leave a message.

"Hey, Hollis. It's Garrett. Give me a call when you get a chance. Hope all is well up north."

The phone is in my right hand; in my left—the bourbon. I seek mercy from either one. Along with the gifts for my children in the bag I've placed on the bar, they are my most valuable possessions.

But mercy is hard to come by these days, and after two hours in deep prayer at this altar, the only good thing to come my way is a cab the bartender hails upon my request. In the backseat, I fasten the seatbelt and instruct the cabbie to take me to the Hyatt. But after a few turns and traffic lights, I say, "I've changed my mind. Take me to St. Louis."

"The city?"

"Yeah."

The old black man looks at me in the rearview mirror with a smile on his face.

"Whatever it is you been smokin," he says, "I'll take some."

"Just bourbon, and lots of it. But seriously, I want to go to St. Louis. I don't care what it costs."

"I think I better just get you to the Hyatt, my friend."

"No, I want to go home to St. Louis."

"That'd take us nine hours. Hell, we wouldn't make it there until tomorrow. How'd you get here?"

"I flew."

"Then you're better off gettin a good night's sleep at the Hyatt and takin a flight home in the morning. You'd probably even get there sooner that way."

Even with more alcohol in my system than there should be, I know the voice of reason when I hear it, and it isn't mine. "Okay, you win. But take me to a liquor store first. There's got to be one around here somewhere."

He looks at me again in the rearview. "What you needin more liquor for?"

"It helps me sleep."

He passes a slower car and makes a left turn that tilts the side of my head against the window. He glances back at me. "Ever try prayin?" I can't help but laugh. The driver can't help but smile. "What's so funny?"

"That's what I was doing for the last two hours."

"In a bar?"

"Yeah, you should try it sometime."

"I got no business being in them kinds of places no more. Been there, seen it, done that."

"I'm just fucking with you."

"I know you is." He brakes for a stoplight. "If you don't mind me askin, and just holler if you feel like this ain't none of my business, but why you puttin your faith in the devil's poison instead of God's hands?"

"You sound like a preacher."

The light turns green and we begin to move as he extends his arm toward the backseat. "I am. Here's my card."

I take it from his hand and try to read what it says, but it's too dark in the rear of the cab. All I can see is a cross and a church steeple.

"Thanks."

I see the hotel up ahead next to Reunion Tower all lit up. Day or night, it's the easiest landmark to spot in the Dallas skyline. No matter how much you've been drinking, you can't miss "The Ball," as the locals call it.

"I take it we're not headed for the liquor store."

"Not tonight, young man."

He pulls up to the Hyatt and requests payment for the fare shown on his meter. I reach for my wallet, hand the man his money owed, and exit the vehicle.

"Thanks for the ride . . . and the advice."

"God bless."

Inside the atrium, I head for the bank of elevators to be taken up to my room—in avoidance of the bar because of the intoxicated thought Agent Vaughn might still be there. As I wait for the chime and the doors to open, I hear a familiar voice.

"Hello, my friend." I turn and see the old cabbie approach. "You forgot this." He hands me the bag of gifts for Will and Jenny that I must have left in his backseat.

"Thank you so much."

"God bless."

* * *

When I awaken, it's daylight, and I grab my watch off the nightstand to check the date and time, which confirms that I did sleep through the night—for the first time in weeks, months, forever. Next to my watch is my phone. Nothing from Hollis. No call, no message. I can't dwell on it, though, because I'm behind schedule for my eight thirty meeting in Turtle Creek.

All day long, I'm behind schedule. From the hotel to the meeting, from the meeting to the airport, from the airport to Jenny's recital, it's a race against time, with no time to let my mind wander places it shouldn't go, other than home, where I am now. It's Thursday night—almost Friday. Hours later, Friday comes, and time slows down long enough for me to wonder why Hollis hasn't returned my call. It's not that I haven't thought about him. That would be impossible. But I haven't speculated any further than him being in an area that doesn't have cellular service, or he just hasn't had the chance to get back to me. He will, though. He always does.

But he doesn't, and it's Saturday morning. He should've called by now. We should've talked by now. Tired of the wait to discuss the next step in our future, I get up from the couch—where Lisa sits next to me—and go to the hall closet to get my jacket. I will take Friday for a short walk and call Hollis. As I put my coat on, I hear Lisa's phone ring. She answers it. "Hi, Helen," echoes out the room and down the hall to me. I stop and listen, though there's nothing to listen to until Lisa says, "Have you called the police?" I walk back into the room. She sees me, sees the same concerned look on my face that I see on hers. I mouth "What's wrong?" She raises her hand to let me know she can't talk to me right now, and she turns away to give Helen her full attention. "I would. Yes, call them again." She turns back to me. "I'll ask him. He's right here."

"Have you talked to Hollis?"

"I haven't. I called his cell Wednesday night, but he didn't answer, and he hasn't called me back. What's going on?"

"He didn't show up for his flight home last night and Helen hasn't heard from him and can't reach him."

Chapter Twenty-Four

The morning sun absorbs what it can of last night's rain, while Lisa and I nest on the couch—in full view of my gun and her cell phone, on the coffee table. She remains afflicted; the consequence of revelation and pre- and post-dawn trauma, including the ambiguity of the club hammer's origins and the notification of Hollis's unknown whereabouts. But I know what we need to do, what I need to do, and if going to see Father Seb is the first step, I will do it. I will do anything to help Lisa and my family. I will do whatever I can to help my friend, Hollis, to help Helen and the kids who've endured the disappearance of their father for the last fifteen hours. An overnight that I imagine for them was as long and trying as the one my family and I sustained. We will go back to Savannah for guidance, and to lend a hand to the Baumgartners. As far as I can see it, that is the only way forward.

"Let's leave today." I stroke Lisa's hair to keep it away from the tears on her cheeks. Like medicine, I wait for my words to take effect before I give her more. "We'll pack up and head to Savannah and see Father Seb and Helen."

She lifts her head from my chest and wipes her eyes. "Why does this feel like it's the end?"

"It's not. It's the beginning, and I promise you I won't let anything happen to you or the kids. We'll come through this okay."

"I'm scared."

"I know you are."

"Do you really want to go today?"

"I do."

"And we'll just get in the car and drive there?"

"Yes. All of us together. The family."

"You're sure about this?"

"I think it's one of your best ideas ever."

"But I didn't say anything about leaving today."

"Not in so many words." I kiss away the last tear on her cheek. "Let's get packing."

In under an hour, we've done what seems like the impossible: we're on the road with the car packed—the kids and Friday fast asleep behind us. Behind the wheel, I'm wide awake with a large cup of coffee to fuel myself for the long all-day drive to Southeast Georgia. Lisa, with book in hand, rides in the passenger seat.

For now, all is quiet as I look out the window the way I so often do on planes, alone with my thoughts. I think about Father Seb; his kindness to clear his schedule on such a last-minute notice and meet with me and Lisa after the 11:30 a.m. mass tomorrow. I think about the backlash from our decision to pull Will and Jenny out of school for a few days. I think about whether or not I turned the thermostat down to save a few bucks while we're gone. I think about the club hammer I found in the yard a few hours ago. But more than anything, though, I think about Hollis.

We cover the open road with speed and efficiency. "Making good time" is the phrase I like to tell the kids when they inevitably ask "how much longer?" When they were little, that question came every fifty minutes on every road trip, but now it only comes once or twice. Today, they only wanted to know why we were in their rooms to wake them, after such a long night. "Mrs. Baumgartner, Graham, and Aimee need our support and company. We're leaving for Savannah and Daufuskie in an hour. Come on, wake up." They weren't happy about the news; about a twelve-hour drive they'd have to endure; about the basketball and dance they'd miss, and yes, school that Will insisted he couldn't be absent from.

But they—Friday included—take one for the team, and allow us to stop only for gas, a bathroom break, or a fast food drive-thru. Through Illinois, Kentucky, Tennessee, and Georgia, we eat, drink, and sleep in the car, and by 10:30 p.m. we arrive at a Marriott in Savannah, much to the chagrin of Helen who insisted we stay with her and the kids at their place in town. I can't impose, though. She has too much on her plate for an additional family of four, and a dog, to drop in late at night. As agreed to, we will see them tomorrow afternoon when we meet to take the ferry to Daufuskie.

It's no surprise that at 2:00 a.m. I lie awake in bed with my eyes wide open. I knew precious sleep would be hard to come by with all the caffeine in my system from the day's drive. But I had still hoped that maybe, just maybe, the wear and tear of being on the road from the heart of the Midwest all the way to Savannah would earn me a night's reprieve from insomnia. Apparently it's not meant to be. Not with the admission of guilt I'm about to confess in the morning. A confession I promised Hollis I would take to my grave. *Where are you, Hollis? God, where is he?*

Those questions turn into prayers, and everything turns into a dream, and when it's over all of us start the new day as Lisa draws back the curtain to reveal the blue sky and amber sun. We rise, and shine, and dress for Sunday mass. After checking out of the hotel, we drive to a little breakfast place in the historic district that Lisa and I know of. The kids are hungry, and they need something to eat before church or they'll make life miserable for their parents. After we've buttered them up with pancakes and bacon, we walk down the road to Forsyth Park. It's a beautiful park in the heart of the city where the kids and Friday can stretch their legs for a while in the warm southern air.

By the fountain, Lisa and I take a seat on a bench and watch the kids amuse themselves as Friday nips at their heels.

"I miss this place."

"I do too," I reply.

"Ever think about what might've been if we hadn't left?"

"Sometimes."

"Any regrets?"

"No regrets."

She reaches for my hand and pulls it onto her white jeans, and rests it there in her lap under the live oaks.

"Doesn't get any better than this."

"It doesn't."

A gentle breeze rolls off the Atlantic and lingers like the Spanish moss it dashes with salt. It's Southern here. Old, too. Old as these trees that stand watch over the petunias that encircle the fountain.

"When I'm old and grey, and you've kissed me goodnight for the last time, I'd like my ashes sprinkled here."

She squeezes my hand. "Don't talk like that. You're going to make me cry."

"I didn't mean it like that. I just love this place."

"What time is it?"

I look at my watch. "Eleven o'clock."

"We should start walking."

The spires of the Cathedral of St. John the Baptist tower over the buildings and trees of the city and guide our way as we walk north on Abercorn Street. Across from the church is a small park called Lafayette Square. There, in the shade of the trees, I find a bench and claim it for my own, to wait with Friday while Lisa and the kids attend mass—sans canine.

But I can't sit for long. I'd rather walk. For almost an hour, Friday and I stroll through the neighborhood of beautiful and historic homes, until we're back on Harris where we stand at the corner and wait for church to let out.

When the doors open, I see them in the crowd of people as they say hello and goodbye to old friends and acquaintances. They see me, and right away the kids come for their dog, while Lisa is much slower to distance herself from the past and trails far behind them.

Her eventual arrival reunites the family and we head back to the sequestration of the Square.

"Is Father Seb coming now, Dad?" Will asks.

"He should be here any minute."

"I'm starving."

"When are you not?"

"Where are we going to eat?"

"I don't know yet. We'll find some place. But Mom and I want to say hi to Father Seb first."

Ten minutes later, I see him. With his five o'clock shadow, jeans and boots, you would never know this fifty-year-old Latino man is a priest. His Roman collar is the only telltale sign. He sees us and waves.

"Why don't you guys take the dog and go play with him over there?" I point to the other side of the small park. "Your mom and I would like a few minutes alone with Father Seb."

"Why? Are you getting divorced?" my devilish Jenny says.

"Actually, we're renewing our vows," I reply. "Now scram."

After she pokes me in the ribs, Jenny takes the leash from me and walks away with Friday and Will as Father Seb approaches.

"If it isn't Jesus himself," I call out.

He smiles and outstretches his arms up to the sky, up to heaven in self-deprecation. A few steps more, and he reaches us. "Welcome back." After embracing Lisa, he hugs me too.

It is so good to see him, to be in his presence once again. On two side-by-side park benches, we take seats. To make eye contact with Father Seb, who's left of me on the other bench, Lisa leans forward and says, "Thank you so much for clearing your schedule for us."

"No problem at all. It sounded urgent." After small talk and pleasantries, he takes on a more serious tone, which he must as a priest with limited amounts of time for duties round the clock. "You've traveled far. What's on your mind?"

I look at Lisa and turn back to Father. "I have a confession to make."

"Okay." He looks at me with eyes that sense the serious nature of my visit. "I'm ready whenever you are."

I take a deep breath and let it out. Before I speak though, I wait for a small tour group to pass by. When they're beyond earshot, I begin.

"Back in October, I went out to Montana to go pheasant hunting with three other guys. On the first day, my friend, Hollis, and I were hunting with our guide and his dog, and when one of the birds flew up out of the grass, I accidentally shot the dog as it leaped into the air for it. I should've waited, Father, for the bird to get higher up, but I . . . I didn't, and I killed the dog."

Father looks at me and doesn't say anything. Lisa does, though. "There's more."

"The dog was mortally wounded but wasn't dead yet. It was wailing and in so much pain, lying on the ground and kicking with his legs. Half of its face was missing. I couldn't believe what I'd done. Our guide—his name was Orrin Gall—grabs my shotgun and shoots his dog with the shell in the second barrel to put it out of its misery." I remember it all like it was yesterday, which chokes me up. "Hang on a second."

"It's okay. Take your time."

I run my hand through my hair, before I continue.

"After kneeling over Truck—that was his dog's name—for a few minutes, Orrin gets up and comes charging at me, yelling and screaming for what I did to Truck. But Hollis steps between us and holds him back from me. While the two of them struggle, Orrin reaches into Hollis's pocket and grabs a shotgun shell. I grab his wrist to try and prevent him from going back toward the gun that's on the ground next to the dog. But he breaks free and goes there. At this point Hollis and I beg him to drop the shell. I even agree to pay him $10,000 for his loss and buy him a new dog. Hollis, though, objects. He thinks it's highway robbery to pay that kind of money and replace the dog, too. Over and over we plead with him to just put the shell down. Instead, he drops to his knees and loads the gun. With a loaded firearm in his hands, our lives are in potential danger. Orrin's back is to us and we don't know what he's going to do next. Hollis bears down on him with his shotgun and one more time demands that Orrin put the gun down. But he doesn't, and when it looks like Orrin is turning to possibly fire at us, Hollis pulls the trigger and shoots him dead."

With the weight of the world lifted from my chest, I begin to cry. To hide the tears—and the shame—I bury my face in my hands. I'm guilt-ridden. I'm relieved. I'm repentant. And what's left of me is in God's hands, and Lisa's that have come to rest on my shoulders.

"It's all right, Garrett. Just let it out," Father Seb says.

As I wipe my eyes and pull my hands from them, I look over my shoulder to check on the kids. They're still occupied with Friday on the other side of the park, which allows my story to go on.

"Hollis and I rush to Orrin and we try to revive him, and we try, and we try, and we try, but he doesn't come back." Another tear falls down my cheek and I wipe it away. "I pull out my phone to call 911 but I can't get a signal. Then Hollis says we need to think about things for a minute before we do anything, because he's worried about the ramifications of shooting a man in the back." I pause to take a breath.

From his pocket, Father hands me a piece of cloth. "Here, take this." I wipe my eyes and cheeks and hand it back to him with a thank you.

"He's all worked up about shooting him in the back, but I tell Hollis it was in self-defense and that we need to call the police and they'll realize we did what we had to do. He doesn't think they'll side with us, though, because they're from Montana and are going to want to seek justice for their own. If I'm going too fast, just let me know, okay?"

"I'm following you."

"We go back and forth. I want to call the police, and Hollis doesn't. Then he confides in me that he's on the verge of financial ruin. He's an oil futures trader and he's made some bad bets. It's the type of business where you can make millions overnight and lose the same amount, or more, the next day."

"I see."

"Anyway, he's brought us to this ranch in Montana because he's going to buy it, and the reason he wants to buy it is because part of it sits on top of a huge oil field. It's his ticket out. He then explains to me that Orrin is a Sioux Indian and that the Sioux are bidding on the ranch, too, and this will only make his actions look even more malicious." I reposition myself on the bench. "I know that was a lot to digest."

"I got it all."

"This is the part you may not get. The bottom line is Hollis wants to bury Orrin and the dog and say that after the hunt Orrin went his way and we went ours, as though nothing ever happened . . . to prevent his deal from going south . . . to prevent a possible criminal conviction from an impartial jury and judge bent on restitution for his constituents, and their friends—the Sioux. And he was of the opinion, that since the man didn't have any immediate family members, there wouldn't be anyone agonizing over his disappearance, or go looking for him too hard."

He leans forward to bring Lisa into the same picture as me. "And that's what the two of you did?"

"Yes, though I agonized over doing it and tried to persuade Hollis into going to the police. That he was thinking irrationally. But I owe him so much, Father. He saved Will's life that day he got caught in that rip current on Daufsukie. You remember me telling you about that, don't you?"

"I do."

"I felt so guilty for not being there, and so thankful that Hollis was."

"I remember."

"And he lost his dad last year, and his wife has gone through hell and back in her fight with cancer. He's my best friend, and he only shot the man to protect me. I couldn't say no to him, Father."

"And no one knows what happened to this man and his dog or where they're buried?"

"That's right."

Lisa intervenes, and says, "You need to tell Father about the other part."

"I know," I reply to her before I turn back to Father. "When Orrin didn't show up at the reservation that night or the ranch the next day for work, the police got involved. As planned, Hollis and I lied to them and said after the hunt we went our separate ways. But they started to poke holes in our story, and when they found his pickup in the river the FBI got involved."

"How did his pickup get into the river?"

"We dumped it there to make it look like an accident, and that he drowned."

"Oh..." Father leans slightly forward, then back to where he was, as though to digest my reply.

"But since there wasn't a body in the truck, and some other things they discovered that didn't quite add up with what we were telling them, they're convinced we haven't been straightforward. I've met with the FBI agent twice now, and the man knows I'm lying."

"I also think you should tell Father about your gun and why you bought it," Lisa says.

"I'm sorry to throw all of this on your lap."

"It's okay. Tell me about the gun."

"For a long time now, I've been worried that someone might be out to get me and my family, so I bought a gun."

"Who do you think is out to get you?"

"I'm not sure, but maybe someone saw us drive the truck into the river, or it could be some people connected with the sheriff's office or Sioux police."

He thinks things over for a minute, then says, "I can't imagine a law enforcement officer would attempt to physically harm you or your family."

"I agree," Lisa says.

"I guess I just have a more trusting viewpoint of policemen and don't see them in that light. Now whether, or not someone saw you drive the truck into the river, I can't give an opinion on that," he says. "But tell me why you became fearful enough to buy a gun. That's what I don't understand, or maybe I missed something. Did Hollis buy a gun, too?"

"Are you asking that rhetorically?"

"Somewhat, perhaps."

"He's told me that he's had his fair share of visits from the Fort Peck Police, which is the Sioux police, the Richland County Sheriff's Office, and the FBI agent. But his skin is much thicker than mine."

"But what about his family?" Father says. "Does he feel like you: that they are at risk and need added protection?"

"That's a good question. And if you're trying to make a point, I get it."

Lisa says, "Garrett did receive a few threatening letters though from an anonymous sender."

Father turns back to me and asks, "What did they say?"

"That I won't get away with it, and the gloves have come off. And one of them indicated that our dog might be harmed."

Lisa jumps in again. "Garrett thinks it's possible the police might be trying to get under his skin, so that he'll confess."

"Part of me also thinks someone may have seen us drive the truck into the river."

"And your gun will do . . . what?"

"I don't like it in the house, Father," Lisa says. "And the other night, when our home alarm went off, Garrett was running all over the place with it thinking someone had broken in."

"Let me back up for just a second, if you don't mind."

"Not at all."

"Your friend, Hollis, where is he and what are his thoughts at this point?"

"Those are more good questions," I reply. "He's been running his oil operation up in Montana and was booked on a flight home to Savannah on Friday night but never showed. He's been missing for several days now and nobody has been able to reach him. He hasn't returned phone calls or texts from his wife, Helen, from me, and a few others."

"That's the other reason we've come to Savannah. We want to be with Helen and the kids. She's a wreck," Lisa says.

"I can imagine."

"To give you more background, and to answer your question a bit," I say, "Hollis has been adamant all along that we stick to our story and deny any wrongdoing. Like I said, he's been repeatedly questioned by the sheriff's office, Sioux police, and the FBI. But Hollis has a much better poker face than I do, and I think that's why they're coming after me more than him."

"And he's been missing for a few days?"

"Yes," Lisa says.

"Have the police been notified?"

"They have. But because of what happened, I'm not so sure how much of an effort they're putting in to find him," I say.

"Hollis's wife, Helen, does she know the whole story?" Father asks.

"I haven't told her, and I don't think Hollis has told her either," I say. "We swore to each other we'd take this secret with us to our graves."

He looks at me. He looks at Lisa. I think he thinks that since I've broken my promise to Hollis, perhaps Hollis has broken it to me and confided in Helen. But he doesn't mention it. Neither does Lisa. "Maybe I should check on the kids," she says.

I touch her knee to let her know that I want her to remain by my side. "I need to add something else, too," I say. "After we buried Orrin, we learned that he'd been diagnosed with Lou Gehrig's disease. And I don't know if I should feel more guilty or less about this, but Hollis and I both agree there was a strong possibility Orrin was turning to position the gun to kill himself, not us."

He pauses, and says, "Is that everything?"

I look at Lisa to see if she has something further to add, before I reply, "Yes, that I can think of."

He looks at both of us. "As a priest, I can assign a penance and impart absolution, but I don't think you're here just for that."

"You're right," Lisa tells him.

"As your friend, and someone who knows the true good in both your hearts, I can give you my best advice, though you're being here tells me you most likely already know what that advice is."

"Maybe," I say.

He shifts on the bench, leans forward again, and rests his elbows on his knees. "It's time to tell the truth and put your trust in God."

I look away at the birds that fly from tree to tree. "I know it is, but I'm so afraid of losing everything we have."

"What do you have?"

"My family, our home, our way of life . . . my freedom . . . it's everything."

"That's not everything."

"I'm sure I could lengthen the list."

"I'm sure you could too, but no matter how much you lengthen it, I'm fairly certain it wouldn't include God." The silence between the three of us runs deep enough for me to hear my kids' voices on the other side of the park. "That's who you don't have now, and that's why you're hurting so much."

CHAPTER TWENTY-FIVE

At Buckingham Landing across from Hilton Head, it nears
4:00 p.m. as we wait to board the last ferry of the day over to
Daufuskie Island. Helen and the kids should be here by
now, but they aren't. She had mentioned they might have to
play catch-up because of Graham's basketball tournament
game, but this is beyond late—they're going to literally miss
the boat if they don't show in the next five minutes.

They don't show, and without cellular reception in the
backcountry bayou of the landing, we have no way to find
out where they are or what's happened to them. With the
small group of people that have gathered with us, mostly
workers and staff for the village of Haig Point, we board the
passenger ferry. My hope is that I'll see Helen and the kids
pull into the parking lot at any moment, which will allow me
time enough to alert the captain.

It turns out to be a pipe dream, though, as we shove off
and motor for the island. Lisa and I take seats in the rear of
the cabin while the kids and Friday choose the open-air of
the bow. Headed for the isolation of Daufuskie, I settle into
the peaceful hum of the diesel. Or maybe it's gratitude I feel
more of—to be with my family for what may be our last few
days together for some time. And so, in a way, I'm glad
Helen has missed the boat and won't arrive until tomorrow,
when I plan to speak to her, and hopefully Hollis, too, about
my impending confession to the authorities. It will give us a

night to be alone, to be with just each other, which there may not be many more of, because when we return from Daufuskie Lisa will drive me to the Downtown Precinct of the Savannah Chatham Metropolitan Police, and I will walk into it, and without the fear of my fate in God's hands, set the record straight once and for all. For all my wrongs, Father Seb could not have been more right. *Hollis, the time has come for us to finally tell the truth.*

Like the ebb and flow of the tide there's a seasonal wave of people that ride ashore on the currents of warming air. Soon, the spring break families will arrive in the low country, and Daufsukie will swell with its fair share of their numbers and ride lower in the water. But until then, there's only the few, like us, here to enjoy the solitude of island life at its bare minimum, the way I like it.

For at least the third time today, I turn to Lisa, and say, "I love you."

"I love you, too."

"Not going to give me an 'I love you more'?"

"I gave you one the last time."

"But not *for* the last time, right?"

"Of course not. Only for this hour."

Side by side we ride the ship homeward, which to us, Daufuskie is and always will be—home. She leans into my shoulder and rests her head there, after we've said to each other, and Father Seb, all that needs to be said for now. For now, I look out the window and see the movie reel that the river and island have become as we head downstream to disembark at Melrose Landing. Frame by frame, the years drift by from infancy to childhood to adolescence. In each one of those years, I see Lisa and Will and Jenny on the beach at low tide, wide and magnificent when the moon's pull on the sea shortens its reach. While they smile and dig in the sand, the children get bigger and bigger like the castles they build, until they get big enough to stop building them. Big enough to tower over anything their hands and plastic shovels and buckets could ever construct. Then off they go, to explore all the other parts of the island on foot, on bike, and the golf cart that Will loves to drive. They go everywhere and leave me and Lisa behind. And it all goes so fast, much faster than the fifteen miles per hour of the ferry we ride.

I will miss this place. I will miss them more than I care to imagine. Without question, Lisa thinks the same of me. I feel it. I know it. We are that close. Close enough to talk without words.

The boat glides into Melrose Landing where we offload with all our belongings. There's much to be carried ashore, which requires Will and me to make two trips back to the boat to get all the luggage and groceries. At the landing, the trolleys await, and after we transfer with our possessions to one of them, we begin the journey to the other side of the two-mile wide, five-mile long island.

On the abandoned road, we travel eastward through the unspoiled maritime forest toward the Atlantic. Its giant live oaks festooned with Spanish moss that drape the setting sun. Here, in the interior of the island, it's as it was hundreds if not thousands of years ago when this was Yemassee territory. For me, I need go back only eight, where on this very stretch of pavement I taught Will to ride a bike in the shade of these trees. And Jenny, two years later. In a peculiar way, as if they know what's on my mind, from the front of the trolley they turn and look back at their mother and father and smile.

We exit the tunnel of live oaks, where the road turns southward and parallels the beach. On this—for the most part—uninhabited island, it's the shore, or nearby it, where the infrequent driveway for homes hidden beyond can be found, which includes ours and the Baumgartner's that we reach after going two miles farther.

I tip the driver and offload our bags with Will, while Lisa and Jenny head inside without us to turn on the lights and open the windows. Upon arrival, it's the first thing Lisa always does to freshen up our four-bedroom Cape Cod.

As the trolley pulls away, the two of us start to carry everything up the steps and into the first floor of the house—a gain of eight feet in elevation on each trip. If I could gain more to be even higher above sea level, I'd take it, but we didn't build the home. We're its second owners.

After they take their own bags up to their bedrooms and change into their swimsuits, the kids venture down to the beach with Friday. From the back porch, which extends the entire length of the house, I watch them run past the pool and through the yard. Just beyond, a short trail cuts through a thin sliver of shrubs, sweet grass, and palmetto that leads to the sand and ocean, where in no time, the three of them are knee deep in water.

As both father and lifeguard, I watch their silhouettes play in the calm surf—silhouettes that are hesitant to take a plunge into the cold sea. "Chickens," I yell at the top of my lungs. Will turns. I think he's heard me. A few more splashes, and he grabs his sister and down below the surface they go. But up they come, even faster. On their feet, they wade with all their might to reach shore as fast as they can, and the heated pool below me—yet to be heated—that calls their names.

Inside, Lisa has put away the groceries and begun the spaghetti dinner in the kitchen.

"Want me to pour you a glass of wine?"

"That'd be great," she replies.

I open the fridge and grab a bottle. "Have you tried reaching Helen?"

"I got her voicemail and left her a message. I'm sure she'll call soon."

"I bet Graham's game was late in starting, or something like that, and they just didn't have time to get to the ferry."

I fill the glass and hand it to her as the kids come back inside wrapped up in their towels. Lisa sees them and the dog, and says, "Don't let Friday in. Not being all wet like that."

Will pushes him back outside and shuts the door that leads out to the porch.

"How's the ocean?"

"Freezing," Jenny says. "And so is the pool."

The two of them take seats on the stools at the kitchen island. "What's for dinner?" Will asks.

"Spaghetti," the cook says.

"When are we eating?" the eating machine says.

"When it's ready," she replies.

The phone rings. Not mine or Lisa's cellular, because there's no service on the island. It's the landline, and Jenny hops off her stool to answer it at the counter behind her. "Ingram residence, Jenny speaking." A pause. "Hi, Mrs. Baumgartner." Another pause, and, "She's right here. I'll get her for you." Jenny takes the cordless phone and hands it to Lisa who's at the stove beginning to boil the pot of water.

"Hi, Helen."

Right away I can see there's a problem. It's written all over Lisa's face. And when she heads for the dining room to speak with Helen alone, there's no doubt to the serious nature of the call. With the kids, I wait in the kitchen and hope for the best.

Two long minutes pass before Lisa returns and gives us the news. "Hollis has been found."

The kids remain silent and wait for me to respond. "And?"

"That's all that Helen would tell me."

"What do you mean?"

"It was so strange."

"Is he okay?"

"I don't know. She thanked us for driving all this way and wanting to help but said she and the kids aren't coming to the island." She stares at me with a blank face. I stare back at her with the same expression. "Something's wrong."

CHAPTER TWENTY-SIX

Through the night we try several times in vain to reach Helen and Hollis on their phones, from which the subjection of voicemail only adds to the oddity of the situation. Stranded on the island like we are, there's nothing else we can do behind closed doors to learn more about Hollis's fate than to dial and hope for an answer on the other end. Though, after numerous attempts, the message is loud and clear that we will be kept in the dark until at least morning when I can catch a ferry to the mainland and pursue my avenues there. While we toss and turn in bed, we speculate. We convince each other that Hollis is of sound mind and body. Anything less, Helen would have said so. We know her well enough to know that is a forgone conclusion, we hope. But what we can't wrap our heads around is why she was unable to confide in her best friend anything further, such as his present location—which I assume to be Montana—and where he's been for the last several days. After we traveled all this way to be here for Helen and support her and the kids, it doesn't add up that she would withhold this type of information and push us away.

My confession to the Savannah Police will have to wait. On second thought, third, fourth, and beyond, it's never going to happen. Not to them. It isn't the right time and place for such a thing, or the right agency. Jakobe Kenton deserves to hear the words come out of my mouth before anyone else. Lisa agrees. She rests her head on my chest and stretches her arm across my torso below the sheet. But Hollis and Helen supersede all others. I need to talk to them first. I need to know what's going on. At daybreak I will catch the first ferry and drive to the Baumgartner's home. There, I will gain firsthand knowledge of what Helen kept from Lisa. And I will confide in Helen what she may or may not already know about the disappearance of Orrin Gall, and my blueprint for restitution. We are all best friends. We are all in this together.

In the dark, my eyes are open. The eyelash that sweeps across the edge of my nipple tells me that Lisa's are too, as though in practice for the long nights she suspects will come. This one is long, but I don't mind. Every minute with my wife is welcomed, because how many more we have together is the great unknown for both of us. In truth, it is a fragile existence, like annuals in the path of a late-spring frost. On the other hand, the truth will set us free, and that is what we've chosen.

At dawn, we rise. There is a chill at the touch of bare feet on the planks of southern pine, though it is minor compared to the oak in our Missouri home this time of year. In full bloom, the Carolina sun conquers all when Lisa pulls back the drapes. I am warmed. I am in her arms. I can see the ocean. But down here things are in constant change, like the tide, like people, and after I am fully dressed, I ebb toward Savannah.

Off the ferry and into our car parked at the landing, the city awaits me. Compared to island life, this is another world when I enter the freeway and speed along like everyone else at sixty miles per hour. Compared to New York City—St. Louis as well—this would be considered island life. It's all relative, and speaking of, I am on my way to see one of mine, though Helen is by choice, not by blood. By the time I arrive, I expect her to be in the kitchen. The good mom preparing to feed her children a warm breakfast.

The drive on the freeway is short-lived, and from there I weave my way to the Historic District-South. Along Gaston St, then Whitaker, to Gordon and I'm there. I expected to see Helen's car out front next to Hollis's, but the street is absent of a Range Rover. Perhaps it is parked in the alley. I find a space on the opposite side of the road and make the quick walk over to the steps of the red-brick colonial. I spring up them and drop the brass knocker hard enough to resonate like thunder against the painted door, black as the godforsaken slaves that once opened it. Several times I knock, but like our phone calls from the night before, each one goes unanswered. The windows with the hurricane shutters to the right and left of the door are too far from the steps for me to lean over and look inside. I go down to the sidewalk and around to the back door, and the steps that lead up to it. The window there offers a view into the kitchen. The lights are off. The galley is vacant. I pull out my phone and dial their landline. The rings penetrate the brick, glass, and wood, and create stereo through my unoccupied right ear. In a recorded voice, Helen suggests I leave a message. Lisa and I have already left several. I hang up and walk back down to the sidewalk, to the alley in search of her car—which isn't there—then to the sidewalk that flanks the north face of the home. From this vantage point, I can view the second-story windows. But there is no sign of life up there, either. No sign of life up in Montana when I call Hollis's cell.

I dial Lisa. "She's not answering the door or the phone," I tell her.

"Is her car there?"

"No, just Hollis's," I reply. "Could she have taken the kids to school this early?" My watch shows it's seven twenty.

"They don't start until a quarter to nine, so I doubt it."

"What if they went to breakfast somewhere?"

"She would never do that."

"I don't know where else to look for them," I say. "Have you tried reaching her on her cell?"

"Still no answer."

"I think I'll catch the next ferry home. There's nothing else I can do here."

"Okay, I'll see you soon," Lisa says. "I'll call you if I hear from them."

"Same here."

"This is so strange."

"I know. See you in a few."

I'm back on Daufuskie by ten thirty, back with Lisa before eleven. From the window I can see Will and Jenny on the beach, until Lisa pulls me down toward the bed. On the nightstand, the phone erupts. Being closer to it than I am, Lisa reaches for it.

"Hello?" Silence. "We've been trying to reach you." More silence. "Are you there now?"

Lisa's phone call with Helen is even shorter than the one from last night. As we sit on the edge of the bed, she tells me that Helen has taken the kids to be with Hollis in Montana. They are in Minneapolis on a layover. "I don't get it," Lisa says. "She told me that we shouldn't expect to hear from them for some time. And that was it. She hung up the phone without even saying goodbye."

Later that afternoon, I say goodbye to my family. I explain to Will and Jenny that I need to go back to Montana to take care of some unfinished business. They inquire further. Yes, I tell them, it involves Hollis. Though I assure them that he is okay and express regret that we won't be getting together with the Baumgartners on this trip.

"When are we going back to St. Louis, then?" Will asks.

"Tomorrow morning," Lisa replies.

"We came all this way for nothing," Jenny says.

I rub the top of her head and she pulls away. With an instantaneous use of her hands, Jenny combs her hair back into place. "Listen," I tell the kids, "be good for your mom while I'm gone. I love you and I'll see you soon in St. Louis."

"How soon is soon?" Will asks.

"Just a couple days."

"Love you, Pops." He wraps his arms around me. Jenny imitates him.

They let go and Lisa walks me out to the street. The trolley is on its way to take me to the ferry.

"I'll be home before you know it. And remember, if you get tired just pull over somewhere and stay for the night."

"I'll be fine," she replies. "Call me when you get in tonight."

"I will, if it's not too late."

"I don't care what time it is. I want you to call me."

"Okay."

When the trolley arrives, I kiss Lisa one last time. As our hands slip away, the diamond on her engagement ring rubs against my finger, and the memory lingers. From my seat at the rear, she remains in view until the road drifts northwest and the live oaks punch my ticket.

I am headed for Denver. It's as far as I can get today on such late notice. From Savannah to Atlanta to the Mile High City, I am routed. I will be tired when I finally get there, but the two hours I gain by going from Eastern to Mountain Time will help. It should be enough to grab some winter apparel that I will need for Montana, and a bite to eat. Maybe even a quick workout in the exercise room at the Hilton before I retire for the night with a phone call to Lisa.

I am tired. These cross-country flights take their toll. With the addition of trollies and ferries, and navigation of the humongous Hartsfield Airport, the infliction is magnified, and by the time the sun escapes our pursuit of it westward I'm as worn down as the tires on my first beater. By the time I land I'm convinced the cold is the lesser of two evils when compared to sleep. Fitness, that is no longer on the list. I must eat something, though. A sleeping pill. That should hold me over. And Lisa's voice, the icing on that diphenhydramine cake.

"Sleep tight, babe," she says.

From room 417, I reply, "I will. You too. Talk to you in the morning."

At daybreak we resume our conversation, but it's brief. Short and sweet, it would be termed. I have a flight to catch and need to hustle to the airport, where I will follow up with her again.

The flight to Williston is delayed, which gives me the opportunity to shop for a coat at the airport. I find a ski parka and stuff it into my carry-on. It will cut the Montana wind for me when I step off the plane there.

But it doesn't. At least not to the degree I'd like. I am not prepared for this Big Land Country environment where the air blows over the snow-capped mountains and frozen plains, a gusty breeze chilled like water poured into a glass of ice. By the time I wheel my bag from the aircraft to the terminal, my fingers are numb. Inside the sliding glass doors, though, does bring instant relief, and to turbo charge the warmth, I blow on my hands. When feeling returns, I head for the rental car counter. With forms signed, payment given, I am on my way toward the freedom of open roads. But not before I pull a navy-blue cotton sweater—intended for the warmer climate of Daufuskie—from my suitcase. Underneath the nylon shell of the ski jacket it will add a thin layer of insulation.

It is 1:30 p.m. Montana time as I head for the Little Wing; a place I never thought I'd see again, in a county and state I swore I'd never return to. There I am, however, on a stretch of two-lane highway that comes right back to me as though it were yesterday. The farms, the homes, the distance that grows between each of them with each mile I travel, until there is nothing left that is human or indicative of human nature. The asphalt, the Camry I drive over it, even they are things that get lost in an imagination absorbed by an endless tract of late-winter Big Sky and Land Country. Or is it spring?

For a moment, civilization returns when I approach the city limits of Sidney. If a road sign can make grey skies blue, this one does it for me. I am back from my trip to the moon, which Williston to Sidney felt like. There are people here. I see them. And these people wave to strangers. I wave back, without the need to remove a hand from a coat pocket and expose it to the elements like they do. The thought alone makes me cold, and I turn the heat up. In about the same amount of time it takes to do that, I am through Sidney and headed for Mars. In the wide open of the white-blanketed tundra again, I can almost smell the isolation out here. But familiar landmarks begin to bring me back down to earth. The old red barn with a slight lean to the left, the grove of cottonwoods, that butte out my passenger window, a mailbox with two horseshoes that form the letter *m* for Montana. I know this place. Up ahead, I see all the trees in a row from north to south like the flow of commerce in this region. Although they are there because their roots access water—not oil—and that water flows in a trough known as the Redwater River. I see the bridge, and with it comes an image of Lawton Mills. I was with him the first time I crossed it. Hollis was with me, too. Soon we will all be together again.

A few miles farther and the Little Wing engages society like a debutante. One day Jenny will be one. Hollis and Helen have laid the groundwork for our daughters to be introduced to eligible southern bachelors. It is tradition in their lineage. Novelty and pomp for ours. Lisa, hesitant at first to such exposure for a young woman and a family of humble origins, gradually warmed to the idea after several wine-soaked luncheons where invitations were revealed to be valued instruments of socio-economic achievement. In the slumber of late-winter, the structure is more majestic—for reasons I can't explain—than when I was last here in autumn. It's bigger, bolder, like everything should be in Big Sky and Land Country.

The pavement silences the rumble and leads me to the circular drive, to Lawton's Jeep parked by the front door. I pull in behind his vehicle and turn the engine off. At the massive timbered door, I'm tempted to knock, but I'm no stranger here and know guests are always welcome, and like Lawton—filled with pride—once told me, just about every one of them returns. Against all odds, now I have done the same. The knob turns in my grip and I enter the lodge.

"Hello," I call out. Noise travels from the kitchen area. I step that way through the dining room. "Hello. Anyone here?"

Footsteps cause the floorboards to creak, which have contracted from the cold. Wood, like people, huddled together for protection from the elements. From the sound of things, it's a man since women tread more like falling snow than hard rain.

"I'll be damned," are the first words out of Lawton's mouth when our eyes meet. He wipes his hands with the dish towel and extends his right arm. "Welcome home."

"Good to see you, Lawton."

"Excuse the mess." He drapes the soiled cloth over his shoulder and nods to the covered furniture still in hibernation during the off season. "Now you know what the place looks like without its makeup on."

"Didn't even notice."

"What brings you up this way? Here to see Hollis?"

"I am."

"Is he expectin you?"

"It's more of a surprise visit."

"The reason I ask is because I haven't seen him in a few days."

In his red and black flannel shirt, he folds his arms across his chest. And in cowboy fashion rocks back in his boots.

"Any idea where he might be?"

"Have you checked the oil fields?"

"No, I came here directly from the airport, hoping I'd get lucky, because I haven't been able to reach him for a while now. To be honest with you, I'm worried about him."

Like the interior of the lodge draped with tarps, something doesn't look right with Lawton, and the honesty I mentioned may not be reciprocal. "I could see how that might cause you to wonder." He unfolds his arms and places his hands in the back pockets of his jeans. "I'd maybe take a drive over to the oil fields and see what you can find out there."

"When was the last time you saw him?"

"A few days ago, I recollect," the old cowboy says. "Seems to always be coming or going."

"Can you point the way to the oil fields for me?"

Lawton walks me out to my car, where I write down his directions. The Redwater and the bridge across it are my points of reference. Just before the bridge, a turn to the left, and two lefts after is an unpaved service road marked with several signs that declare: NO TRESPASSING; PRIVATE PROPERTY OF PERMEX ENERGY; AUTHORIZED PERSONNEL ONLY.

"Take care of yourself," he says.

"Likewise."

He heads back inside as I pull away, again with thoughts that it's for the last time. Past the grasslands on either side of me, I stare straight ahead in avoidance of the memories that are out there in them. I prefer the beaten down path of this dirt road out my windshield and the continual dust cloud it balloons in my rearview mirror over anything else. Blinders, I wear them. I follow Lawton's instructions and make the turn just before the bridge. After a mile another dirt road takes me north and another one takes me west and another one takes me who-the-hell-knows where. I am lost, and I stop the car and review what Lawton told me. In my mind I retrace my steps, and I believe I'm where I should be. It would be nice though if there were some others here, too. But there is nothing but more of the same old same old white land and patches of brown the size of putting greens where winter has yielded to the threat of spring. With renewed confidence I continue. The road narrows and I am squeezed into the ruts and mud pits that I would like to avoid at all possible costs, which causes me to regret declining the SUV upgrade for an additional thirty dollars per day. Patience and caution persevere, though, and I crest a slight ridge where I get a glimpse of danger on its fast approach. A black dually stampedes toward me. Its extra wheels and extra chrome exhausts that chimney each side of the pickup throw out steam like a mad buffalo. With nowhere to go, I brake. The horn comes next. The high beams. The horn once more. Without breaking stride, the man behind the wheel with long hair the color of his truck drives his vehicle off road and into the field like he's done this a million times before. In an instant he is past me and back on the road like nothing ever happened. I, however, am shaken as I lift off the brake and get the car on the move. To steady my nerves, I look at the positive side of things and the suggestion from the workhorse that almost killed me that I may be on the trail of a construction site.

I am. There are signs up ahead. There are more pickups, too. A derrick that broadcasts its whereabouts like a cell tower. As the ground levels, trailers appear at the base of operations. I see PERMEX written in green letters on the side of the road, and with that, all I can think of is my friend. I'm ecstatic to see him. God, I hope he is here. A few men in hardhats wander about, like me in search of a place to park where I won't get stuck. At the first trailer I find a clearing with the imprint of a motor vehicle the way deer flatten grass they lie in. I shut off the engine and exit the car.

"Excuse me."

"How can I help you?" one of the two men headed toward the derrick replies. He stops, but the other doesn't.

I approach him and say, "I'm looking for Hollis Baumgartner."

"Haven't seen him today."

"Do you expect him anytime soon?"

"I have no idea when he might be here. Check with the office."

"Where is it?"

He extends his arm and index finger. "That trailer there."

"Thanks."

Up the three aluminum steps, I grab the handle to the door and open it. Two men sit at their desks. Not the type of desks found in an office tower, or the type of people who work in them. They are a different breed out here. Everything is. Inside and out, though, the genetic link of the roughnecks employed at Permex is more than transparent.

One of them looks at me. "Can I help you?"

"I'm looking for Hollis Baumgartner."

"And you are?" the other one says.

"Garrett Ingram." My smile goes unreturned. "Hollis and I go way back."

"He's not here."

"Do you know where I might find him?"

"He's taken a leave of absence. That's all we know."

CHAPTER TWENTY-SEVEN

The International Inn in Williston becomes home for the night. But it's far from home in more ways than one. At all hours the roughnecks come and go. The oil boom has caused a housing shortage and companies pay extra for their workers to double up. That's what I've learned. It is just the opposite of an overcrowded prison where low-level, nonviolent offenders are turned loose. Here, the roughnecks are incentivized to live on top of each other while the oil flows and money is printed faster than amounts-owed can be typed, and accommodations can be built. Compared to those above, below, and on either side of me behind these walls, I have it good.

I have tried to reach Hollis on his cell. Lisa has tried to reach Helen. I have done all I can, short of enlisting a private detective to help with my search. There is no need for that, though. At this juncture, I know what I will do when morning comes. With or without Hollis and what I had hoped to resolve between us and remain in solidarity, my confession is imminent. I had wanted us to do it together, to come forth together. Lisa and I thought that would be the best way. I think Father Seb would agree. But I'm left to go it alone. Unless my phone rings, and Hollis is on the other end, which I doubt will occur.

Nothing occurs through the dark hours, except the sound of doors down the hall opening and shutting. The flush of toilets. Valves that allow water to flow through pipes, and those same valves that shut it down. The world around me is busy. I am anything but. But another sleepless night is nothing new to me, and I prevail in my prediction that another day will dawn, and I will rise with it.

Which I do, and now it is my turn to make some noise. Now it is 7:00 a.m. I turn the shower on and wait for the temperature to rise. But it moves upward as slow as the sun. I wait and wait and wait, until my patience wears thin as the stubborn layer of snow that remains on the ground and I give in to the realization that my fellow occupants have drained the International of its hot water.

The rinse is quick. Toweled off and dry, I shave and dress as best I can to fend against the forecast of high winds and arctic air pushing down from Canada. No confusion about what to wear. Layers it is, and the ski parka. In consolation, high pressure will keep the skies clear and bright, which I deem a formidable counterpunch.

Downstairs, I pay my bill and wheel my carry-on out to the rental that's been dusted with frost. Buckled into the driver's seat that's as cold as the shower I just took, I start the motor and crank the defroster. Without a scraper, I will have to wait until the windshield has been thawed before I can go anywhere. And before that I need to plot a course to get me there. I pull the map—given to me by the car rental agent—out of the glovebox and spread it open. The Fort Peck Reservation draws my eye. The roads to it, of which there aren't that many. The Missouri River that outlines the southern boundary. The town of Poplar, one hundred miles west, my destination.

My hands thaw at the same time as the windows, and I'm off. With each turn on the streets of Williston that take me east, I'm blinded by the sun. For protection I lower the visor, but anguish over the checklist I'd failed to create in Daufuskie. Had I done so it would've included sunglasses. On Highway 2, however, just outside of town, I'm able to put my troubled vision behind me. On a road I hope will put my troubles behind me too, I drive the sovereign Plains that rule all seeds of life. Grass, that's all the life there is, as it slumbers out of dormancy. The only trees reside along riverbanks, and rivers are few and far between. Buffalo, they were once here. In numbers so vast—Lawton told me—that their grazing had just as much of an impact on trees from taking root as the wildfires and droughts. He is of the opinion, though, that the bison decimation will be the bur oak and cottonwood's gain. However, other than telephone poles, I don't see any evidence of timber. This is a savanna. From one to the other, I have traveled.

The drive-thru town of Culbertson is the beginning of the end in more ways than one. It's the last American outpost, and not long after, I cross Muddy Creek and enter the Fort Peck Reservation. There is no difference in the landscape, though, the absence of humanity, the absence of trees, or the prevalence of snow and wheat grass in their struggle for domination like winter and spring, like Big Sky and Big Land that have settled on a compromise and meet each other halfway. I glance at the map on the passenger seat. The outlined boundary of the reservation has a shape that looks familiar. I pull the map onto my lap. With a closer inspection, which is easy to do on this arrow-straight highway, the reservation is a spitting image of Montana, one hundredth in size. I name it Little Big Sky and Land Country.

My wife and children are on the highway, too. It was good to hear their voices before I got on this one. Though the call wasn't long enough, it was enough to keep me headed in the direction of restitution. Tempted as I was to turn around and drive into the sun, I didn't. I kept going. I continue to keep going. For them. For God. I can't live without both. I take that back. I *can* live without them, but it's miserable. It's a miserable existence that's as barren and flat as this land covered in a thin film of snow.

It is lonely out here and gets lonelier with each mile. I travel twenty more and feel it deep within, where the urge to be with Lisa, Will, and Jenny keeps tugging at me. Once again, I'm torn. I don't want to go any farther away from them. I don't want to go away from them, period. But I fight the impulse to upend what I know must be done. A sign for the town of Brockton—next exit—toothpicks the side of the highway. At 65 mph, the decision to turn around or keep going is imminent. With a lift of my right leg, I let off the gas, decelerate, and roll into the Fort Peck hamlet. Population: 247. Right now: 248. Ten seconds later: 247. I'm now headed east on Highway 2. Back to where I came from. I can't do what I thought I could. *Yes, you can.* JESUS SAVES the little homemade sign in the grass field reads. *Then save me*, I reply.

If that's what a U-turn on an empty stretch of highway reveals, I'm as blessed, or unblessed as they come. Without the sun in my eyes, I've once again drawn a bead on the western horizon. With tunnel vision I push down on the pedal to reduce the amount of time allowed for temptation. Just get me there, God, and let's get this over with.

With His part of the bargain upheld, I see Poplar up ahead. From the looks of it, it is Brockton on steroids. Perhaps a population of six hundred, maybe even eight hundred. As the light traffic slows to 35 mph within the city limits—at the high point of the road—I scan the undernourished metropolis. North of town, there is a brick structure, an institution of some sort like a school or municipal building. I take a right and follow the road that winds its way to the Tribal Headquarters of the Assiniboine and Sioux. In more ways than one, I've arrived. I park the car and pick up my phone from where it rests in the cup holder. One more try to Hollis, I decide. Then, and only then will I one day be able to look him in the eye with the knowledge that I did everything I could to reach him, to discuss with him what I felt I had to do (we had to do) before I did it. The signal, weak as it is, or even non-existent to begin with, disappears from the screen. Today, there is no stay of execution.

On my walk from the car to the main entrance, the tailwind of what feels like the jet stream gives me an extra boost. As he exits the contemporary one-story building, an older man holds the door for me. "Thank you," I say. Inside, I reassemble my disheveled hair and walk toward the American Indian woman who appears to be someone who could direct me.

"Excuse me," I say to her. She looks up from her paperwork. "Where would I find Jakobe Kenton?"

"Down the hall in Law and Justice."

In khakis and hard-soled loafers south of my ski jacket, I'm overdressed. This is jeans, cowboy boots, and gym shoe country. Some work boots, as well. All the men and women I pass wear them, and all of them are Native Americans. If physical appearance was the stick that measured who does and doesn't belong here, I wouldn't qualify. I am the sole Anglo Saxon. At the Law and Justice Office, a woman takes notice as soon as I enter her domain.

"Can I help you?"

"I'm here to see Jakobe Kenton."

"Is he expecting you?"

I avoid the question. "Could you just tell him that Garrett Ingram is here and would like to speak with him?"

She avoids eye contact. "Have a seat."

I step over toward the two chairs in the lobby and lean against the wall—I would rather stand than sit—and watch her pick up the phone. She speaks, then hangs up. If I wasn't nervous before, I am now. I am now wet under the arms. My light-blue starched cotton button-down would be a far darker shade there if I could see it, which I can't. But I can feel it, and it's uncomfortable.

He sees me; I see him. We give each other acknowledgement with a slight tilt of our heads. I stay where I am and let him come towards me from the back of the office. But then I think of Big Sky and Land Country, and how they meet each other halfway—at the horizon—and that's what I do.

"What brings you out here today, Mr. Ingram?"

He looks just as he did months ago. Same jeans, cowboy boots, and tan shirt with insignia of the Sioux Nation and

Fort Peck Police. Maybe the belt buckle's different. Maybe it's not—as big. "I'd like to talk to you."

"After all this time?"

"I understand."

"No, you don't. Because you'll never know what it feels like to stand in our shoes."

"Nor you in mine."

He grins a condescending grin. "I don't think it's equal footing, Mr. Ingram."

Though I'm inclined to think his statements are more from an historical perspective, there is the very real possibility that he speaks of the current troubles afflicting the Sioux from the unknown whereabouts of Orrin Gall, which I induced. Either way, it's a good opportunity to segue into my reason for being here. "I can shed some light that I hope will ease the sorrow."

"Rather convenient of you to offer that now, wouldn't you say?"

"I'm not sure what you mean by that."

"Well, if you're here to tell me what I think you're going to tell me, that light has already been shed."

"Care to elaborate?"

"That's what you're here to do, right? Not me."

"Okay, I get it. I see where you're coming from," I reply. But I will soon find out that I don't. "Is there a place we can sit down and talk?"

Next to the hard feelings on his tawny-skinned face, there is disdain. Within the lines on his forehead, there's contempt. Both are justified. "Follow me."

Through the side door and down the hall, I stay on his heels. Midway down he opens a door and asks me to have a seat. "I'll be back in a moment," he says.

The small room is four beige walls, a ceiling, tiled floor, a metal table and three matching metal chairs. I sit on the side of the table with the one chair. It's cold—both the seat and the room. In response, I zipper up my jacket, fold my arms across my chest, and cross my legs. And wait. And think. Alone with my thoughts in a sterile room, I am the patient whose blood is waiting to be drawn.

Fifteen minutes go by before Kenton returns and takes a seat opposite me. The legal pad and pen he places in front of himself. I lean forward. The less of me that touches metal, the better. I'm ready. He's not. And now I know why. A man the size of a bear enters our cell.

"Mr. Ingram, this is Jim Winters, Chief of Police."

I stand and make the man's acquaintance. After his acknowledgement of me, he places the recording device on the table and plugs it into the outlet in the wall. With a few words, he tests the equipment and plays it back for all to hear. The time, the date, the location, all those present and accounted for. For posterity, each of us take a turn and state our names into the microphone. Per the man's request, I let it be known that I am here of my own volition and volunteer the information forthcoming.

"Five months ago, while a guest of The Little Wing Ranch, I was guided on an upland hunt by Orrin Gall. I was one of two hunters that Orrin was guiding. The other was my friend, and trip organizer, Hollis Baumgartner. Hollis has hunted pheasant and quail all his life and was a frequent visitor of the Little Wing. It was later in the morning, when

Truck—Orrin's dog—sniffed out a bird and got on point. I was anxious to finally shoot one and moved into position. As I moved toward the bird and began to mount my twenty-gauge Beretta Silver Pigeon, I stepped on a stick in the grass and the crack of it spooked a rabbit. The rabbit ran towards the bird, and the dog gave chase. This flushed the pheasant. In my excitement, I aimed and pulled the trigger before the blue sky was completely around the bird, which Orrin had told us to wait for. It was one of the first things he told me when we met. I don't know why I didn't wait. I wish I had. I really do. But I didn't and I pulled the trigger too soon. I didn't see the dog until it was too late. I hit both the pheasant and the dog, and they just dropped to the ground. I was shocked at what I'd done. The dog was on the ground wailing. Orrin rushed to its aid. The dog continued to yelp and wail and then Orrin got up and stomped toward me. I can still see the look of rage in his eyes. He reached for my gun, but out of instinct I held firm of it. Hollis told me not to give it to him. Orrin told Hollis to stay out of it and he kept tugging. My finger was close to the trigger, I was worried the gun would go off, so I let go of it. To protect me, Hollis aimed his gun at Orrin. Orrin spun around and headed for his dog. He stood over the animal and fired the other shell in my over-under to put the dog out of its misery."

I'm out of breath, and I pause to catch it. They say nothing. There's no reaction from either of them. It surprises me to see them this way. I expected more emotion, from Kenton, in particular. Something—a question or a clarification of a detail. Squeezed into his chair like he is, like he would be as an airline passenger in coach, a man who tips the scales at 280 pounds or more, perhaps it is too much effort for the American Indian police chief to intervene. I look at Kenton and hope for a facial expression that gives even the slightest hint for me to continue, that he appreciates my truthfulness and that at last I've come forward. But there is none. Maybe they just want more.

"He grieved over the loss of his dog. I couldn't believe what I'd done. Over and over I kept telling Orrin how sorry I was. He rose from his knees and marched toward me. He started yelling at me. 'I told you no low shots, you sonofabitch.' Hollis stepped between us and told Orrin to back off. That it was an accident. He was big and strong and pushed Hollis into me. I told Orrin that I was willing to pay him whatever he wanted but he said the dog was irreplaceable. I can't remember exactly, but eventually Orrin settled down and accepted my offer of $10,000 plus a new dog. Hollis thought this was way too much, though. He knew that the price of a new bird dog was $5,000. Orrin and Hollis exchanged a few heated words, and there was more pushing and shoving between all three of us, and that's when I noticed Orrin steal a shell from Hollis's coat. He broke away from us and headed back toward his dog and my gun on the ground next to the dead animal. Hollis told him to drop the shell. But Orrin held on to it. With the shell in his possession, he could load the gun, and with a loaded gun anything could happen. I was nervous and, without a gun, defenseless. Hollis kept demanding that Orrin drop the shell. But instead, Orrin dropped to his knees and loaded the shell into the shotgun. The man had his back to us and started chanting. Hollis gave him one last warning to put the gun down. Because our lives were in danger, Hollis had his shotgun aimed at Orrin. I didn't know what to do. But when Orrin began to turn his body, I ran. And that's when I heard a gun go off."

Jakobe Kenton turns his head to the left. In reply, Jim Winters turns his to the right. Face-to-face, the two men communicate in a silent language all their own. Then they speak in their native tongue. With what seems like the power of hydraulics, Winter's massive arms lift his body from the constrictive metal chair, and he repositions himself in it. Now, his upper torso has a slight lean toward the door.

"Please continue," Kenton says.

I'm spoken to, which I take as a positive sign, and continue with my story. "When I stopped and turned around, Orrin was facedown on the ground with a bloody wound in his back. Hollis put his gun down and raced to him."

"Are you stating that Orrin Gall was shot by Hollis Baumgartner?" Jakobe Kenton asks.

"Yes," I reply.

"Okay."

"Hollis turned Orrin over and began CPR. He kept pumping his chest over and over and over, but there was no response. I pulled out my phone to call for help but I couldn't get a signal. Hollis kept at it and wouldn't give up on trying to revive Orrin. Finally, though, he tired, and he stopped. We checked for a pulse. Nothing. There was no breath. There was no life. Orrin had passed away."

Every detail of the story that I can remember, I tell them. From the tools we used to dig the grave, to the pickup we drove into the Redwater, to the reasons I did what I did for the benefit of my friend. Accurate, honest, and remorseful, my confession is given to the representatives of the Great Sioux Nation that I believed needed to hear it before anyone else. I owed them that much, at the very least. With the expectation of a cross-examination that has yet to arrive, and to my surprise never does, Jakobe Kenton instead keys-in on that ever-familiar critical piece of jurisdictional precedence when he says, "From the Little Wing Ranch headed for the bridge of the Redwater, was Orrin Gall shot and buried on the left or right side of the road?"

"It was the left."

"Mr. Ingram," Kenton begins, "there's nothing further we can do for you. We have no authority to investigate crimes committed off the reservation."

"I didn't come here looking for help. I just want to set the record straight and accept responsibility for what I've done to a member of your tribe."

"Awfully convenient of you to do this now, don't you think?" Winters says.

It was the same comment Kenton had made earlier, and I give the same reply. "What do you mean by that?"

They both give me a once-over, the way people do when they size you up. For the criminal investigator, this was done months ago when we first met at the Little Wing, so I think it odd that he would need a second look. He did not strike me as the type of person handicapped by indecision, then or now.

"At this point, I'm going to turn the recorder off, Mr. Ingram. This concludes your statement to the Fort Peck Police Department," Kenton says, and he pushes the button to neutralize the device. "Between the two of us, I think you missed your opportunity to cut yourself a deal with the feds long ago, and I think you know that, too, and that's why you're here. You won't get any sympathy from me."

"What are you talking about?"

"Is it coincidence that you happen to make a confession three days after Hollis Baumgartner made his?" Winters says.

"You're a day late and a dollar short," Kenton adds.

"Hollis told you what happened?"

"Not to us," Winters says. "He went to the feds and got a cooperation agreement from what I hear."

"He did what?"

"Special Agent Vaughn wants to string you up by your balls, Mr. Ingram," Kenton tells me.

"You're going to need a good lawyer," the chief says. "But then again I'm sure someone with the kind of money you have won't have any problem getting one."

I bite my tongue and ask, "What's a cooperation agreement?"

"It's using a little fish to catch a big fish," Winters replies.

"Did Hollis point fingers at me?"

"That's a question for Special Agent Vaughn," Kenton says." I'm not at liberty to speak about an ongoing federal investigation. I'm just here to do what you asked—to listen."

I want to wake up from this nightmare. I want to wake up in the arms of my wife and children. In a city park where the grass is green and flowers bloom. Where the sea is a short walk away. Where it's warm and the rain and sun grow trees big enough to throw shade on all four of us. I can see it all so clear; the life I had. They sit across from me and speak

Sioux as though I am as nothing to them as they think they are to me. But I don't think that way about them. I've never looked down upon the Sioux, or any tribe. And yet they have every reason to look down upon me. I just want them to know that I'm sorry for everything. I was in the wrong place at the wrong time and had no business to be in the possession of a loaded gun with the intent to aim and fire in the blink of an eye at a bird taking flight. I am here to right those wrongs.

Hollis, what have you done! Is it true what they say?

Chapter Twenty-Eight

I walk out the doors of the Fort Peck Tribes municipal building a free man, though it appears those days are numbered. Maybe hours. It will be two until Special Agent Vaughn arrives from the FBI satellite office in Glasgow, Montana. I was advised by Kenton and Winters that the Feds were on their way. Cadaver dogs, too. As a token of hospitality, I'm offered water and shelter for the time being, but I tell them I want to stretch my legs.

What I really want, though, is to call Lisa. As I head toward my rental, I happen to pick up a faint cellular signal. Without moving another foot—for fear of losing the connection—I dial. But she is out of reach. Somewhere on the highway, somewhere between the Atlantic and the Mississippi she travels homeward with our kids on a stretch of road down south that has yet to be updated with cellular towers, which is tenfold up here. That is my line of thought. I've never felt so helpless. I've never needed her more. I wait five minutes and try again from inside my vehicle—as refuge from the jet stream—that I've driven to the south end of the parking lot to pick up reception on my phone. However, the result is no different. For now, she is unobtainable, and I have no choice but to accept this, and the frustration that accompanies the drumbeat.

I can't sit still, and I'm not one to remain idle in a time of need. If I can't reach Lisa, maybe I can reach Hollis or

Helen. They are my second and third choice for conversation, for questions that I'd like answers to. If a knife has been shoved into my back, the confirmation of such a betrayal would best be heard directly from the horse's mouth, or its mare. Still, I can't believe that Hollis would do such a thing. But there's no reason for Kenton and Winters to tell me anything other than what they know to be true because my confession was voluntary. In return for it, they promised nothing, other than to listen and record. Perhaps, though, their strategy and hatred for me extends beyond professional boundaries, like anonymous notes taped to porch beams and windshields.

As expected, neither Hollis nor Helen answer my call. I hang up and try Lisa again, and this time she answers.

"Hey, you."

"It's good to hear your voice," I tell her. "Where are you guys?"

"Somewhere in Tennessee." There's worry in her intonation. I can hear it like the wind that attempts to breach the rubber trim around the windows. "How are you, and where are you, and tell me everything. I've been trying to reach you."

"I won't sugarcoat it for you. It's not good."

"Do I need to pull over?" It's her way to let me know that if we need to talk in private, she'll find an exit with a gas station where she can step out of the car far enough away from the kids. But I don't want her to stop. I want my family home as soon as possible. That's where they belong, where I produce an image of us all there together.

"No, keep driving. Just talk quietly when you need to."

"Okay, tell me what's going on."

"I met with the Sioux Police and told them everything, and they said the case is out of their jurisdiction and is being handled by the FBI."

"We know that, don't we?"

"In part," I say. "What we didn't know, and what I'm still trying to find out more on, is that Hollis went to the FBI and has gotten a cooperation agreement from them."

"What do you mean by that?"

"He's entered into an agreement to help the FBI in their case against me. And in return, he'll get a lighter sentence or immunity maybe."

"Are you kidding me."

"I know. I can't believe it either."

"But he's the one who shot that man, right?" she whispers.

"Yes."

"So how can he help the FBI against you?"

"That's what I need to find out."

"Are you sure about this?" she asks.

"It's what the Sioux Police told me."

"Maybe they're lying."

"Could be," I reply. "But I can't figure out why they would."

"Do you think that's why Helen hasn't returned my phone calls?"

"Looks that way."

She takes a deep breath. When she exhales over the mouthpiece on the phone it sounds like the hurricane that batters my Camry. "Where are you now?" she asks.

"I'm in Poplar. In the parking lot of the police station."

"So what's next?"

"The FBI agent is on his way here."

"And what's going to happen?"

"Everything is going to be fine." I sugarcoat it.

"I'm worried."

"We're doing the right thing. We know that we are."

"Are we?"

"Yes, and what do we always tell the kids . . . if you do what's right, you can't go wrong."

"I know, I'm just worried."

"How are they?"

"They're fine," she replies. "Do you guys want to say hi to Dad?"

I hear Jenny in the background call out first. She asks where I am and when I'll be home. She asks about Mr. Baumgartner and if I've found him yet. The liar that I was and have become again throws white lies her way, and then at her brother. Content on both ends, I am transferred back to Lisa.

"I miss them," I tell her, which also is not the truth, because, what I feel is that, without them, and Lisa, I'm dying a slow death out here. To say I miss them isn't anywhere close to the truth. Without them, it has become hard to breathe.

The conversation has taken an emotional turn. She knows she needs to change its direction or we'll both be unable to go any further, and that's the last thing we need right now. We need to keep going. "I think we need to talk to my brother."

Lisa's brother, Jay McClelland, is an attorney in Chicago. "I thought about that, too." He's a partner in a big firm there. Criminal litigation is not his specialty, but there's no question he'd connect us with one of the best in that field. "I'll call him."

"Would you rather I do it?"

"No, that's okay."

"Are you going to call him now?"

"Yes."

One last goodbye to the kids, and another broken promise—a lie—to them that I'll be home soon, and I hang up and dial Jay's number. Even though I'm family, he's unable to take my call. I inform his receptionist that the matter at hand is of an urgent nature and that I would appreciate a return call as soon as possible. As an attorney who spends most of his time in the corporate tax and business side of the legal system, I hope that the unusual solicitation from his brother-in-law will lead him to believe my issue is of much greater magnitude than something like a random audit letter from the I.R.S., and prompts him to get back to me right away.

I wait in the car to make sure I can hear my phone when it rings. I would like to walk somewhere instead of being held captive like I am inside this vehicle, but the wind whips through this land with a voice that drowns all others, and I can't afford to miss the call. Thankfully, I can afford a top-notch attorney. Though for how long and to what extent is yet to be determined. There is only so much of my hard-earned income that can be justified in a redistribution of wealth from my pocket—my family's pocket—to someone else's, no matter the education, experience, and skill set of the lawyer hired to represent me. I intend to plead guilty, which I assume has been done in the form of my taped confession. To what charge, and to what extent I'm held accountable is the reasonable price I must pay for my defense and dispensation of punitive damages.

Hollis, Hollis, Hollis. Talk to me. Tell me what you've said and done. I wait for a reply. There is none. I wait for the phone to ring. It doesn't. Impatient and unable to stay put, I start the car and drive out of the parking lot. At the intersection of Highway 2, I turn west. There seems to be more of the town in that direction. But there isn't. There isn't much of anything out here. Some homes, a gas station, a school. Trees, however, have managed to proliferate along each side of the road like they would a stream. Without leaves, though, they're skeletal imitations of fertile life. The gas station with a small convenient store is the only place I can find open to the general public. I pull in. With my phone on vibrate in my hand, I make the short walk from vehicle to dwelling. Inside, the American Indian woman behind the counter smiles and says hello. I do the same. Across from the doorway, a man in a cowboy hat has his back to me as he fills a large plastic cup at the soft drink dispenser. Other than the two of us, the store is empty. The shelves in the three aisles are somewhat empty, as well. I walk up and down each of them in expectation of something to purchase. In reciprocation for the shelter from the wind and cold, it's the least I can do. Though with an appetite that mirrors the lack of inventory, I'm unable to project a consumption of anything more than two packs of peanut butter crackers. I grab them and head for the fountain drinks. My thirst is far greater than my hunger. But with a phone in one hand and crackers in the other, I'm presented with the dilemma of which to put in my pocket so that my cup can be filled with Coke. I choose the phone. Anything other might be construed as shoplifting. I fill up and walk over to the counter. I'm behind the cowboy who roots through his pockets in search of change. He has plenty of it and unloads both wheelbarrows full onto the Formica top. Some of the pennies make a run for it, but he's quick enough to break their fall. One by one, the woman begins the count. This is going to take a while, and it does when he rushes over and grabs a bag of chips to add to the soft drink. To add to the pennies, he scoops nickels from his jeans.

"Sorry about this," he says to me.

"No problem."

But there is. "You're thirty cents short," the woman says.

He digs deeper and hands a few more coins to the clerk. They're copper, though, and they are far short of thirty-two.

"I'll cover for him," I tell the woman.

"No, I got this," he says. "Hang on, I'll be right back." He goes outside and roots through his truck. As I watch him through the glass door, a man in a Chevy Tahoe passes by at the restricted city speed limit on Highway 2. The man is familiar to me. The chlorine-tinted hair. The profile. My memories from the airport in Sidney and the hotel in Dallas. In Poplar, Special Agent Curtis Vaughn has arrived. We will meet again soon.

The door swings open and the cowboy enters. But the wind and the cold beat him to the counter.

"Pardon me," he says, and places a few dimes at the head of the one-man line I reside in.

The woman picks them up and pushes back a few of the pennies. He grabs his drink and snack, and says, "Keep the change."

In all of this "excitement" I have missed an important phone call. The price I pay for switching the ringer to vibrate, and for getting the Coke and crackers I didn't need but felt obligated to buy.

In my car, I listen to Jay's voicemail. He's at O'Hare to catch a flight to Seattle, where he has business for the next two days. Right away, I call him. The call gets dropped. I look at the phone. One bar appears, then disappears, then reappears. I start the car and drive down the road with one eye out the windshield and the other on the phone. Two bars appear and I pull over and dial Jay. He doesn't pick up until after the fifth ring. "Hi, this is Jay McClelland. Please leave a message and I will return your call as soon as I'm available. If you need immediate assistance, please contact my assistant, Beth Bowers, at—" *Blah, blah, blah, blah, blah.* I call Beth. She answers and lets me know that she gave Jay my message as he headed out of the office for the airport. It disappoints me that she makes no mention of the urgency I had conveyed to her when we spoke last. To hand her boss a note as he passes her desk on his way to the elevators is a far cry from the effort I expected from her. I'd presumed she would track him down and let it be known that I needed to hear from him as soon as possible.

"Do you know what time his flight for Seattle leaves O'Hare?"

"I don't," she says. "Sorry about that."

We part ways and I'm back on the hunt for Jay. Voicemail is the closest I can get to him, though. If he's taxiing on the runway or airborne, it will be hours before I can connect with him, and I don't have hours. I only have minutes. I gave my word that I would remain in Poplar and wait for the feds to get here and take me into custody, if that's what they choose to do after Special Agent Vaughn listens to my taped confession. But I would like to speak with an attorney first, and Hollis before anyone. I try him one last time. As expected, there's no answer. I'm sent to voicemail and hang up without leaving a message.

On the empty highway in the empty town in the middle of somewhere between the past, present, and future, I'm as committed to my destiny as I am landlocked. From what I can see all around me, there is no escape from Big Land Country. It stretches to infinity—beyond the flight of birds— and there isn't enough gas in my tank or tread on the tires for me to outrun it. From habit, and for no one, I pull down on the lever to activate my turn signal. I go left and follow the road as it doglegs right. When I reach the parking lot of the Fort Peck Tribes municipal building, the space I had occupied earlier remains vacant and I pull into it as though it were the one assigned to me at work. I do all I can physically and mentally to stay the course. I take a quick look at myself in the mirror—another habit—then reach for the door handle and step into the windstorm.

With big strides for Big Land, I cover terrain at the pace of an airliner's shadow and take haven behind brick, glass, and steel before the wind has the chance to enslave me like litter on a highway. I straighten my hair and walk to the counter. The same woman as before sees me make my approach, and she picks up the phone. She speaks a few words that I can't hear, then hangs up and comes to the counter, where we meet again.

"Just have a seat, Mr. Ingram. They'll be with you shortly."

"Thanks."

With the acknowledgement of my name, I feel more the honored guest than I was on my last visit. Good or bad, it's professional at the very least, and as a businessman, I appreciate the heightened level of awareness. That is what I focus on. This is the mindset I've adopted. I'm here to take care of business. I've always done what I've needed to do. I've never shrugged my responsibilities. For myself, for the companies I've worked for, and most of all, for my family, I've always given one hundred percent and met or exceeded expectations. This transaction will be no different. *Stay the course.*

Special Agent Vaughn comes through the side door as though he's on a mission. "Mr. Ingram, please follow me," he says. We exit through the doorway I'd come through and we walk past a lobby and down a hall. With intent and purpose, he moves at a good clip, and I push myself to stay within arm's reach of his FBI-emblazoned navy-blue windbreaker that is unzipped and flaps in the air behind him like a cape. Superman's perhaps. At the end of the corridor, there's a door on the right and he opens it. "Have a seat."

The small conference room has an oval wood table and six leather chairs. An overhead projector is mounted to the ceiling. A briefcase, a satchel, and a legal pad and pen rest near the south end of the table. There are several water bottles as well. Opposite each other, we take our seats. On the wall behind him is a large, glass-framed map of Montana that catches my reflection on the descent. As it catches my eye, I find Poplar and project myself into that part of the Big Sky universe. I am here. And here is where I'm meant to be. *Stay the course.*

"Shall we get down to business?" he asks. But it's not a question. Not in the least, and he reaches for the pen and pad and places it in front him.

"Yes."

"I've listened to the recording that you voluntarily produced for the Fort Peck Police," he begins. "I'd like to inform you of your Miranda rights. You have the right to remain silent. Anything you say can be used against you in court. You have the right to talk to a lawyer for advice before I ask you any questions. You have the right to have a lawyer with you during questioning. If you cannot afford a lawyer, one will be appointed for you before any questioning if you wish. If you decide to answer questions now without a lawyer present, you have the right to stop answering at any time."

"I understand this, Agent Vaughn, and I'd like to continue." I reach for one of the water bottles. "I'm in the process of finding legal representation, but I'm here to tell you the truth and can do that without an attorney by my side."

"Very well, then. Let's begin." He removes his jacket and places it on the back of his chair, which reveals a striped button-down underneath a brown wool sweater. And I can't help but notice the lighter shades of fiber in it that pull from the strands in his hair where the chlorine resides. "As I mentioned, I've had the opportunity to listen to the recording you provided to Criminal Investigator Jakobe Kenton and Chief of Police Jim Winters of the Fort Peck Police Department. Your version of events of what happened to Orrin Gall differs greatly from that given by Hollis Baumgartner."

"What did he say?"

"He states that you shot Orrin Gall and it was you who insisted on burying him and fabricating the story of going separate ways after the hunt."

"That's a lie."

"Is it?"

"Yes, it is. Hollis was the one who shot Orrin, but it was self-defense. You heard what I said on the tape, and that's exactly how things happened."

"According to Mr. Baumgartner, you were worried about the consequences of shooting a man in the back. He said that you told him, and I quote"—he looks down at the legal pad and reads from it—"'Out here in Montana everyone is related, and I'd never get a fair trial if it came to that.'"

"That's bullshit. That's what he was worried about and that's what he said to me."

"He asserts that the bird flew left of twelve o'clock, which made it his bird. But the bird stayed low and he should not have fired. However, he did, and he hit the dog as it leaped for the bird that was spooked by a rabbit. Just as he fired, you fired too. But you were out of position and had no business going left of twelve o'clock. Your shot struck Orrin

Gall in the back and he died. Isn't this the truth, Mr. Ingram?"

"It's not. It's the complete opposite."

"Isn't it the truth that you were so concerned about what a criminal investigation and possible trial could do to your career and the harm it would cause your family if you were terminated from Boeing, that you pleaded with your friend, Hollis Baumgartner, to bury Orrin Gall and his dog, drive his truck into the river, then act as if nothing ever happened."

"Nothing could be further from the truth," I say. We stare at each other. "If you don't believe me, I'll take a polygraph to prove it, if that's what you still want."

"I *did* want that. But you refused. You lawyered up and the offer went off the table. However, Mr. Baumgartner accepted my offer and took a polygraph."

"And?"

"He passed," the agent says. "And he and his family are now in protective custody."

"From who?"

"From you."

"What?"

"He said that you called him and told him about the nine-millimeter you purchased and that if he ever spoke a word to anyone about what happened to Orrin Gall, you wouldn't hesitate to use it on him."

"That's outrageous."

"Is it?" he replies. "We checked the records and saw the transaction in your name for a nine-millimeter Berretta a few months back."

"I can't believe this is happening."

"I knew you were lying the first time I met you, Mr. Ingram. I just couldn't prove it," he says. "Now I can."

"You're going to take Hollis's word over mine?"

"Yes, and in my opinion, so will a jury."

"This is such unbelievable bullshit," I lean forward in my chair and rest my elbows on the table to be closer to Special Agent Vaughn, so he can see the disbelief and exasperation in my eyes. "Hollis was the one who was worried about his deal with Lawton going south. How he needed it to go through because he made some bad trades and lost almost all his money, and the oil was his ticket out."

He ignores my statement and meets me on the table. "That won't hold up. We've confirmed he has a net worth of over twenty-million dollars," he says. "Mr. Ingram, you were given multiple chances to cooperate and come clean, and you chose not to. Hollis Baumgartner chose a different path—the right path."

You lied to me, Hollis. You greedy fucking liar.

"I don't think I want to answer any more questions without my attorney present."

"You came to Poplar to set the record straight, or something to that effect, I believe is what you told the Fort Peck Police."

"I did."

"A jury is going to have to choose between coincidence and reaction." He pulls back from the table and makes more use of his chair than I do. "And what I mean by that, is that three days after Hollis Baumgartner gave the FBI a full account of the events that transpired with you, him, and Orrin Gall, you come forward to the Fort Peck Police—not the FBI—and claim that Hollis Baumgartner held the smoking gun and coerced you into concealing the truth from the state of Montana, the Fort Peck Tribes, and the United States Government. Do you really think a jury of your peers will see this as coincidence, or a reaction from you in response to what you may have suspected Hollis Baumgartner would do under threat of violence from you, or an inability to keep buried what most men of morals simply cannot?"

"You're never going to believe me, are you?"

"Your cellular phone records, most notably the numerous calls you made to Hollis Baumgartner immediately after our meeting in Dallas, and the numerous attempts you've made to reach him these last few days, your purchase of a firearm and the private training you obtained to learn how to fire it, your numerous lies to me, which constitutes a felony, your lies to Jakobe Kenton, your lies to Deputy Sheriff Trevor Maultsby, your lies to Lawton Mills, and the list goes on and on," the Special Agent says. "I'd be a fool to believe you. A jury will be no different."

"But you believe Hollis?"

"I do," he replies. "His story is more palpable than yours, and he passed his polygraph. But make no mistake about it, he's going to do some time for what he's done. However, you're going to do hard time. That's what it's called when you're sent upriver for years." He clasps his hands in his lap and waits for my reply, which is long in coming because I am at a complete loss for words, and thoughts, other than to seek legal representation.

"If you've made up your mind, then I guess there's nothing I can say or do to change your opinion of me." In closing, I say, "I'd like to speak to my attorney now."

As though indifferent to my request, he says, "About the only thing you can do to gain any goodwill is to help us locate Orrin Gall's body."

"Whether you believe me or not, that's what I came here to do."

"Two days ago, we searched the fields with Mr. Baumgartner's assistance, but we were unable to locate the body," the Special Agent says. "If you want to help, and possibly help yourself, we'll set out at first light in the morning with cadaver dogs. From the satellite pictures I showed you, we know the starting point."

"I'm willing to cooperate."

"You would've made it easier on yourself had you told me that months ago," he replies. He reaches into his satchel, pulls out a piece of paper, and puts it in front of me. "The Richland County Sheriff's Office has issued a warrant for your arrest."

CHAPTER TWENTY-NINE

I've been down this road before, I tell myself. And I have. Maybe as many as a thousand times. This morning, though, it's different. It's not something that continues to playback over and over in my head. This isn't a dream. I had those all through the night, and they were nightmares. These SUVs and pickups and dogs and voices are real as the land is big. I am here and now, in Montana, not in my dreams.

Brakes squeal, shocks rumble, and snow and mud are stamped with tire tread; some of it for the second time this week. In one of the ruts, I plant my feet. Yes, I have been here before. These dogs haven't. For them, this is virgin territory and they act like it as they tug hard on their leashes to mark their scent on the frivolous blades of wheatgrass they wish to call their own. Called by their masters, Lewis and Clark sit upon command. I feel like them. The dogs, not their masters. I turn the collar up on my county-issued corduroy coat and wait for my next directive. The exit from the vehicle was just one of many this morning after I awakened in the Richland County Jail. In this crowd, there are no faces I've seen before, except for Special Agent Vaughn. Several of the men wear the markings of the Richland County Sheriff, one of which is the Sheriff, and several are in plain clothes and boots like the ones that have been loaned to me. To my surprise, there is a woman in the group, and if I had to make an educated guess, she is Sioux or of Sioux ancestry. Perhaps a relative of Orrin Gall or a representative of the Sioux Nation. I look at her. She looks at me and turns away, in disgust it seems. In the light wind her long black hair lifts off her shoulders. She pets the German shepherds and keeps her back to me.

"Sheriff Thompson wants you up front," a deputy says to me. I follow him. He stops next to the Sheriff, a fifty-something-year-old cowboy who's talking to one of the dog handlers. "Just wait here."

The group tightens and the talking subsides. "Mr. Ingram, when you've gotten your bearings, lead the way," Thompson says.

Behind me, stout men walk with shovels and pickaxes, and a handful of other tools to break through the first few inches of earth that remains frozen beneath the thin layer of latticed snow, should the grave be found. Behind them, at the rear, trails Agent Vaughn and two other men whom I now believe to be crime scene investigators. Beside me, two men walk with their dogs untethered. With their noses to the ground, Lewis and Clark remind me of Truck. Everything out here reminds me of Truck, Orrin, and Hollis. I can't get any of them out of my head, and it's been months. From the road to the grave, I've made this journey with them enough times to follow my own footprints in the snow. And before there was snow, it was the trodden grass that guided my way. In the dark of night, as though blindfolded, I'd lie awake and make the trek without the slightest deviation from the proper coordinates. I've done it that many times.

Within thirty minutes, I spot the tree. The one whose twig I stepped on in the grass and spooked the rabbit. I know that tree like I know the back of my hand.

"We're close," I turn and say to Thompson who is on my left heel in Wrangler's, boots, and his brown sheriff's jacket. "That tree there, I recognize it."

"Lewis," the dog handler in his duck coverall shouts. The dog stops and gives his master his full attention. "Over here."

"Clark, here boy," the other man says.

Both dogs race ahead of me, and I quicken the pace to keep up with them. They are onto the scent. From sixty yards away and several feet below ground, death has reached them. Other than the dogs that I'm downwind of, I don't smell a thing, and it's my assumption the olfactory nerves attached to the rest of my platoon are no more or less talented than mine. What I have over them though, is my vision. I can see below the snow and into the soil beneath it, all the way ahead of us to where Lewis and Clark have begun to paw at the ground. I can see the remains of Truck and Orrin Gall. The skeletons of man and man's best friend where Hollis and I laid them to rest. To warm the image, I clothe Orrin, like he is in my dreams.

"We've got something," the handler says to Sheriff Thompson.

In her puffy grey ski pants that swish from nylon friction, the woman rushes to the lawman. "What did he say?"

"The dogs may have found what we're looking for," he replies.

Agent Vaughn pulls out his cell phone, but I know all too well it is of no use out here. "Sheriff Thompson," he says, "are you able to get a signal?"

Both Thompson and the deputies check their phones. "Negative," the Sheriff replies. "Anything boys?"

"Nothing," his subordinates say in unison.

"Want the two-way?" Thompson asks.

"That's okay," Vaughn tells him.

Like a wolf pack we advance across the tundra that thaws in coordination with the sun's continual elevation in the Big Sky. Fueled with expectation, we close the distance to the grave in no time. There, the handlers leash the canines and pull them back from the pock-mocked snow they've put their signature on.

"Sit, Lewis."

"Sit, Clark," the handler in the coveralls says. He lets go of the leash and takes his foot to mark an outline of the grave based on the dogs' tracks in the snow and dirt. "This is it," he tells Thompson. "From the way they're acting, I'm ninety-nine-point-nine percent sure this is the gravesite."

"Look familiar?" Agent Vaughn says to me.

"It does," I reply, loud enough for all to hear.

"Let's get digging, boys," Sheriff Thompson says. With an extra pickaxe handed to him by one of his employees, Thompson is first to strike the earth. "Rock hard," he exclaims. "But we'll bust through it."

With the strength and determination of Montana men as tough and hard as this moon they've lived on for years, the frozen layer of soil a few inches thick is vanquished by the sheer force of powerful swings, over and over. Into the soft soil, they switch to shovels, slow their work, and proceed with caution. Not only is it a grave, but it's also a crime scene, and the evidence must be preserved as well as possible.

"At two feet we'll be close?"

"Yes, and the dog is on top," I tell the Sheriff for the second time this morning.

When they reach that depth, they lay their shovels down and dig with hand spades and gloved-hands, like gardeners.

"I've got bone," a deputy says. He takes a trim brush out of his coat pocket and gives it to his boss.

Thompson fans the soil to make more visible the bones of death and decay. Same as the others without tools, I step forward to see it with my own eyes. A glimpse, and I'm overwhelmed. I step back, and from there I step back to that fateful day, when Big Sky and Land Country held me in wonder and amazement with its beauty. Truck's too. But I go no further. To go down that road one more time—the dead end that it always is—will yield nothing more than pity and sorrow and remorse, none of which can change the course of history that is slowly unearthed before me. I've put my faith in God's hands, my attorney's, and soon, I will be in Lisa's.

I'm escorted back to the road by a deputy whose name I've yet to discover or ask for. Perhaps the cool air has numbed my appetite for social interaction. That, or the image of skeletal remains I try to leave behind, like regret. At the SUV, I'm handcuffed and placed into the backseat. The vinyl is cold. The steel around my wrists is colder. He starts the car and I make my first request of the day. "Could you turn the heat up?"

"I will when the engine warms."

We drive away and I look at our tracks in the snow that trail off to the ridge on the northeastern horizon. Later they will be trounced with all-terrain vehicles and other equipment needed to exhume and transport the evidence of my crime—handled with great care for the forensic specialists to examine, and prosecutors to inflict charges upon me; from which, I will accept a resolution based on the truth. Anything other than that will be met with my best defense possible for myself and my family. Deep inside, though, I hold out for the chance that Hollis will recant, because I still can't believe what he's said—and what he's done to me.

My arraignment is scheduled for 2:00 p.m., at which time my attorney, Jonah Corcoran, expects bail will be set on the charge of negligent homicide. In our brief discussion over the phone, a plea of not guilty will be entered. There will be more charges, he expects, and we will be meeting in a few minutes to discuss our legal strategy. But all I want right now is my wife. She is on a flight to Williston, and from there she'll make the drive down here to Sidney. Will and Jenny have been left behind under the care of their grandmother. They are still in the dark, like me in many ways.

Down the hall I hear a door open, and the jailer's steps that carry the transmission from there. The key slides in, my door opens. We walk together a short distance. In a detention center for twelve or so inmates, space is confined, in stark contrast to Big Sky and Land Country. He opens a door and there alone in the room seated at a table awaits Jonah Corcoran. We've never met, and I've never seen a photo of the man, but I know it's him.

"Jonah." I extend my hand and walk toward him while he rises from his chair in his blue suit and crimson necktie. "Thank you for coming and thank you for representing me. Jay spoke highly of you."

"My pleasure," the lawyer replies, and as though he knows my most desired wish at the moment, says, "First of all, let me tell you we will be getting you out of here today."

"That would be nice."

"And secondly, they don't have a chance in hell on the charge of negligent homicide."

It's a huge relief to hear this wise old man tell me what I want to hear. But he's not that old. More premature gray and an overexposure to the Big Sky sun than what he appears to be in years. Early-sixties, I presume, in conjunction with Jay's accolade of the man being one of Montana's best criminal defense attorneys with a plethora of experience, which would put him somewhere in that age group. On the table in front of his sturdy build, a briefcase and papers sit. On the lower bridge of his nose, are bifocals to read them.

"That is even better news," I say, though I'd like to hear his reasons for such a bold statement.

"I've listened to the tapes and they know as well as we do this is a he said/he said case. It's your word against Hollis Baumgartner's." He leans back in his chair and crosses his legs. He's comfortable and relaxed, and if the demeanor was intended to rub off on me, he is successful in the transfer of body language. "Either way, for them to prove you acted recklessly by firing at a bird in a flight path in line with your hunting guide . . . no way, and they know it. Again, I'm well aware that it wasn't you who pulled the trigger."

"Can you keep the good news coming?"

"I can." He leans forward in his wooden chair and reaches for one of the papers in front of him. "As stated in this transcript of your recording, the evidence will show that the dog was shot twice, not once as Hollis Baumgartner professes. A shotgun blast to the dog's ribcage at point blank range will be an easy assessment for any medical examiner assisted by a veterinarian. Once the forensics on the animal have been completed, the negligent homicide charge gets tossed and they'll take aim at your 'friend', not you."

In my eyes, the man is brilliant for his quick study of the evidence, and for the simple fact of the matter—which I overlooked in my worried state of mind—of one shot versus two that divides one man's word from another's. "I presume the Sheriff and the FBI and the prosecutor are aware of this?"

"Absolutely." He returns the piece of paper to the oak table. "That's why Special Agent Curtis Vaughn wanted your assistance with finding the grave more than he probably let on."

I recall my time in Poplar with Vaughn, and it sinks in. "I get it."

"They are banking on their cooperating witness."

"And he's lying."

"And we'll prove it." He looks at his watch. "Just checking to make sure we're on schedule." He reaches into his open briefcase and pulls out two pieces of paper. "There are one or two other charges I expect will be forthcoming, such as making false statements and possibly abuse of a corpse if they want to go that far for extra bargaining chips, but let's put those to the side for now and just concentrate on today's arraignment and a homecoming of sorts with your wife."

"Let me ask you something."

"Go right ahead."

"For what I've done, there's no way around some type of incarceration, though, is there?"

Chapter Thirty

Five days pass. In that time, crocus emerge in our flower bed. I look at them—in appreciation for the permission granted by the court to leave the state of Montana—through the living room window while I wait for my phone to ring. Jonah Corcoran has sent word that he will call by 4:00 p.m., in response from the prosecutor's office that the coroner's preliminary report is ready and is being sent to him. I turn, and turn my attention from the flowers to Lisa, who sits on the couch with her legs tucked underneath her. A shawl drapes her shoulders. A wool blanket covers her lap and the empty space next to her that I've vacated to pace the wood floor along the exterior wall of our home. She waits with me. For five days, she hasn't left my side, nor has the fire that needs another log. I feed it then take my seat.

"It's going to be okay," she says, then reaches for my hand, the one that doesn't hold the phone. I tilt my head to acknowledge the faith I have in her—her reassurance of the path we chose—and I leave it at that. A reply isn't needed, and if it was, it would be the same one I gave her an hour ago, and the hour before that. But she squeezes my hand because she wants one.

"There's nothing to worry about. It's Hollis who should be worried, not us."

It's a front. I'm a front. I can't help but worry. It's all I do. I sit and worry, and when that isn't enough for me to fill my addiction to anxiety, I get up and pace the floor by the window and root for the crocus to win their battle, to rise up through the soil and change the world from black and white to color.

I can't sit. I let go of Lisa's hand and walk over to the mantle. On it rests candles and two pictures of the kids at the far-left end. Above it, is an oil on canvas that is Lisa's favorite—a French landscape. I'm drawn to the pictures of Will and Jenny, whose footsteps I hear above me when they take turns to run the hallway with Friday, who beats them to the tennis ball every time. The painting cost me thousands. But the pictures are priceless. A few steps and I'm in front of them. One at a time, I pick them up and hold them like the babies they are in the photographs. As I place Jenny's on the mantle, my phone rings.

"Hi Jonah." I return to the couch.

"Hello, Garrett," he replies. "I'd hoped to have better news for you, but I don't."

My heart sinks. "Then what do you have for me?"

"The results of the autopsy on the dog are conclusive," he says, without a trace of Western or Montana dialect in his speech. Because he is not from there. He is from the Bay Area. Stanford grad, Harvard Law, and a career with a big firm in San Francisco where he made partner before he moved to Montana with his wife after their kids left the nest for college. "There is no gunshot wound to the ribcage, or any other part of the body."

"That's impossible. I saw it. I saw him shoot his dog, Jonah."

"I believe you," he replies. "Let me just tell you what the results say then we'll discuss things in more detail."

The nightmare continues, and I can't wake up. But I can take a deep breath. I exhale. He hears it and encourages me to continue to calm myself down. "Okay," I reply when I feel more stabilized.

"All parts of the body show no sign of penetration or disfigurement. No sign of impact from ammunition fired from a shotgun, no matter the gauge, twelve, twenty, twenty-eight, or four-ten."

"This is just unbelievable."

"The middle intermaxillary bone, the nose bone, and the upper intermaxillary bone all show signs of damage that would be consistent with that caused by ammunition from a shotgun, such as number six lead shot," he says. "These are the bones above and around the mouth area of the dog."

"I'm goddamn speechless, Jonah."

"I expected that much," my attorney says. "Canine and incisors, as well as parts of the mandible show signs of impact, and of course we all know about the missing canine tooth found in the bird. The report goes on to include the forensic process and other things that really have no bearing on our case. It's standard practice and procedure type of stuff, and so I don't think that is an area of discussion for us now. What we need to focus on are the possibilities for what could've taken place for the results of the autopsy to be as they are."

"I saw what happened. Clear as day," I plead my case with him. "I shot Truck and he went down. Then Orrin stood over him and put him out of his misery."

"But is there any chance Orrin could have missed?"

"At this point I'd like to believe that's possible, but the answer is no," I reply. "I saw what happened, and I helped bury that dog. And it had a hole in its side the size of my fist. There's just no way. The autopsy has to be wrong."

"We can't go down that path, Garrett. But we can look at the potential of it being the wrong dog."

I sense a sliver of hope. "What do you mean?"

"What if Hollis Baumgartner exhumed Truck and buried another dog?"

This man is bright; bright as Hollis. I wouldn't have thought of that in a million years. But I also wouldn't have thought my friend ever capable of putting the two of us in the position we find ourselves in now. Long before I'd ever be able to come to a theory of this sort, I'd be far down the road of hallucinatory history that had me in the firm belief that what Hollis said I did, I did. Eyes have been known to play tricks on those they belong to. The mind as well.

"Would the coroner or whoever be able to determine that?" I ask.

"I think a vet and medical examiner would be able to determine the breed and age of the dog."

"What about the time of death?"

"That too," he replies. "But my guess is that if Hollis Baumgartner took things this far, he would've buried a dog similar in age, and not long after Truck was buried. And certainly, the same breed."

"What about DNA? Is there any way that could help me?"

"It would if we had a good sample from Truck, but we don't. Even if we were able to recover some of Truck's hair from Mr. Gall's old residence, which is a longshot at best now that it's occupied by new owners, a small quantity of dog hair is problematic when it comes to DNA testing," he says. "I wish that Sioux policeman had found the nose and tooth the day he went to the Little Wing Ranch to recover them."

"So do I," I say, with a vivid memory of when Lawton and I sat at his bar and he confided that same bit of information to me; evidence at the time I was glad to have learned had been discarded, but which now has come back to haunt me, like so many other things. "Where do we go from here?"

"I'll request a confirmation of age and breed," he replies. "If they're confirmed to be the same as Truck's, then we can pursue our own investigation."

"What would that entail?"

"We'd have to hire a P.I. to try and track down where Hollis procured the replacement pointer," he says. "But that could take some time, and from what I've seen so far of this man, he goes to great lengths to cover his tracks and the truth might never be discovered."

We spend another five minutes on the phone before we exchange goodbyes. We will spend more time again on the phone tomorrow. Lisa is on edge to hear all that has transpired from the Montana end of the call and has me tight by the arm. We talk, at great length. She asks questions. I answer as best I can. All of them, and all of them that spew hatred for Hollis's betrayal of our family. "Why would he do this to us?" she asks. "How could he do this?" When her anger finally diminishes, she says, "What's going to happen to us?"

"We need to sit tight and wait for the confirmation that Jonah is going to request." I try to be the voice of reason and calm, a trait I always admired in the friend I once had. "And nothing is going to happen to us that we can't handle."

Chapter Thirty-One

I think of Montana every day. With it right out my window here in Deer Lodge, it's impossible not to. In this field of vision, far in the distance the Flint Creek Mountains reach for the sky—the Big Sky—and sun that shines quite often on Mt. Powell's snow-capped peak, beaming and imperfect like my life once was.

There's no denying the beauty of Western Montana, and this valley I now call home. For me though, I was never meant to be here. Maybe Hollis, but not me. It's too far from the sea. It's too cold. It's too far from my family, whom, these days, every day and every minute and every second of them, is almost all I can think about. Everything else, well those thoughts come and go like the guards here, and at best, offer nothing more than a brief escape from reality. Sometimes it's Hollis. I'll just stare out my window and wonder if he's thinking about me too, in deep thought from shame and guilt. Anything's possible. I know that as well as anyone.

But I also know something else. Something that conquers all my self-doubt, fear, and misery and lets me fly out this window and soar over the mountains on a wing and a prayer. I'll make it. I'll get through this. The day will come when I'm reunited with my family for keeps. It won't come soon enough, but it will come. Of that, I'm certain. And when it does, I will walk out of this prison and into their arms, to be held by them beyond my wildest dreams.

For now, though, darkness and loneliness are at my door as the lights go down until the sun comes up again. In the dead of night while I lie awake on my bed, they'll enter and land on my chest like shovel loads of graveyard dirt. For six wretched months I've been incarcerated in the Montana State Prison. As part of my plea bargain—an arrangement between Jonah Corcoran and state, and federal authorities—I have thirty more to go, which I try not to think about. To think about how far away two-and-a-half years is can cripple you. Already these walls, this door and this tiny window have held me longer than I could ever imagine possible.

The first night here it was so bad I thought those shovel loads might bury me alive, without the chance to ever see my family again. They visit me, though, which are those good days that I mentioned. Opposite my window is a steel door that opens and closes with a key or a push of a button. Not my push. When they come, it opens and out I go, escorted through more steel doors and concrete block hallways to a room with a row of stools, impenetrable glass, and phones. There, I'm placed at one of them and I pick it up.

Most times Jenny talks to me first, followed by Will, then Lisa, with signs of resiliency on display to assure me of their happiness to be back in Savannah. Then they're gone. Just like that. It's unbelievable how fast time passes by when they're in front of me on the other side of the glass. And it's unbelievable how slow it ticks away when they're not. So, I think of something else. Something other than the amount of Mountain Time ahead of me. I go beyond that, where I've set my sights squarely—which my eight-by-six-foot cell is not—on the future. Down the road, though far it may be, it's there waiting, and it's bright. As bright as hope and faith could ever be for someone who has both. A man who's learned to breathe with the extra weight on top of him, to shut his eyes and pretend he's somewhere outside these walls where he can root his way through the soil and into the sunlight like a blade of grass, like the dawn of a new day that never fails to arrive.

* * *

That dawn, it is here. The buzz, the noise, the steel doors, they awaken you if you're not already. In anticipation of the likelihood that I will see Hollis today, I've been up for hours. Word has reached me that he has been transferred here to serve out the remainder of his sentence. For his "cooperation" with the feds and Richland County Sheriff, he was sentenced to eight months. Four in a minimum-security federal prison camp in Montgomery, Alabama, and the other four here. My assumption is that he will find life a bit more difficult and less pleasant in a state prison than the "Club Fed" from which he has been reassigned. I don't wish him pain or ill will, though. He has to live with himself, and I would think that would be punishment enough.

There are two times and places I expect to first make his acquaintance again: breakfast in the mess hall or rec hour in the yard. Unless, of course, Hollis still feels the need for "protective custody" from me and has filed for that request. I can't imagine though anyone would believe the necessity for such a thing, as there are six levels of custody that inmates here are grouped into, and I am in minimum with the others who pose the lowest risk. With only four months to serve and no prior record, I would be shocked if Hollis isn't in amongst us. In addition to my other qualifications for the lower tier security threat designation, I have long since given up possession of my firearm . . . and my wife, my children, my career. In short, I'm not someone a fellow inmate should fear. In here, respect is all that is required, and in return, it is given by most.

The buzzer goes off, but the game isn't over. It has just begun, and one by one the doors open. I step out into the hallway for roll call. When completed, we walk single file to the mess hall for the morning meal. Hours and hours, I have waited for this moment, and before that it was days and weeks and months. Upon entry into the large cavernous room—all rooms are, compared to my cell—with rows and rows of tables and chairs, I search for Hollis amid the inmates in the serving line and those already seated. But with all of us in the same clothing he is camouflaged like the pheasants we once hunted. To stay head and shoulders above the fray, I ward off the blue and khaki-colored clothing. I am the lion. They are the zebra's stripes. No, it's not him. The man turns in the serving line and the resemblance isn't anywhere near as strong as first glance. I continue with my floodlight along the perimeter fence. Midway across the room, something catches my eye. Same hair style, same length, and just a bit grayer than when I last saw him, this could be Hollis. I take a step to my right and manage a brief snapshot of his profile, only to determine it's not him either.

On my tray, I place two slices of white bread, margarine, oatmeal, milk, and head for my table. The others seated there are regulars, too. We converse while we dine. It's standard fare, both the subject matter and the food, neither of which, I give much attention. It's the faces and the backs of heads of every inmate in the room who's busy at work in the consumption of sub-human provisions that I'm consumed with. After each one has been given a thorough examination, I'm disappointed to conclude that Hollis is not present and accounted for and would've been by now if he was going to eat breakfast.

Two hours is nothing. It's easy time compared to the hard time of thirty-six months. In my cell, I digest my meal and wait for rec hour in the prison yard. Out my window it's a morning in so many ways like the one Hollis and I spent with Orrin and Truck. The season, the land, the sun to our backs, the light frost, and the blue sky big and bold, they are in direct proportion, and in every sense, equal in inspiration as they were that day. When they're all you have, their novelty never wears thin.

With memories and expectations, time passes, and the next chapter of my daily routine begins its repetitious birth. The buzzer sounds, the doors open, roll call, then down the hall we go. I haven't felt butterflies like this though since my first day here. However, back then they weren't insects with wings. They were insects. This is something different because the only fear I have is that my "friend" has been segregated from the general population (and me) and it will be some time before I'm able to speak with him, if ever. There's also the remote possibility he's been placed into a different custody level than me, although with only four months to serve I can't imagine they'd consider him anything other than minimum.

For the yard we make a left turn at the end of the corridor, through another set of steel doors, past the commissary, past the chaplain's office, and out we go into Big Sky and Land Country Club, which the yard is anything but. I just like to call it that to help remove the trepidation that always comes with those first few steps into it—from that first time, which tends to linger. Again, the world is a shade of blue and khaki like that fateful day in Eastern Montana. Just beyond those first few steps, I step into his gaze. It is my "friend." He sees my eyes connect with his, and I change course to let him know I accept his invitation, whether he's sent one or not. In the yard, it is common courtesy to respect each other's space, and an intrusion of that is not taken lightly. Be that as it may, this is a circumstance without precedence that I'm aware of in my short but hell-filled tenure at this correctional institution. Without hesitation, I proceed toward him. Thirty, twenty, ten, five feet and one step further and I stand before him.

"I didn't see you at breakfast this morning and wondered if maybe you thought you still needed protective custody from me."

"I ordered room service."

"Should've figured."

"How are you, Garrett?"

"Numb, most days," I reply. "Feel like stretching your legs?"

"Sure."

In our blue clothing, we walk side by side along the perimeter of the yard. "How are Helen and the kids holding up?"

"Fine," he replies. "Heard Lisa took Will and Jenny back to Savannah."

"It's home."

"I hope one day they'll all talk again."

"Like us?"

"Yes, like us."

"Then you have a lot of explaining to do." I bring the two of us to a stop, to look him in the eye.

"Reach for the sky," he says.

"What?"

"Put your hands up."

I lift them up to my chest and he pats me down. "Do you really think I'd wear a wire?"

"No, but you never know."

"Isn't that the truth." I wait for him to reply but he doesn't. With a swing of my left leg, I continue our tour. Hollis follows my lead. "Why'd you do it?"

"Do what?"

"I guess I do probably need to be more specific because the list is long." Again, he ignores the jab and remains silent. "How could you go so far as to put the blame on me?"

After a few steps, he says, "We swore an oath to each other, and you broke that oath."

"I couldn't live with myself any longer."

"We promised to take our secret with us to our graves. Remember that?"

"Yes, but I never wanted any part of it. I did it for you."

"And I did what I did to Orrin, for you."

"But everything afterward was for the money, wasn't it?"

"The bottom line is that it all comes down to our families and doing what we have to do to take care of them."

"I agree, but not at the expense of ruining your friend's life and causing an enormous amount of pain and suffering for his wife and kids."

"You broke our pact and left me no choice."

"What about the truth? Wasn't that an option?"

"Maybe it was, at the beginning, but we chose another path."

"You chose it."

"If that's the way you want to look at it," he says, still somewhat careful with the words he chooses. "As businessmen, we both know a deal is a deal, and you signed off on it."

"I didn't want to."

"Then I guess you shouldn't have."

"You should've let Truck rest in peace."

He stops. I stop. "That was my intention, but when you 'panicked' over the notes left on our porches and the one on the windshield, and then the issue about Truck's nose and tooth, I knew I was going to need an alibi if and when you broke down and went to the police."

"Before any of that, though, you lied to me."

"About what?"

"You said you were very low on funds and needed the deal with Lawton's ranch to save you from financial ruin."

"I don't ever remember using the words 'low on funds' or 'financial ruin.'"

"Spin it whichever way you want, Hollis, but you deceived me on that."

"If I stretched the truth to convince you to help me out, then so be it."

"I think you were more concerned about the deal for Lawton's ranch going south than you were about the consequences of shooting a man in the back."

"Think what you like."

"You place a much greater emphasis on the almighty dollar than you let on."

"And you on the Almighty," he says. "Going to the priest didn't do you much good, did it? All it did was make him look like a pawn for a last-minute cover-up, same as your home invasion charade."

"It was no charade, and I said what I had to say to Father Seb because I would rather spend thirty-six months in hell than a lifetime in it. Unlike you, it had nothing to do with money."

"Don't' be so naïve," he replies. "The Bakken play is a once in a lifetime opportunity. It's going to turn ranch hands into millionaires and millionaires into billionaires."

"While I rot away in prison."

"We're both paying our dues."

"For your lies, I'm paying a much bigger price."

"All you had to do was stay silent."

We walk a few steps and dogleg left of a group of younger inmates who have their eyes trained on an eagle gliding on the thermals across the valley. "But you confessed before I did."

"Rumor had it that you had reached your breaking point, which turned out to be true. So, I cut the best deal I could for me and my family."

"Knowing I'd be the one who'd unwittingly find the grave to solidify your alibi."

We walk to the south end of the yard. There we have nothing left to say, and no time left to say it. The buzzer sounds, the game is over. I watch him as he quickens his pace to enter the building ahead of me, aware of the fact that the two of us will never speak to each other again.

ABOUT THE AUTHOR

 *The Silver Pigeons* is Jeff Howe's second novel. Jeff is a Cincinnatian, born in 1963, the son of James and Marjorie Howe and the youngest of nine children. He was raised Catholic and attended Catholic grade and high school. In 1985 he graduated from the University of Cincinnati.

Upon graduation he moved to Aspen, Colorado where he worked for KSPN radio station. When the ski season ended, he moved to Los Angeles for a brief period before returning to Cincinnati, where he went to work for his family's manufacturing and distribution business. After a few years he grew restless and left the company to travel and pursue other interests. Eventually settling down, he rejoined the family business, married, fathered two children, and lives with his wife and kids in Cincinnati.

An avid fly fisherman of both freshwater and saltwater game fish, Jeff has a true passion for being connected to the water. In addition to his outdoor pursuits, which also include upland hunting, he plays piano and guitar.

www.jeffhowebooks.com
jeffhowe@jeffhowebooks.com

9 780578 654249